Dagny,

or a Love Feast

Dagny,
or a Love Feast

Zurab Karumidze

DALKEY ARCHIVE PRESS
CHAMPAIGN / LONDON / DUBLIN

Originally published in English by Siesta, Tbilisi, 2011

Library of Congress Cataloging-in-Publication Data

K'arumize, Zurab, 1957-
Dagny, or, a love feast / Zurab Karumidze. -- First Edition.
pages cm. -- (The Georgian literature series)
"Originally published in English by Siesta, Tbilisi, 2011."
Bilingual text. Georgian and English.
ISBN 978-1-56478-928-0 (alk. paper)
1. Juell, Dagny, 1867-1901. 2. Authors, Norwegian--19th century--Biography. 3.
Berlin (Germany)--Intellectual life. 4. Kraków (Poland)--Intellectual life. 5. K'arumize,
Zurab, 1957---Translations into Georgian. I. Title. II. Title: Dagny. III. Title: Love feast.
PT8903.J84Z43 2014
839.821'6--dc23
[B]
2013037161

Partially funded by a grant from the Illinois Arts Council, a state agency

Georgian Literature Series is published thanks to the support of the
Ministry of Culture and Monument Protection of Georgia.

www.dalkeyarchive.com

Cover: design and composition by Mikhail Iliatov
Cover image: Konrad Krzyżanowski (1872–1922),
Portrait of Dagny Juel Przybyszewska (detail),
Ministry of Culture and Art, Poland

Printed on permanent/durable acid-free paper

To my wife Nina, who dreams of Norway . . .

PART ONE

I'm afraid my English is inadequate for the task I now face—I'm not a native speaker. Besides, I'm not quite sure what makes me write about a mysterious woman from Scandinavia coming to my hometown in the South Caucasus to be shot dead by one of her admirers more than a hundred years ago. Moreover, I'm a bad man—*I don't know what love is*—and there's definitely something wrong with my liver, because I drink too much . . . actually, maybe I drink because I don't know love, or maybe I don't know love because I drink? Hear hear!

Saint Paul, the thirteenth of the twelve apostles, spoke the tongues of men and angels and knew what love was. A long time ago he wrote to the Corinthians: ". . . and though I give my body to be burned, but have not love, it profits me nothing." And more importantly: "Love suffereth long and is kind . . . Love doth not rejoice within iniquity, but rejoiceth within the truth."

Well, what can I draw from this knowledge?! I personally rejoiceth within alcohol, which certainly might contain some truth, as the Latin saying has it, though mostly it contains some regular stuff distilled from grapes, barley, grain, berries or whatever, which bathes, enshrouds, and buries my brain . . . and yes, love is also in it, but as much as I can taste, it amounts to less than one percent of the forty per volume, especially if one drinks alone. Thus, to borrow from Saint Paul himself, the way I understand love is almost the same as how a sounding brass or a clanging cymbal understand the sounds they make, or, to be more precise: my knowledge of love equals the knowledge of love "experienced" by, say, Eric Dolphy's flute, when the guy played the old jazz standard "You Don't Know What Love Is" on that very same instrument.

Undoubtedly, the flute as a musical instrument is extraordinary: it was invented by a theriomorphic creature, a half-goat, half-god, to celebrate the moment when all physical matter went mad over the course of a single, golden afternoon. As some Gaelic bards suggest, the best flute is made of bone taken from the thigh of a heron crazed by the moon. Maybe this is why nearly all flute players are slightly nuts, like the most famous of them—Jethro Tull's Ian Anderson. And yet, the maddest of all was a Russian one—Vladimir Mayakovsky. Once he even dared to play his spinal column like a flute. Just imagine him balancing on one leg, the other one raised, and with his eyes wide shut blowing into his vertebrae—

Flying so high, trying to remember . . .

May I suggest here a musical-biological definition of love? Love is when her/his breath fills up your spinal column with sounds . . . the gentle wind moving silently, invisibly . . . indescribable love . . . hear hear!

Oh yes, Dagny Juel Przybyszewska must have inspired this kind of love: she would play the spine-flute of the men around her, stirring jealousy in with excitement, mixing orgasm with death, and transforming sexual fear into the destructive aesthetics of the *fin de siècle*. The "Nordic Sphinx," they called her. She would strangle them with her dazzling riddles, like fetuses strangled inside the spectacular belly of Our Lady of the Life-in-Death-and-Death-in-Life-as-Art. The high priestess of Berlin bohemia, the midwife of the terrible beauty that was then being born; she was their Androgyne and their absolute source of ecstasy, madness, and inspiration. And they all desired her, desired this Botticellian-Rembrandtian-Rosettian vampire of the soul—curly, silken, fine, convoluted, airy, overpowering, aristocratic, atmospheric, bloody, murky, shady, tall, lean, supple, dry, stiff, bristling—rejecting innocence for that real selfhood reflected in dark mirrors . . . and she was shot dead by a neurotic young admirer, who shot himself afterwards . . . screeeeam!

"You had to experience her to be able to describe her," said Edvard Munch, her fellow Norwegian and painter of *The Scream*. Munch was allegedly the first to "experience" Dagny, as one experiences the odor of a freshly picked flower. Actually, the smell of a deflowering is far more intricate—like the smell of Lebanon, perhaps? I don't remember myself; it was many years ago . . . either way, as Dagny Juel was killed in a hotel room in Tiflis, Russia (read: Tbilisi, Georgia), as long ago as June 1901, my chances of experiencing her, and, respectively, of "capturing" her, are rather slim.

What brought this mythical woman with a roaring past to the major artistic centers of Europe, and then to the town of Tiflis—"near the Black Sea," as she wrote on a postcard?! Tiflis has never been "near the Black Sea"—it's hundreds of kilometers from the city. Sure, some tens of millions of years ago, the sea covered the whole of Transcaucasia, and Tiflis at the bottom of it was inhabited by the usual prehistoric creatures. But the same is true of many other cities, like, say, London—as some scholars have proved recently. Actually, the sea at Tiflis, or Tbilisi, is not black but wine-dark, as people drink a lot here, and in fact I am one of the ancient, surviving species—something of a fossil.

Was it poverty or despair that pushed Dagny Juel to come here? What is the force that makes animals wander, to explore ceaselessly, driving leopards to end up on snowy hills? Hey, more than thirty years after Dagny's murder, a tiger was shot in Georgia near Gori, incidentally the birthplace of Joseph Stalin (yes, the "gory" guy came from such a town). The thing is, tigers have been extinct in this country for centuries. This particular tiger obviously came from Persia, having covered a huge distance. À la Salman Rushdie, one may presume that the tiger was Dagny Juel's reincarnation, coming back for revenge. If so, she got the wrong place. She should have gone to Poland; some feminist biographers hold that her destruction began there. It was her husband, the demonic Polish writer Stanislaw (Stach) Przybyszewski, who shattered the poor thing psychologically. Oh, that male chauvinist *piggyszewski!*

Tiger, tiger burning bright, in the forest of the night . . . yes, from time to time, some transplanted wild cats show up in Georgia, dead or alive. So far, the most celebrated of them was a dead one, arriving in the form of a panther (or tiger) skin, adorning the apparel of a strange knight, who shows up as a "Sacred Outsider" known as *The Knight in the Panther's Skin.* This medieval romance, about a pardivested[1] seeker of lost love kidnapped by dark and evil creatures, is a Georgian national epic—just like the Constitution with its Bill of Rights is for Americans. As it happens, some stanzas of the poem's Russian translation were even edited by Uncle Joe himself—you can see the manuscripts in his museum in Gori.

But what was Dagny to Stalin, and Stalin to Dagny? In 1901, young Koba (Stalin's nickname) was engaged in underground proto-communist activities in Tiflis, showing up from time to time among his class enemies in taverns or restaurants. Perhaps on one such occasion, he caught sight of Dagny's patrician profile at the next table and felt a dialectical urge to expropriate the expropriator in the missionary position (but hadn't he been expelled from the local seminary?!).

Even having done my research, how can I describe Dagny Juel as the woman really was? She has been mythologized enough, and yet it is the myth that fascinates me more (forgive me) than her writings or her life, with the exception of her last three weeks, which she spent in Tiflis, and of which we know almost nothing.

And yet, this "almost nothing" will form the gist of my story.

---

1. "Pardivested," or the wearing of a leopard or tiger skin garment, is a coinage by Wim van Binsbergen. For more on leopard symbolism, see his *The Leopard in the Garden of Eating.* "Sacred Outsider" is his coinage too.

But my God, what an untimely ambition it is to make something out of almost nothing! In today's world, who buys those texts driven by sheer obsession with that nothing called fiction?! Today when friction is all and fiction is nothing?! Let's get this straight, my friends: after the 9/11 attack, the spectacular outbreak of the War on Terror, and the ruthless *shahid* counterattacks, creative writing lost its reason. (For various other reasons too, which I would rather not delve into here.) Alas, the highest awards and *Palmes d'Or* are today bestowed upon mere documentaries, while autobiographies peppered with social criticism and outlandish behavior top the bestseller charts. But how about fantasy, which sells by the millions?! Well, we all know fantasy is for young adults—but won't they inherit the earth?

Therefore, and for the sake of being up-to-date, I wish to take a stand and declare that I'm not going to write about Dagny Juel Przybyszewska—no, I'm going to *eat* her instead. Yes, I'll eat her flesh and drink her blood, and through this act restore the animal in me, or "re-territorialize" it, to speak philosophically. Henceforth this very special woman is going to feature as a very special food for my special thoughts on love . . . and you, reader, are most welcome to my Love Feast! Hear hear!

> I once had a girl, or should I say, she once had me
> hey tra la la la
> . . .
> isn't it gooood, Norwegian wooooood . . .
> this bird has flown . . .

Dagny Juel was found fully dressed on a chaise lounge between 1:00 P.M. and 1:20 P.M., just after having had lunch. Her killer probably poured sleeping potion into her wine (for he had been planning the murder for a long time, as her sister Ragnhlid wrote in a letter afterwards), and then, as she lay there with her right hand under her neck assuming exactly the same posture in which Munch portrayed her as the Madonna, he shot her in the back of the head. She felt somebody's kiss on her powerless mouth, the sleeping earth opening its wide womb to flow forth seething floods; the bullet penetrated her skull like a star sinking back into her soul, and she saw the glowing flower of death grand as a rainbow dripping blood and fire. She was thirty-three.

An aristocrat by birth and character, Dagny Juel was like fresh forest air to those men who were breathlessly seeking their identity in the arts and life. She was the queen of the artistic crowds that flocked to the *Schwarze Ferkel* tavern in Berlin at the end of the nineteenth century. She inspired such celebrities of fledgling European modernism as August Strindberg (who had hated her, and depicted her in his plays as a femme fatale); Edvard Munch, as already mentioned; Gustav Vigeland, the erotic sculptor of marble; and Stanislaw Przybyszewski—the guy who fucked the muses of his dramatic and lyric poetry just like he would fuck any woman available to him, as his obsession with gratifying his desires was almost as strong as his obsession with the nationalist New Poland movement. The great Nobel Prize-winner of Norway, Knut Hamsun himself, also discovered the diamond called Dagny; in his 1892 novel, *Mysteries,* the female protagonist, a subtle and alluring young beauty with Dagny's name, was inspired by her.[2]

She had more admirers—lesser known, or less important—less significant as artists and thinkers than Hamsun was, for instance, but these men also roamed in the forest of Dagny's enchantment. "She had green eyes, a red dress and danced for us, and we all desired her," Gustav Vigeland recalled.

What about her family background? Her father was a

---

2. Knut Hamsun visited Tiflis in 1899 and stayed in a hotel next to the one in which Dagny would die two years later. What sort of premonition brought him there?

physician and on several occasions treated His Royal Majesty of Sweden, while her uncle ended up the Prime Minister of Sweden, or something like that. She played the piano and took lessons in Paris and Berlin; Grieg was her favorite composer. One of her three sisters became a singer—probably "Solveig's Song" from *Peer Gynt* was the main item in the girls' repertoire. Oh yes, her Norwegian backdrop: the fjords and the gloomy sea; the misty look in the eyes of those reasonable Northerners, torn between puritan morality and the allure of free love as practiced by some in the capital city of Christiania, now known as Oslo.

Dagny wrote poetry and left behind several plays. Deadly love triangles, i.e., "the coming together of predestined lovers and the death (physical or psychological) of the socially legitimate lover at their hands," was her area of expertise; she played with such triangles in her writing and suffered from them in her life, making others suffer too. Her first triangle materialized right after her marriage to Stach in 1893, though this one was sort of "retroactive": several months after the wedding, Stach's mistress Marta Foerder, who had borne him two children, committed suicide. (Stach had to go to prison after that, staying there for a couple of weeks abandoned by everyone except Dagny, of course.) The last triangle in Dagny's life was formed in Tiflis, and this one killed her—but we'll touch upon that later.

For now, what about tracing the origins of cubism in the destructive geometry of love triangles instead? A curious consideration, though cubism aimed exactly at restoring something to its true nature through destruction . . . Given the social and moral restrictions of that period, Dagny Juel would have seemed to polite society almost as destructive as female suicide bombers from Chechnya do today. For a woman of the late nineteenth century, as Dagny was, stepping into the triangular terrain of erotic love equated the destruction of her sociobiological role as a wife and mother, and the restoration of her original nature as a demonic creature who would communicate the obscure message of gods to men (perhaps this is what makes some men so religious).

Such women are sometimes referred to as "larger than life." Maybe this is why female declarations and actions occasionally seem foolish. But this has nothing to do with their alleged "intellectual disabilities." They simply have to deal with something totally irrational—the transcendent whims of immortal beings that never sleep—and pass their desires on to us in the language that we speak, which is the most difficult and complicated form of translation, dating back to the high priestesses and temple prostitutes of ancient times. Those women were the genuine hermeneuts, who in their dreams would straddle menstrual rivers of dirty, clotted blood, and with natal fluids in their heads speak the Word of the Gods. The task is more difficult today, as those ancient gods have abandoned us (though some maintain that they are still to return).

It occurs to me that even in Dagny's time, triplicate eroticism, or love triangles, could take a woman beyond commonly observed rules and standards and into a fourth dimension—the one of change and transformation. This is exactly what love is all about: the great change, the transformation of identity into difference— through which process, for example, a bat feels itself torn between being a mere rodent on the one hand and being free as a bird on the other. Correct me if I'm wrong, folks, but the same shit must happen when crude matter is transformed into pure energy, just as when a moth is consumed by the flame of a burning candle.

By the way, Edvard Munch has a portrait of Dagny—*A Portrait of Dagny as a Young Bat*, as I myself call it—and I should say that yes, there is something bat-like in the look of her shoulders against the background of the dark blue sky . . . In one of her poetic fantasies, Dagny writes of her "gray sister," a huge bat staring into her mind, which is just an empty cavity, into which the sun pours its golden flood. Yes, she "drank from the deep wells of her men, and their power became poison in her veins," as she herself puts it elsewhere. All this symbolism could be boiled down to mere pornography, consummated by the banal act of ejaculation . . . though excuse the trite psychoanalysis; I'm dealing with a woman who was "larger than life," and as life is larger than language, from time to time I must go beyond the verbal images suggested by pure poetry.

Dagny used to drink and, yes, she smoked too. "She was like an angel with a cigarette in her mouth"—this description of Dagny's character (which I think is the best) came from a friend of hers. Next comes Strindberg, swallowing his own venom in order to describe her: "The face is singular, aristocratic, and winningly full of life. There is something searching in it, something testing the air; there's a trembling around the nostrils, she holds her eyelids lowered but the eyes still stare out audaciously."

An angel with a cigarette in her mouth: the interplay of love, which hates identity and abides in difference—or, to put it in terms of animal symbolism, the juxtaposition of the Lion and the Leopard. The Lion, an even-colored, texturally homogeneous feline, symbolizes identity, while the speckled and variegated Leopard is difference. The Lion personifies reason, moral authority, state power and law, while the Leopard is love—sheer love disseminated over time and space, covering and pervading all.

Maybe you remember that rhyme by Lewis Carroll: "The Lion and the Unicorn were fighting for the crown . . ." The origin is ancient, and once read as follows: "The Lion and the Leopard were fighting for a Cow."

Now, let me tell you a true story.

Genes are to biological organisms as so-called "memes" are to human ideas and values (following the analogy of geneticist Richard Dawkins). On the other hand, Hegel had it that history is the dialectical juxtaposition and development of ideas and values. So here is my suggestion: human history is a dialectical play, a juxtapositioning, a competition between two memes: the Lion Meme and the Leopard Meme. These memes originate as far back as the Upper Paleolithic period, and were brought to earth by some celestial body. Both memes share the same origin: the Ur-Leopard Meme. The leopard subsumes the lion (or leo) and also the panther or tiger (the etymology of the word "leopard" testifies to the fact that ancient cultures once believed the leopard a hybrid species of the latter two). To put it back in theoretical terms, difference is given and identity is made up from it. Difference comes before identity, just as love comes before everything else. Hear hear!

The rupture within the Ur-Leopard Meme and the breakup into two genii happened when fire was stolen. Until then, fire was regarded by humans as a holy tongue, the ardent state of a numinous intercourse between mortals and the immortal gods, the nexus of supreme fusion, uniting earth and sky where the speckled angel called *Poesis* brings beings forth from non-Being.[3] But after it was stolen, a man named Dhemi Urgush started using fire as a tool to make other tools. And he became the first identity forger. The Lion Meme developed through him, channeling power from the golden angel called *Techne*.

From then on, across millennia, the Lion Meme would materialize amongst generations of men who rejected affection and dedicated themselves to power and reason. On its own, the Leopard Meme would incarnate in those generations of men that rejected power and devoted themselves to the sublimity of art in all its varieties. From now on, I will refer to the descendants of the two branches as the *Pardimemes* and the *Leomemes*.

The Leomemes often developed into groups, brotherhoods

3. "Supreme fusion" was later rendered "meta-fusion" and eventually misinterpreted as "metaphysics."

or organizations; think of the architects and high priests of dynastic Egypt, the patriarchs and kings of Israel (except King David), the Knights Templar, the Rosicrucian, the Freemasons, multinational corporations, etc. Contrary to this, the Pardimemes never congregate or form groups; they remain scattered and roam on their own (as the speckledness of the leopard skin suggests). Some people among this race I call *Shamanic Individuals.* Such individuals show up throughout history from time to time, in the West as well as the East. Consider the ancient Greek shamans, like Heraclitus, Sophocles, Socrates; various gnostics and heresiarchs like Mani, Nestorius, etc.; then comes Meister Eckhart and Dante Alighieri in medieval Europe; and Jalal al-Din Rumi, or Omar Khayyám in the medieval Orient—among others. Later, in modern times, we see such types as, say—C. G. Jung (the best apprentice of the "Shaman of Vienna"), James Joyce, Bakunin, Sikorsky, John Coltrane, Charlie Chaplin, Gilles Deleuze and Jimi Hendrix.

There are also those known as the so-called *false shamans,* who misappropriated the shamanic art in their lust for power, and for this treason were cursed by the angel *Poesis*: Lenin, Hitler, Stalin, Mao, etc. Akin to them are the *debilitated shamans*—suicide bombers and various charismatic idiots.

I have also identified some marginal cases, indicative of obviously tragic misconceptions. Take Mozart: though a natural-born shaman, a man of amazing genius, his flamboyant personality drove him to defect to leomeme-based Freemasonry. His last piece, *The Magic Flute,* demonstrates this defection: one supporting character, the bird-man Papageno, is a clear-cut shamanic person who is manipulated by King Zarastro (a purely leomemic representative of wisdom and of the brotherhood of the great architects of the world). Papageno is represented as an ignorant, crude, short-tempered simpleton, whose interests are limited to copulation and drinking. Such a parody of shamanism in favor of Freemasonry must have been the sole cause of Mozart's decline and death—he must have been punished by an anonymous shaman, who poisoned the composer and then took away his body (nobody has seen Mozart's burial place). Undoubtedly, the killer could not have been Salieri, who was a typical leomemic person and obviously a Freemason himself.

Or take Goethe, who ended up as a secret counselor and cabinet minister for the Grand Duke of Saxe-Weimar-Eisenach—or Yukio Mishima, who misappropriated the shamanic art of dying and committed a merely traditional suicide on behalf of the Emperor. Among those who dealt with the Leomemes, it was only Richard Wagner who succeeded in preserving his shamanic nature, meanwhile dazzling Ludwig, the King of Bavaria.[4]

Now, to return to Lewis Carroll's rhyme, the two memes are supported by a third—an ungulate, or a Cowmeme, which historically has materialized in the huge but passive masses of people, today classed as consumers, who are happy in the same way that all happy families are happy . . . *the young in one another's arms* . . . though, let's get back to our predators.

It is well known that lions and leopards shun each other—leopards especially try to avoid the hunting areas of a lion pride. However, they occasionally become deadly rivals for the same prey. This goes for the Pardimemes and the Leomemes too. While they usually "hunt" in different places, when it comes to sharing the Cowmeme people, the Leomemes always banish the Pardimemes, just as a lion pride would oust a leopard, with the lionesses being the most aggressive. (A similar dynamic is evident

---

4. I would tender Che Guevara as a modern example of misguided shamanism: he fought against power his whole life, but politicized affection too much, and thus sapped its force. The same could be said of Bill Gates, a man of pretty decent shamanic knowledge, which he nevertheless exhausted in his leomemic adventures. There is also an extreme, deranged wing of misguided shamanism, which encompasses the so-called "shamaniacs"—the serial killers and rapists (like Jack the Ripper, Charles Manson, etc.).

in the king-queen-knave triangles of popular Russian card games.) Besides, the Leomemes are preoccupied with controlling as many people as possible, while the Pardimemes are staunch individualists. To an extent, this is an indirect competition and the aforementioned case of Mozart should be attributed to the whim of a deranged shaman.

And yet, there comes a time when the Pardimemes are driven towards each other and towards the Leomemes too, as if by the residual energy of the Ur-Leopard Meme or by some extraneous threat. They seek a rapprochement, an intercourse, a sort of reunion. However, they usually fail to achieve this, as often happens in nature too—lions and leopards can breed, but only in captivity and yielding morbid offspring.

There is no way back to the Ur-Leopard; thus, those few isolated meetings between Shamanic Individuals held throughout history—intending to develop something grander that also included the Leomemes—were disrupted by various disasters, both major and minor.[5] Such failures totally discouraged the Pardimemes, and there were almost no attempts towards another possible meeting made for hundreds of years. And this went on until 1901.

By the beginning of that year, quite a few Shamanic Individuals, though scattered around the world, had a so-called Pardimeme Premonition of a very big threat approaching: "A Cow will fly to the moon!" The cry was heard throughout the shamanic underground, through dark cells and coppices; it was a mixture of whimpering, lamentation, and sarcastic laughter.

One hundred years later and with the benefit of hindsight, we can easily decipher this weird, almost nursery rhyme-like statement. As a matter of fact, those chosen Pardimemes had a

---

5. The meeting in Telgte during the Thirty Years War can also be considered a shamanic-pardimeme venture. Regrettably, as Günter Grass attests in *The Meeting in Telgte*, it was disrupted by fire.

premonition of oncoming disaster that would plague the Earth in the new century: masses of people would go mad! Led by false shamans, they would rebel and rejoice in massacres! (But no room for repeating the tragic facts of the twentieth century, and no sense in it either.) However, the picture which Shamanic Individuals then divined was horrible, even for those who had traveled to infernal spheres and the land of the dead, or surveyed wars and calamities of the past. Some of them could not recover from this visionary ecstasy and got lost; some were hit by lighting and burnt to ashes; some jumped into their most abysmal thoughts and were destroyed. One of them, over-intoxicated by this revaluation of all values, died of madness: his name was Friedrich Nietzsche.

"All that's sublime in art will lock itself up in an ivory tower, and the natural curative power which comes from it shall be exhausted, and the crowds knowing art no more will wage wars on each other!" Thus also spoke the Pardimeme Premonition, foreshadowing the estrangement of the masses and the spread of lying as a form of knowledge. Yes, the pied pipers of totalitarianism would draw the Cowmeme crowds away, and the wild shaman of Piccadilly would go unheeded; he died around that time too, with words of wisdom on his lips—"Art should never try to be popular; the public should try to make itself artistic!"[6]

In their ecstatic visions, the Pardimemes realized that only a gigantic discharge of the sacred substance *Askokin*, which on the Planet Earth is known as the *Love that Moves the Spheres*, could stop "the Cow from flying to the moon." And this discharge had to come from the Ur-Leopard. But the shamanic capacity to channel Love would not itself be enough, and therefore the Pardimemes would need the Leomemes and *their* channels to

6. Oscar Wilde was destroyed by a Leomeme-manipulated Cowmeme— Lord Queensberry, acted upon by his son, Alfred Douglas, a handsome but spoiled English aristocrat who had some hidden pardimeme biases towards the love that dare not speak its name . . .

obtain the desired effect. Thus, to initiate a conclusive restoration of the Ur-Leopard Unity, the Pardimemes had to act together with the Leomemes: they had to make a synchronized effort, accomplishing a rite known as the Cosmic Agape, or the Celestial Love Feast.

This rite can be conceptualized as an ecumenical-universalistic communion, a trans-religious enactment of divine passions through the passage of identity towards difference. On the one hand, it engages the mystery of the Leopard as simultaneously the eater and the provider of food—since humans used to be scavengers and would feed upon predators' leftovers—while on the other hand, the rite enacts the transubstantiation of a sacrificial creature into the body of Love. And this very body of Love, through various symbolic correlates, was to be devoured at the Cosmic Agape.[7]

Through ecstatic networking, the Pardimeme Voices passed on a message to convene the Agape and a special site was fixed on the verge of the Occident and the Orient, a place where extremes meet and abide in difference: Tiflis, a city in Russia's southern province of Georgia.

I still have a problem understanding why the shamanic-pardimemes chose this city. There were so many other places where east meets west, or north meets south. What about Constantinople, the great old Byzantium with its "sages standing in God's holy fire . . ."? (W. B. Yeats, or "silly Willy," got pretty shamanic too as he grew older . . .) Either way, even if these Leopard men got fixated on the South Caucasus, why not in Baku? Baku would have been very good city to choose, since

7. Incidentally, some physical anthropologists claim that the consumption of scavenged meat caused a substantial increase in the volume of the hominid brain, thus making proto-humans superior to other apes. Such a qualitative change in diet could also have contributed to the formation of archetypal rites involving the consumption of "sacred flesh," which in Christianity developed into communion.

the Pardimemes needed to attract the Leomemes, and oil is a typically leomemic matter . . .

Forty-two years after the event I am now describing, another Shamanic Individual, Salvador Dalí, would highlight the location once again in his famous *Geopoliticus Child Watching the Birth of the New Man*. In the painting, a colossus is being born from an egg-shaped globe, while a woman with a child (the "geopoliticus") is standing by with her arm outstretched toward the scene, regarding it. The colossus is emerging from North America, its left hand leaning heavily on the British Isles, while the "geopolitical mother" points at one of the regions of the globe, marking the exceptional importance of that area. The area is between the Black Sea and the Caspian Sea, with Tiflis located in the middle. Obviously, Dali was not yet born in 1901, and so was in one of his pre-prenatal phases, contemplating fried eggs without a frying pan . . . he had to learn much later about that pardimeme effort.

But look at the painting again: the ambiance is gloomy, pierced with the sharp regret of a missed opportunity. Alas, the Tiflis agape failed due to negligence and a dirty trick played by false shamans, whom I will not name just yet. It failed, and the Cow did "fly to the moon," causing the death of millions and millions of people; the bread was poisoned and the air polluted![8] But getting back to the motivation behind the shamanic decision to hold the Cosmic Agape in Tiflis—a glance at the pardimeme tradition in Georgia will help us understand it. Let me focus selectively on three examples only—the fourth comes in 1901.

The origins of the tradition date back to one of the first female Pardimemes—Medea of Colchis, who was an enchantingly

8. The "flight of the Cow" did have some positive side effects, such as the successful American and Russian space expeditions in the sixties and seventies. As a matter of fact, Shamanic Individuals inspired the greatest achievements of modern science; take Einstein, who once acknowledged how much he learned from Dostoevsky.

beautiful sorceress.[9] She had a tragic love affair with Jason, who came to her land to purloin the Golden Fleece—the very fabric of the pure, Pardimeme nature (though the leomeme descendents of the Knights Templar very much revered it in later ages). I can see this mysterious woman, who betrayed her country and her royal family for love, driven by that very Ur-Leopard urge for reunion with the Lion men. She helped Jason with the theft and ran away with him to Greece. I can see her in the full moon, picturing her aunt Pasiphaë copulating with a bull in the esoteric enactment of the "sacred marriage"; I can see her performing fertility rites and earthly orgies in anticipation of Georgios, the martyr who would be most venerated by her people in times to come—Saint George, who let himself be dismembered, and then came back in the full glory of Love. I can see her, delirious, killing the children she bore by Jason—punishing him for his infidelity, and shedding tears of grief, since her desire for the Ur-Leopard reunion had destroyed her; finally, I see her transformed into a panther and running away into the wilderness.

The next example brings us to the fifth century AD, when there lived a man called Peter the Iberian, who in the rest of the early medieval world was celebrated as Pseudo-Dionysius the Areopagite. Peter was of royal lineage too; his grandfather on his mother's side was the great sage Bacurius. On his father's side, his grandmother was Osdukhtia, whose brother Pharsmanios enjoyed great favor with Arcadius, Emperor of the Romans, occupying the rank of general in the army. But Peter renounced his royal position for an ascetic life. He was acquainted with many prominent personalities of the time, including the famous patriarchs: Nestorius, Juvenal, and Timothy the Cat. As Pseudo-Dionysius the Areopagite, Peter in his shamanic meditations transcended his era and observed the solar eclipse at Christ's Crucifixion, looked upon the Life-begetting and God-receiving

9. Colchis is the ancient name for western Georgia, as Iberia is for eastern.

body of the Virgin Mary, encountered the Apostles Peter and James, and wrote letters to Saint John the Evangelist. The corpus of Peter's writings was later designated the *Areopagitica*, consisting of four treatises and ten letters (one of them to Saint John). The most significant of these is the text called *De Divinis Nominibus* (or, *On the Divine Names*), in which the traditional shamanic invocation of proper names in order to cast magic spells and perform compassionate acts of healing was elevated to the heights of superb theological mysticism. The underlying idea of the text is as follows: Love, the one being, transcends "all quality and predication, all affirmation and negation and all intellectual conception, by the very force of its goodness gives to beings outside itself their countless gradations, unites them in the closest bonds, keeps each by its care, directs in its appointed sphere and draws them again in ascending order to itself." Dante Alighieri was Peter's disciple—and the revelations of Peter-Dionysius inspired the Tuscan's transcendent travels through infernal reality and his thoughts about the sacred celestial mechanics of Love. And yet, more than a century before Dante, Peter-Dionysius reared a disciple from his own Iberian homeland: the poet, iconographer, and author of the seminal pardimemic poem *Vepkhistqaosani,* or *The Knight in the Panther's Skin*—Shota Rustaveli.

The information available on the life of Rustaveli is extremely scanty. He must have been of noble lineage, as according to some sources he served as treasurer at the court of Queen Tamar (1184–1216). Popular tradition keeps alive the legend that Rustaveli was in love with the Queen, but when he disclosed his passion, he was banished from court and country. I doubt the validity of this sentimental legend though. The court of Tamar was pretty flexible about love and sexuality, and such a refined sentiment would hardly have been regarded as punishable. However, it is also true that Rustaveli was banished, and that he ended his life in Jerusalem, in the Georgian Monastery of the Holy Cross (his fresco is still there, though defaced recently by some jealous Greek monks). But here is my point: his exile could have been due to the disclosure of his pardimeme affiliation, as the country at that time was run by the Leomemes, particularly by people who were closely associated with the Knights Templar. (As a matter of fact, the leomeme tradition in Georgia is much older than the following examples demonstrate; it dates back to the times of legendary blacksmiths and the first men to forge bronze and iron—the Chalybes mentioned by Homer, and the Tubals, who were direct descendants of Dhemi Urgush.] The Knights of the Temple were influential in Georgia since the time of Tamar's great-grandfather, David the Builder. In 1119, Baldwin of Jerusalem came secretly to Georgia, seeking an alliance with this magnificent king. Due to agreements arranged at that time, Tamar's son, King Lasha-Giorgi, took part in the Crusades; his addiction to wine lead to the failure of this adventure.

Rustaveli himself makes several allusions, both direct and allegorical, to the leomemic lineage of Tamar; as said previously, he remained her ardent admirer. But after all, isn't pardimemic scope and sensibility more comprehensive than the leomemic preoccupation with identity? Either way, as soon as the text of Rustaveli's poem got into courtiers' hands, he would have been banished as a shamanic-pardimeme (with the lionesses being the most aggressive, to be sure).

To the academic eye, *Vepkhistqaosani* is a mixture of Areopagitic wisdom and Sufi mysticism. The literary genre of Persian Romance strongly influences its formal elements, but this is not what interests us here. Written in superb verse, the poem is permeated with love, although this is more than just religious-mystic sentiment—it goes beyond these limits and takes us to the realm of inexhaustible longing for the Ur-Leopard Unity.

The central characters of the poem are divided into two pairs: the pardimemic ones (Tariel and Nestan) and the leomemic ones (Avtandil and Tinatin). Tariel, the knight clad in the leopard skin, is also endowed with clear-cut shamanic attributes, frequently fainting and losing consciousness in fits of ecstatic visions. Nestan shares similar qualities—she's a shape-shifter, occasionally revealing to Tariel her true form as a panther. After ending up a hostage to evil spirits, Tariel and his friends perform marvelous stunts in order to retrieve her.

Queen Tamar is the prototype for Tinatin, the female of the second pairing. She is a royal lioness, worshipped by her chief general, who is another lion-type person—Avtandil. However, the special thing about these two is that they, as Leomemes, get transformed and take up pardimeme paths. The first half of the poem is about their obsession with the idea of finding that strange knight in the panther's skin, Tariel, whom they encounter suddenly while hunting (as lions do), although he escapes them (as a leopard should do). Could it have been as follows: by describing such a transformation of Leomemes, Rustaveli divulged Queen Tamar's clandestine sympathy towards shamanic-pardimemes, thereby sentencing himself to exile? Possibly: the Queen might have been fascinated by the idea of Ur-Leopard harmony, but as a royal ruler, she would never have spoken about this openly.

Written in an age of highly developed feudalism, which coincided with the acme of the Leomeme rule in Georgia, *Vepkhistqaosani* abounds with shamanic references. With regard to the Ur-Leopard mystery, most suggestive is the passage in which Tariel tells Avtandil the story of killing a lion and a panther, right in the golden middle of the poem (chapter thirty-eight, according to the modern numeration). Roaming in a forest, Tariel encounters a lion and a panther, which seem to him "enamored."

As a matter of fact, they are making love, and "sport gaily." The knight envisions an idyll—a harmonious union of differences and an edenic state of all-embracing Love before the "fire was stolen" (to put it in the terms of our narrative). Then suddenly the rupture comes: Tariel tells how the two break into a fight: "embittered they struggled, each striking the other with its paw." The panther, losing heart, is fiercely pursued by the lion, which would have killed it if Tariel hadn't intervened and stabbed the lion with his sword ("I killed him, I freed him from this world's woe.") Having done this, Tariel attempts a pure, shamanic gesture: he tries to embrace the panther and kiss it, declaring, "I wished to kiss it for the sake of her for whom hot fires burn me." But this embrace of love ends with the death of the panther.

Rustaveli was one of the best minds of his generation, superbly read and educated. He could have thrived as the Leomeme ideal and favorite. But he chose to burn himself down in the flames of Love. The passage above is as illustrative of the pardimeme Weltanschauung as the primal scene—when a child suddenly witnesses his parents copulating—is for the psychoanalytic paradigm. One can clearly discern in this passage the trauma of the dissolution of the Ur-Leopard Unity, the breakup of the face-to-face between mortals and immortals, and the separation of earth and sky, as felt by Tariel; since then, the forgers have been in the ascendant and Love has had to recede.

To cut a long story short (as Rustaveli himself suggests in the prologue to his poem), we can presume that the pardimemic drive has been historically strong in Georgia. Take another, supplementary, example: *The Lay of the Huntsman and the Panther,* a folk ballad recited by local highlanders. It is about an encounter between a beardless youth and a panther, ending with the death of both of them. The final part of *The Lay* is most demonstrative: the mother of the youth goes to the mother of the panther, seeking to share their grief and the "loud lament":

So quickly will I go to her
And strive to soothe her sorrow deep.
She'll proudly tell me of her child,
And we in common grief will weep.

Could it be that some hidden message carried in these poems—the refined one and the crude one—made the shamanic-pardimemes identify Tiflis as a possible site for performing the Cosmic Agape in 1901? I now suggest another story about a hidden message which might help us to clarify the question at hand.

There is a fourth-century Gnostic text rewritten in the middle of the tenth century by Ioane-Zosime, or John-Zosimus, a Georgian monk of the Mount Sinai monastery. A hymn, it is entitled: *The Praise and the Glorification of the Georgian Language.* It goes like this:

Buried is the Georgian Tongue until the day of
His Second Coming to bear witness,
So that God shall charge each of the tongues
with this very tongue;
And this tongue is asleep until today and in the
Gospel it is named Lazarus,
And Nino of Good News converted it and Queen
Helen:
Those are two sisters, like Mary and Martha.
And the Amity was spoken hereto, that the whole
mystery is buried in this tongue;

And the four-day dead was said by David the
Prophet,
because of "a thousand years as one day."

And in the Georgian Gospel by Matthew there is inscribed a letter, which is a letter with a number making up four thousand, and these are the four days.

And the four-day dead, and therefore buried with Him through baptism into death.

And this very tongue, adorned and blessed by the Name of God, humiliated and oppressed, awaits the day of the Second Coming of the Lord.

And as a token of the miracle, it has ninety-four years ahead of other tongues from the coming of Christ until today.

I'm sorry, my friends, I'm afraid we're getting kind of "lost in translation"! Let me just go back and tell you what the whole story is about:

The mystery hidden ("buried") in the Georgian tongue is the mystery of the resurrection through the word of infinite love. The mystery was inscribed as a cipher on the Golden Fleece, which originally had the power to bring a dead man back to life. The magi, and the orphic mystagogues of Colchis, both of whom spoke the "wild" tongue of the wine-drinking panthers living in Asia Minor, inscribed the cipher onto the fleece. The panthers were the sacred animals of Dionysus—the dying and resurrected god of wine and tragedy. The panthers were known for the "sweet smell of their roar," and also because the words they spoke would transform into things, and things would transform into the words they spoke. Thus, the tongue the panthers and, respectively, the magi spoke can be identified as a modification of the language spoken by Adam in Paradise, when he was naming all the beasts of the fields and the fowl of the air, and death had no dominion. The etymological affinity of *Paradis-Pardis/Panther* is also noteworthy: it refers to the Ur-Leopard phase of existence. After the Fall, the primary tongue of Adam was inherited by Noah as he passed through the esoteric initiation rite of being buried through baptism into death, which on the surface (exoterically) was manifested as his drunkenness and nakedness after the flood. This very same tongue was inherited by his son Japheth, whose descendants populated the vast territory from the Pyrenees to India long before the Indo-European invasion (as recorded in Genesis, 10:5). The sacred tongue was spread amongst the Japhetic peoples, and today is known as Proto-Iberian, a language lost during the *Confusio Linguarum* (or, the Confusion of Languages) after Babel and the Indo-European invasion circa the beginning of the second millennium BC. Proto-Iberians densely populated Asia Minor and the Caucasus, from which they migrated westward and eastward, splitting up into several linguistic groups (Basque, Gallic, Ligurian, Caucasian, Dravidian, etc.).

As mentioned previously, the Sacred Tongue was lost, as was the Golden Fleece with its secret cipher. However, the cipher was rediscovered on the maggot-eaten body of Lazarus when Martha and Mary Magdalene bathed him after his resurrection. Mary wrote down the cipher on a tablet, which she then carried with her as she followed the Virgin Mary on her way to Cappadocia. When the Virgin Mary ended her earthly life there, Mary Magdalene buried the tablet at the site of the Virgin's ascension near Ephesus and continued her journey to the land of Gaul.

Three hundred years later, a young woman from Cappadocia, Nino, had a vision that made her go to Ephesus. The Virgin Mary visited her there, passing her the tablet inscribed with the mystery of the Resurrection and ordering her to go to Iberia (the land allotted to the Mother of God) where she was to preach the Word. Hearing about Nino's vision, Queen Helen of Rome, wife of the Emperor Constantine, assisted Nino in her journey to the designated land, where remnants of proto-Iberian (i.e., Georgian-Caucasian) were still spoken. Nino came to Mtskheta, the Iberian capital, and preached the Word of God to King Mirian and Queen Nana, who in 337 AD converted their people to Christianity. As Mirian was of Iranian origin and did not speak Georgian, Nino bequeathed the Sacred Tablet to a local, unknown Gnostic; it was likely he who, inspired by the Golden Fleece Code, composed the *Hymn to the Georgian Tongue*. After that, Nino had another visitation from the Virgin Mary, who ordered her to bury the Tablet in the land allotted to the Mother of God in a place near Mtskheta. Ever since then, all trace of the Tablet was lost and a legend arose in its place—the Legend of the Holy Grail. Yes, it's obvious that the Holy Grail was neither a chalice nor a woman beloved by Jesus; etymologically, the word "grail" comes from the medieval Latin word for "flat dish," *gradal.* "Flat" because it was a tablet, and "dish" because it provided the Bread of Eternal Life. As simple as that!

The rest of the story of the Sacred Tablet brings us to the twelfth century. As mentioned earlier, in 1119, Baldwin, King of Jerusalem, paid a secret visit to the king of Georgia—David the Builder, who during the Crusades was also known as John the Presbyter, or the Priest-King. This happened a year after the Order of the Knights Templar was established in the Holy Land, a period of severe trouble for the Crusaders. Historians interpret the secret visit as an attempt on Baldwin's side to attract King David to the Crusades, which, if successful, would definitely have augmented the Christian forces. However, the question remains: would the powerful king of Jerusalem really cover such a long distance in secret, merely to seek military alliance with the local king no matter how important it was strategically? Men of lower hierarchic position, such as envoys or messengers, could have done it. A likelier answer involves something beyond a military alliance. It was the newly established Knights Templar that sent Baldwin of Jerusalem to King David, as the latter was in possession of the so-called Holy Grail, which as a matter of fact was the Sacred Tablet carrying the Cipher of the Golden Fleece! Alas, this was Baldwin's last chance to save his Crusade. And he got it—his "Holy Grail!" It is not clear how he managed to talk David the Builder into giving away the Tablet; was it possible that cunning Baldwin obtained it in some surreptitious manner? I don't think so. As if a token of his gratitude, Baldwin left behind several hundred of his knights, who served King David and even rode by his side in the glorious victory over the Saracen coalition at the Battle of Didgori in 1121. But how and why did David exchange the life-giving treasure of the Grail for a battalion of skilled warriors? Is it not a repetition of King Aeëtes' original loss of the Golden Fleece?! Or a repetition of his daughter Medea's loss, when she shared the hidden treasure with the "other" and thus gave it away? In any case, the Tablet ended up in Jerusalem, where it disappeared yet again for almost another hundred years.

It was rediscovered in the early thirteenth century in the Georgian Monastery of Jvari (or the Holy Cross) in Jerusalem by a monk and iconographer who had stayed there for a decade and whose secular name was . . . Shota Rustaveli! As mentioned previously, he was exiled from Georgia because of his love of the Queen, but found sanctuary in the Holy Land. It is indisputable that the Tablet was deciphered and read by that very Georgian shamanic-pardimeme-poet, the descendant of the Proto-Iberian Magi. He not only deciphered it, but managed to weave the Sacred Code of the Golden Fleece into the refined texture of his magnum opus—*The Knight in the Panther's Skin.* The Georgian tongue is at its best in this poem, and reading it, one can hear the sweet-smelling roar of the wine-drinking sacred panthers, and the fiery Word of the dying and resurrected god—which is Love, which is God!

Rustaveli's genius substantially transfigured the Golden Fleece

Cipher—or the Lazarus Code—"buried" in the Proto-Iberian-Georgian tongue. He elaborated upon it in such a meticulous and supple manner, that the original message became scattered through the multiple verses of his text, turning the text itself into a cipher of inexhaustible meaning. Having accomplished this . . . Rustaveli destroyed the Tablet! No, it was not an act of revenge because of his exile: a shamanic-pardimeme would never harbor the sentiment of revenge, unless he'd become touched by madness. The destruction of the Tablet was due to the shamanic-poet's creative drive and the preoccupation of his wit with the semiotic play of esoteric symbols and mystifications. From then on, Rustaveli's poem remained the only source of recovering the lost Cipher of the Fleece.

Now you tell me, my friends, what could be a better place than Tiflis to set the scene for the Celestial Love Feast?! Paris? The Louvre, with *Mona Lisa* as the hostess?! Come on! In Tiflis at that time, you could approach any peddler in the street or any shop assistant indoors, and he or she would proudly declare, "Tiflis is a small Paris, my friend!" And truly it was (although this is not the case now). Like the writers of today who, according to J. M. Coetzee, claim at the Gate of the Law to be "secretaries of the invisible," the shamanic-pardimemes of olden days would always follow the directions they got from the "Voices" they heard, painstakingly trying to interpret them. In 1901, some of them heard those very "Voices" referring to some place in between the two seas, and the Cipher of the Golden Fleece. However, there still must have been somebody local who could attract the others to Tiflis—somebody who would act as a liaison man. Without a doubt, the maker of the Sacred Dances, the man of the Fourth Way, George Gurdjieff, alias the *Black Greek*, alias the *Tiger of Turkistan*, could have been just the man.

Gurdjieff's autobiography indicates that he left the Caucasus as early as 1887 and for twenty years, i.e., until 1907, traveled in

Central Asia and the Gobi Desert, "meeting remarkable men." Thus, he could not have been in Tiflis for the Celestial Love Feast. But never trust a shaman telling his/her own life story— their creative imaginations won't let them stick to mere facts. As Gurdjieff scholars have noticed, the memoirs are "innocent of consistency, Aristotelian logic and chronological discipline." Notoriously problematic are the "missing twenty years." The journals of the epoch's great Central Asian geographers (Sir Aurel Stein, Albert von Le Coq, Count Kozui Otani, etc.) do not provide collateral support for Gurdjieff's accounts which, here and there, is understandable. As a matter of fact, Gurdjieff spent half of 1901 in Tiflis, leaving briefly for Livadia, in Crimea, only in July, where he was presented to the Russian Emperor Nicholas II in the guise of a Transcaspian Buddhist.

Thus, Gurdjieff was the liaison man for the Pardimeme "gathering" in Tiflis that spring. And he was not the only one. At that time in the Georgian highlands, there lived a man whose shamanic skill and art by far exceeded Gurdjieff's. He called himself Vazha-Pshavela.

Dagny Juel Przybyszewska arrived in Tiflis on the eighteenth of May, accompanied by her five-year-old son Zenon and her suicidal soon-to-be murderer, Wladyslaw Emeryk. Two other males accompanied her in her thoughts: Stach Przybyszewski, the husband she had left a year earlier, and a young, half-French, half-Polish poet called Wincent Brzozowski, with whom she had carried on an affair after her split with Stach. Dagny and Wincent had moved to a hotel in Krakow, although Wincent poisoned himself several months later. When Dagny heard of his suicide her response was refreshingly simple: "*Ja, er hat das getan*" ("Yes, he has done it"). It was as if she had learned something special about dying and had divulged that knowledge to Wincent. Incidentally, before he took the poison, Brzozowski had left his revolver to Emeryk—the same revolver which would fire in the Grand Hotel in Tiflis, ending Dagny's life. *Yes, he had done it—* and left her a fiery kiss from beyond the grave, because love is as strong as death.

What about Wladyslaw Emeryk then? He was a Pole of Russian extraction: a sensitive, idealistic, emotionally unstable good-for-nothing, the son of a wealthy businessman from Warsaw. It was thanks to his father's support that he ventured to open a salt mine in Georgia, which thanks to his own ineptitude, had gone bankrupt by the time he took Dagny to Tiflis.

Emeryk adored Stach and admired Dagny (or "Ducha," as the Poles called her). At that time, Stach was a celebrity in Poland—a bohemian drinker, a talented writer, and a public intellectual in the avant-garde New Poland movement, which reflected the wave of nationalism then washing over Russia's Central and Eastern-European colonies. Stach and Dagny were the king and queen of the Warsaw bohemiams, and Emeryk's admiration would occasionally materialize as substantial financial support. I would not say this was philanthropy—more like the devotional offerings of a sycophant.

The belief that Dagny followed Wladyslaw Emeryk to Tiflis as his lover had nothing to do with the truth. They definitely did not have a sexual relationship. Just like religious enthusiasm is not enough to receive God's grace, admiration towards a particular woman, no matter how passionate, is not enough to get her into your bed. As it is written—"many are invited, but few are chosen"! In a sense, Emeryk was a castrated priest in Dagny's sacred grove. And insanity was the religion he professed.

Before killing Dagny, Emeryk wrote several letters—to Stach, to Zenon, and to his own friend in Tiflis, Anton Keller, whom he'd meant to arrange Dagny's funeral. "She was not of this world, she was far too ethereal for anyone to understand her true nature . . . That she was an incarnation of the absolute, that she was God, you will learn from others. I only want to tell you that she . . . was a saint. She was goodness itself, the kind of goodness that is called regal and that arises from contempt," he wrote to the five-year-old Zenon. To Stach, he wrote: ". . . I'll have to postpone the whole thing and kill her at a moment when she least expects it . . . *She knows I am going to kill her* . . . she sees it as the only way out, that it has to happen. Stach, I'm killing her for her own sake."

It looks like Emeryk had read too much of Dostoyevsky's *The Idiot*, in which an extraordinary woman is also killed "for her own sake." Art had a far greater influence on fragile minds at that time than it does today. Or he might have come up with his paranoid motivation because of the unconscious eruption in his psyche of an archaic, primordial image of killing and dismembering a goddess in an act of cosmogony—the creation of the World.

Could Dagny herself have inspired this madness in him? Emeryk would never have dared to disclose his intentions to her. Then how would she have realized that he was "going to kill her?" Why did she see it as "the only way out," and "that it had to happen"? Well, women like Dagny Juel who are *larger than life* have a special relationship with death. Or maybe death treats such women in a way that only the beloved are treated? As I cannot speak for death itself, let me speak instead of the extraordinary men who were attracted to women like Dagny Juel.

The train slowly entered the Tiflis railway station like a stream of lava, its breathless steam engine stuttering to a stop. Emeryk was the first to step onto the platform. He waved his hat to Anton Keller, who was hastening towards their car attended by a porter, a local Kurd with a thick mustache. Zenon skipped down the steps, followed by Dagny, who was trying to hold him by the sleeve.

"Careful, my love!" she said.

"Ducha, meet Anton Keller, my partner and friend, my *Peter— the Rock* on which I can build my *Church*." Emeryk introduced his friend to Dagny, who stumbled down the train's iron steps, her dress caught on something there.

"Welcome to Tiflis, Mme Przybyszewska!" Keller blushed with excitement, and attempted to kiss the lady's hand.

"How wonderful to meet you, Mr. Keller!" said Dagny. Shunning his gesture of modest admiration, she embraced him instead in a sisterly manner. "Wlad has spoken so fondly of you ..."

"Don't swoon, Anton," Emeryk said. He seemed to become slightly jealous at this gesture of Dagny's. "Let's look to the luggage."

"Oh yes, certainly." Keller turned to the Kurd and ordered him in colloquial Russian to be more careful with the suitcases.

"With his gorgeous mustache like two huge fangs, this porter resembles Friedrich Nietzsche, doesn't he?!" Dagny's observation made them laugh.

"Mama, I'm thirsty!" Zenon pulled her dress.

"Me too, darling," said Dagny. Turning to Emeryk, she asked, "Do you think they have a buffet here at the station? Could we find a glass of lemonade?"

They walked towards the station building, passing through the variegated and noisy crowd. Some people were dressed in European suits, some in the uniforms of postal workers, policemen, and railway officers. The rest were dressed in traditional apparel, with the men wearing huge fleece hats and leather boots and the women in embroidered vests over satin and silk. Nuns passed in total black, followed by peddlers carrying sweets and candies.

It was cooler and calmer in the buffet; the sounds of a mechanical piano mixed with the sounds of the various languages spoken there—Russian, German, Turkish, Armenian. The Georgians were the loudest—four of them sat in a group drinking champagne.

"Isn't it rather early for champagne at this time of day?" asked Dagny.

"When it comes to drinking, these people lose any sense of time or duration, my dear," explained Emeryk.

They took seats at a table next to the bar and ordered lemonade. Sipping the sweet, refreshing drink, Dagny suddenly felt somebody's gaze *passing* through her. She looked towards the opposite end of the counter and saw a man standing there, leaning on his left hand, his eyes riveted on her.

"Another enormous mustache . . . it seems these gentlemen cannot breathe without bushy hair beneath their nostrils," thought Dagny, and looked away from him.

The man's dark black mustache was really very thick, with its tips curling upward. His eyes were also huge—shining, almost popping from his high forehead; swollen veins stood out on his muscled temples. He wore an angled Turkmen hat on his shaved head. His colored shirt was stained, as were his vest and pantaloons. Nevertheless, he did not look like a tramp—more like a man who had traveled a lot. Neither did he seem to be very poor; responding to the buffet server's question, he ordered French Armagnac and Armenian *basturma*. When he was younger, he was known as the "Black Greek," but after spending a decade in Central Asia, his traveling companions gave him a new name: "Tiger of Turkistan." In another couple decades, he would become famous as George Gurdjieff, a teacher of sacred dances, also known as movements, and of the harmonious development of man.

That day, in the buffet of the Tiflis railway station, the "Tiger of Turkistan" (who had just returned from that very place) was waiting for an acquaintance of his to pick him up and take him to where he was going to stay while in town. The acquaintance's name was Tigran Poghossyan, a twice-removed cousin of his childhood friend Sarkis, with whom he'd discovered the ruins of the "Sarmoung Brotherhood," a school of wisdom founded in ancient Babylon. Tigran was an active member of the Armenian nationalist Dashnak-Zoutyun party, with whom Gurdjieff had once been affilitated, being half Armenian himself and needing money, which the organization did have. As a matter of fact, he'd traveled to Switzerland and then Rome as the Dashnak political envoy, though he'd quit before long because his interests were not strictly nationalist.

In a way, standing there at the counter and drinking Armagnac, Gurdjieff was celebrating his homecoming. He'd worked as a stoker for this railway as a teenager. Earlier, he'd failed to enter the Archdeacon's choir in the Tiflis Religious Seminary—his extraordinary musical talent was meant to manifest itself in a more *universal* way. To this end, he'd studied human and plant biology and a couple years later visited Constantinople, where he befriended Ekim Bey and was introduced to the Bektashi Dervishes and the art of Mevlevi. Afterwards, having discovered a map of "pre-sand Egypt," he redirected himself to Alexandria, where he split up with his friend Sarkis and met Prince Yuri Lubovedsky and professor Skridlov, with whom he visited Thebes, Abyssinia, Sudan, Mecca, Medina, and the remains of Babylon in Nippur. The prince, the professor, and Gurdjieff sought esoteric knowledge, calling themselves the "Seekers of Truth." To facilitate wider travels in Central Asia, Gurdjieff ventured back into politics, and as a Tsarist Russian political agent, established close contacts with high-up Tibetan officials. There in the monasteries of Tibet, he listened to the lamas and learned what he had heard before from Persian Dervishes and would hear again in India, though spoken in different languages; he learned about the Ur-Leopard Unity and its rupture. And it was near Boukhara, in the secret Sarmoung Monastery, that he rendered this knowledge into the tongue of the Divine Individuals, developed his insights about the Endlessness, and conceived his sacred dances. In 1898, while exploring the Gobi desert with Skridlov and the Seekers, Gurdjieff first experienced hints of the Pardimeme Premonition regarding the "Cow's flight to the moon," although the images were extremely vague. The Premonition came back when he was in Baku studying Sufi mysticism, and it was also there that a Daghestani silversmith told him of a shaman living in the central Caucasus highlands in Georgia who called himself Vazha-Pshavela. Afterwards, in Ashgabat, he set up a "Universal Traveling Workshop" and earned large sums of money. On his way through the Pamir Mountains to India, he heard Voices calling for the Cosmic Agape, but once in India the Voices got stronger. Gurdjieff abandoned his companions, the Seekers, and set out for Tiflis.

Now, standing at the counter of the railway station buffet, he felt himself *falling*, as everything existing in the world tends to fall to the bottom of its nearest stability, where all forces arriving from all directions converge. And he saw this point of stability—where his cosmic-erotic forces converged—in the woman sitting with a little boy and two men speaking Polish at a table opposite the counter. *The words, of which our contemporary languages consist, convey, owing to the arbitrary thought people put into them, indefinite and relative notions . . .* in this parenthetic manner, Gurdjieff understood that there was something more to this woman than the words that came to his mind conveyed.

He was beginning to feel some sacred vibration coming from her planetary body, which inundated her entire presence and filled him with trepidation. He felt inside him the crystallization of his pleasure-seeking senses somewhere at the base of his spinal column, in the very rudiments of that special organ described in ancient Gnostic teachings as the *Kundabuffer*, which was once understood to be the chief source of man's deceptions and illusions.

She can't be Polish, he thought. *She looks more Scandinavian . . . and rather aristocratic . . . her aura is magnetic, fed by an excess of unchanneled energy, which she has accumulated from others . . . yes, she has loved a great deal . . . a misguided sufferer, struggling with the*

*heavy mechanics of being human . . . she drags me down too . . . asking
for help . . . shall we dance . . .?*

The woman stood up, casting a glance at him—they were
leaving. As she passed by him, he bowed to her and she responded.
One of the men attending her looked at him with a touch of
irritation around his lips. Gurdjieff made an even deeper bow to
him, too. They left.

"Still glancing after beautiful women, Black Greek?" Gurdjieff
felt somebody's hand on his shoulder. It was Tigran Poghossyan.
"Welcome, my friend, it's been too long."

"Tigran-jan, what a pleasure to see you!" They hugged each
other and kissed three times.

"What brings you to Tiflis? I thought you'd have found a
better place in your travels," said Tigran.

"What brings me here, my friend? Voices brought me, but
they are not clear yet," Gurdjieff explained.

"I see, so you are still talking to ghosts and shaitans?" Tigran
joked.

"They are real, my friend . . . come now, no more. Have some
Armagnac with me."

"No, no, I insist you come with me, I have some excellent old
Kakhetian wine," Tigran countered. "Besides, you must be tired."

"I'm never tired, you know that, Tigran-jan, but let's be off."

"You have nothing else with you—just this sack?!"

"I have much more with me, but you cannot see it," said
Gurdjieff, with a flicker of mock-mystery in his eyes. "Besides, as
Mullah Nassr Eddin, the greatest of wizards, put it: you should
never carry more than you need." They both laughed.

"You'll never change, my Black Greek!" said Tigran as they
walked towards the door.

"I do change, Tigran-jan," Gurdjieff replied. "Only ignorant
people do not change."

Hailing a coach at Railway Square, he saw her again; her

whole group was settling into a carriage. She had the little boy on her lap. "To the Grand Hotel!" someone by her side shouted to the departing coachman.

"How far is the Grand Hotel from where you live?" Gurdjieff asked Tigran. "It must be new. I have not been back here for years . . ."

"Almost fifteen years, my friend! The Grand Hotel is on the Mikhail Bridge; we'll be passing it," said Tigran, turning to give the coachman his address.

"Good, and do you also know the German Garden?" Gurdjieff inquired with a flicker of interest. "Could you walk me there, say, tomorrow?"

"Certainly, but tonight we will visit my reserves of Kakhetian wine, that is the only condition," Tigran maintained.

At the time of Dagny Juel's visit, Tiflis was a very nice and cozy place to live—a sort of small, modest Tower of Babel, a melting pot of nationalities, languages and styles. But—*a melting pot*?! No. As one of my colleagues recently clarified for me, Tiflis was more like a bowl full of salad, in which different cultures were mixed, though still maintaining their individual identities.

Dagny's ride to the hotel encompassed her private thoughts and worries, and some instances of sightseeing with Keller and Emeryk as her guides. They took Mikhail Street, which had a couple of theaters and hotels on it, as well as lots of shops and taverns. They passed the German chapel, and then turned off towards the Vorontsov Embankment, from which a panorama of the city opened up.[10] "The hunchbacked Tiflis," as Osip Mandelshtam, the Russian-Jewish poet-martyr, would later call the city.

It was a gorgeous afternoon: green trees in golden sunshine with blue patches of sky in between. Dagny had never been this

10. The German chapel in Tbilisi was pulled down during World War II, and the Germans living in Georgia were deported to Kazakhstan.

far east before, and she noticed how different the sun felt, and how mild the air. What if she stayed here for good? Iwa, her sweet, sweet Iwa, her little daughter—she should have brought her here too, but how? It was as if she'd left her on another planet . . . yes, Norway and her sisters were worlds away from here . . . *Now in a land sunlit and far away / Bathed in sun I sit and watch / And feel the power in my heart* . . . no, she was a woman without an existence, with nothing . . . Wincent was dead . . . she was nobody . . . she didn't even have a bureaucratic identity on paper. Stach was supposed to arrange passports for her and Zenon, and send them to Tiflis . . . she was nobody . . . she would love to get lost in this sunshine, in the leaves—leaving her identity behind . . . she needed to write Stach and ask for the passports . . . she didn't sleep well on the train, it was stuffy and noisy, but the air now was so refreshing . . . *Sleep! Sleep! / The angry voices grow silent. / As if the day has spoken far too many words* . . . could she start over again with Stach? He'd promised to join her, and they could stay here, together for good, reunited, for good, and with Iwa also . . . yes, he'd join her as soon as he was fed up with Jadwiga . . . Stach, that screwing and drinking piglet . . . she'd met him in the *Schwarze Ferkel* (the "Black Piglet"), a tavern in Berlin where all the artists went . . . she saw the same kind of wine-bags here . . . the black piglet wine-bags . . . the owner of that tavern must have been from Tiflis . . . they said he was Armenian . . . oh, just look at this horseman passing by—what a triumphant posture, as if he had conquered the whole world! Dressed like a Cossack . . . those white things on his chest were for bullets, she assumed. She glanced over at the hot-tempered and arrogant Georgian next to her. Emeryk was so funny—he was jealous about everything to do with her. He looked slightly mad . . . so pensive and nervous . . . a weak man . . . it is through such weakness that a man might come up with murder one fine day . . . no, how could she think of him like this? She was such an ungrateful woman . . . we all are weak—all of us. She was getting older—she'd be thirty-four soon. *The last dance* . . . but that man in the railway station buffet! His eyes were like strong, muscled hands squeezing her, *wrapping her in queen's robes and setting a queen's invisible crown on her head* . . . his had been a truly occult gaze. Wincent was also crazy about the occult sciences . . . had it been Wincent who had looked at her then, from the beyond? Could she still attract men? Those weak-nervous-pensive-drinking-screwing-piglet-men? She'd been clinging to one such man, trying to hold her world together . . . how stupid, how childish . . . you can't hold the world together with a man like Stach. Now she was clinging to Emeryk—God! How infantile she was! Lovely chapels in this city . . . so many of them . . . the people here must be very pious. She'd once meant for her house to be the house of love, but Stach had made it into a den of bigots . . . she was called "the love queen" by friends back in Berlin: the love queen of little black piglets. They preached "free love" and masturbated before cultivated scenes of punishment for the sake of that very "freedom."

They were passing a mysterious mountain with a railroad and a small chapel on the slope. Emeryk told her it was called Mount Salvage, the "Holy Mountain." Dagny felt her salvation would be there . . . the mountain looked as strong as the gaze of that man in the buffet . . . for love is strong as death . . . she'd thought that as he was looking at her, there in the station . . . and she felt herself slipping deep into the wine-dark waters, *her golden hair a wreath of fire!*

"The Grand Hotel," Dagny read aloud from the top of a five-story building opposite the bridge they were crossing. There were mills along the river, a big white chapel with three domes, houses, and caravansaries . . . the bridge was crowded with pedestrians and carriages; there were shops on both sides . . . the bridge! Eddie Munch had painted that screaming face on this very bridge . . .

this bridge would take her where *my pale dead meet in festival /
their moon-sick faces giving birth / to a new and lasting peace for
them and me* . . .
 Looking up, she caught sight of the striped dome of a big
temple—a Russian Orthodox temple in the Moorish style, how
eclectic . . . why was she in this place? Mamma . . . Iwa . . . what
was this careless course of action she'd chosen? Her sisters Astrid,
Gudrun and Ragnhild . . . what was going to happen to them?
Might she stay in this city for good?
 Yes, Dagny Juel would stay here for good—but in the local
cemetery.[11]

That spring, Vazha-Pshavela began working on his masterpiece,
a poem called *The Snake-Eater*. He was forty and living in the
highland village of Chargali, where he combined "creative
scribbling" with hunting, teaching at the local elementary school,
and fistfighting. He also spent much of his time talking to
plants, animals and rocks—having obtained knowledge of their
sacred tongues ten years earlier, when he contracted anthrax and
exchanged his eye for the honey of poetry. This came to pass in
the remotest of mountainous villages, "as lovely to behold as a
woman's breasts," as he himself put it elsewhere.
 The Snake-Eater was conceived by Vazha-Pshavela in order to
narrate his own experience as a shamanic-Pardimeme. He chose
the Faustian paradigm, portraying an "exalted insider" whose
initiation took twelve years, during which he had to stay with
demonic creatures and eat snakes with them, and through this
receive the multiplicity of tongues spoken by non-human beings.
The story takes place in the time of Queen Tamar—and thus the

11. Buried in 1901 at the Koukia cemetery in Tiflis, Dagny's body was re-
interred in 2001 in a small pantheon there, not far from the tomb of another
victim of deranged male violence: Tamriko Chovelidze was only seventeen
when she was killed by Soviet troopers during a punitive operation to disperse
a nationalist independence rally in Tbilisi on April 9, 1989.

hereditary link with the acme of Georgian Pardimeme tradition was reestablished.

Vazha-Pshavela wrote in the austere language of highland folk poetry, using compressed syntax and an abrupt, dislocated narrative style. Through this very crudeness, he imparted a gloomy message of the isolation and loneliness of a mind haunted by transcendent worlds. The fact that plants and animals speak in his writings can by no means be identified as a so-called "pathetic fallacy"—the term John Ruskin coined to describe the tendency of some poets and painters to ascribe to nature the feelings of human beings. No, the "pathetic fallacy" is a mere artistic device, while in Vazha-Pshavela's case we see how a shamanic mind *translates* the supra-human language into a human one: his is a painstaking hermeneutical attempt to overcome the total misconception through which humans deal with nature; or how a man as *Being-there* deals with the *Being* as it unfolds.

In a short narrative poem ("The Wounded Tiger," written in 1890), Vazha-Pshavela tells the story of his encounter with the mystery of the Ur-Leopard. A hunter, roaming hungry in the forest, seeks game that never appears—a cursed hunt. Suddenly he catches sight of a tiger lying by the river, its paw bleeding, the blood tinting the waters red. This totally exhausted and vulnerable creature asks the hunter for death, but the hunter cures its wound instead. The tiger runs away, and then a mysterious phenomenon begins: each animal the hunter shoots dead turns out to be that very tiger, the ubiquitous and polymorphous giver of life.

Pshavela was also able to trace and read various inscriptions scattered across forests, meadows and mountain slopes. Once, on Christmas Eve, he was staying with some lumberjacks. When a pine tree was chopped down, he suddenly saw ink coming out of it, spelling words in the snow. The words were written in a childish hand, in which somebody invisible entreated the men to abstain from their greed and heed the forest's creatures that were dying at the men's hands.[12]

Pshavela was obsessed with the rupture of the Ur-Leopard Unity, after which the leomemic preoccupation with power and the dominion of law and tradition would crush Pardimeme individualism, with its fanatics of Love and wizards of letting-be. In his bitter narrative poems, *Aluda Ketelaouri* and *Host and Guest*, he hypostasized himself into the rebellious individuals who would break up the commune's imperative and therefore be destroyed. They were not destroyed because they fell into that old classical hubris—no, it was the Leomeme rulers of the Cowmeme commune who proved hubristic in their determination to maintain the established rules and regulations (such as the imperative to cut off the hand of one's defeated enemy). Thus Mindia the "Snake-Eater" is destroyed too, since by providing for his family, he had assumed Cowmeme responsibilities, and later acted as a leomeme chief-commander during the war of his people against the invaders. These actions deprived him of the magic powers he'd received, and out of sheer disenchantment, made him commit the gravest sin for a Pardimeme—suicide. In the poem's final passage, which depicts Mindia's suicide, Pshavela almost opens up his own wounds as the mouths through which non-human nature speaks:

> The moon shed its light upon the ridge,
> Where alone the wild goats live,
> And fixed in its beams the suicide
> With the hue of a mourning girl.
> And the soft breeze wafted to and fro,
> Carefree, singing a peaceful song.
> It brushed its wings on the sword's sharp point,

12. Pshavela witnessed several episodes of this kind. In 1909, he described one of them in a poem called "Christmas Carol."

Which jutted out, a bright red tongue
Stained by the juice of the human chest.
It began to frolic over the green,
Whistling cheerfully, proud and free.

That year, drafting the first stanzas of his new poem, Vazha-Pshavela observed the birth of spring—the first spring of the nascent century. He fasted a lot and rambled ascetically, driving his wife and children to quail at nights in the cowshed, *where the Cowmemes were supposed to stay*, so that none would distract his unleashed mind. And that was the time when he had the first clear flashes of the Pardimeme Premonition.

First he saw a wounded speckled eagle, warring with crows and ravens and dragging one wing on the ground, its chest bleeding. Since ravens are shamanic birds themselves, this was a clear omen of the coming war between the false shamans and the Pardimemes; he sensed repressions, exiles and the execution of free and creative minds; the solid color of the attacking birds implied the onslaught of a uniform and totalizing identity upon the variety of difference.

Next, Pshavela saw a roe deer fawn being slaughtered by a hunter, his hands and his knife stained with its blood. The hunter peeled back the poor creature's skin, put salt on it, and hung the hide on a tree. There, on the hide of the roe deer fawn, he read words spelled out in tiny speckles: "The Passion is the Passage!"

And then he saw himself speaking to a lovely violet, telling it that worms would come and eat it up; that if the violet believed life to be an open door to paradise, it should not come into this world, and should stay hidden in the earth; he begged the earth to protect the violet, and to be a parent to it, as was its wont.

After this, he saw giants at a wedding feast eating boiled human flesh and inviting him to eat it too . . . he wept, and saw a woman's breast burning bright, and a bleeding cut-off hand squeezing it. And then he saw a panther with sparkling stars on its back. The panther said: "To the Lowland City go!"

Later his wife found him lying in a swamp, feverishly murmuring, "The Cosmic Agape! The Celestial Love Feast!"

It took Vazha-Pshavela seven weeks to recover. One gorgeous morning in mid-May, he rushed out of bed, and, grinning at his wife from out a rudely awakened face, stuffed some manuscripts into his saddlebag, mounted his horse and made straight for Tiflis.

You haven't been to Tiflis until you've been to the Tiflis baths—even the Shah of Iran, Agha Mahmad Khan, who destroyed the city in 1795, went there straight after the battle (even though, having enjoyed them very much, he later ordered the baths burnt down). Praised by Pushkin and Alexander Dumas, the Tiflis baths are unique in their combination of inferno, purgatory and paradise; if only Dante could have come here, he would have seen the three in one. The hot, sulfuric, subterranean water smells like hell; the heat together with the special felt-glove *qissa* massage purges you of filth both physical and existential; the deep breath of cool air taken after coming out into the antechamber, along with the sip of tea or beer or whichever beverage they serve, makes you feel like the lead voice in a choir of saints.

Poor or wealthy, sick or healthy, everybody goes to the Tiflis baths! After all, this is the site where the city of Tiflis was born—out of this hellish sulfur smell and the hot natal waters filtered down from its mother-fortress, the Narikala. As a matter of fact, the founding of the city fifteen centuries ago is associated with another Shamanic Individual, though in reality he was a king and thus must be regarded as a Leomeme. However, the Georgian King Vakhtang Gorgaslan (Gorgasali), the founder of Tiflis, obviously had werewolf powers. Known as the "wolf-man" or the "wolf-headed king" not only because he wore a wolf-inspired military uniform, he could turn into a huge wolf on the battlefield and cast terror over his adversaries. Besides, Vakhtang was also an unsurpassable hunter, just like his spirit animal. It was precisely during the royal bird-hunt that the city was founded. A falcon launched by the king was chasing a brilliantly colored pheasant, when both birds fell into a spring of hot subterranean water. Carefully studying the site and taking in the healing powers of the hot spring, Vakhtang the "wolf-man" decreed a city should be built there and named it Tbilisi, as *tbili* is the Georgian for "warm."

That's how the city was founded, and due to the magic of its name, the inhabitants of Tbilisi or Tiflis are neither hot nor cold but always warm. Yes, such a positioning proved to be the city's destiny. "Tbilisi is like a kind of Janus: one face towards Asia and the other towards Europe," as some travelers would later write in their journals.

The Black Greek had had too much red Kakhetian the night before and his head felt heavy. The Azeri masseur was ruthless; scraping with the *qissa*, he almost peeled off Gurdjieff's swarthy skin, weather-beaten from the Gobi desert winds and the muggy air of the Indian jungle. Bending and twisting Gurdjieff's limbs, stretching and squeezing, the Azeri seemed to have the sole intention of turning Gurdjieff into a piece of dough and then baking him. Moreover, he even dared to stand on Gurdjieff's back, but beginning to slip, he stepped down. Telling Gurdjieff to lie face up, with both hands the Azeri pressed his client's breast-bone just like a medical man would in order to make a stopped heart start, and Gurdjieff's heart did go—with a new charge of frightening energy. Next came the bucket of hot water to rinse off the threads of dirt rolled up by the felt glove. No matter how often you shower or bathe, the *qissa* glove will always detect the invisible uncleanness of your body. Finally, the Azeri appeared with a kind of silk bag resembling a pillow case, put a lot of soap on it, filled it with air like a balloon, and then, squeezing it out, produced a cloud of foam over Gurdjieff's head and body. The soap smelled of lilac and it was very soft against his skin . . . he felt drowsy, though was awakened by yet another bucket of hot water, and then it was over.

"I've been in this trade for more that twenty years," the masseur said, "my father did this, my grandfather, my great-grandfather . . . we, the Azeri, are the best *qissa*-men."

You certainly are, thought Gurdjieff, making his way over to a basin in the floor filled with sulphurous water. Getting slowly into the basin he told the guy: "The money is on the table, thank you very much my friend, take care."

"May the power of Allah stay with you, Agha-jan!" said the Azeri, and left humming a tune about the love of Lyla and Majnoun: "From stillness dance arises . . . we enter the silence of our own presence, relaxed of body and mind . . . we enter stillness . . . when we turn our attention to stillness, a new energy will arise in us . . . when we move this energy the body will follow . . . and the dance comes alive in us . . . "

Sitting wrapped in white sheets and sipping very strong tea from a Turkish *ince belli*, or slim-waisted, glass, Gurdjieff enjoyed the stillness around him, letting it linger. The thought of the dance and the dance of the thought arose in his still mind.

Movements make up the universe—the movements of opposites, of contradictions. Through sacred dance, man will regain his position in the cosmos as the maintainer of the moon and *Anulios*—the unseen satellite circling around planet Earth. But if the "Cow flies to the moon" and the masses go mad, the correspondence shall be lost, at least in this solar system. Man must come up with adequate *movements* to match the movements of the universe; he needs music that matches the Music of the Spheres . . . Pythagoras . . . he needs music because he needs meaning, since only music provides maximum meaning in the least materiality.

But what meaning? The Voices that had sent Gurdjieff to Tiflis had spoken of a Love Feast, of a Cosmic Agape . . . what had this to do with the Dance and the Music? That woman at the railway station he'd met yesterday—she'd stayed in his mind all night, and the red wine opened up the way to that woman in his veins and muscles and testicles and penis and through the rudiments of his Kundabuffer upwards through his spinal column, filling it up with celestial sounds . . . he thought of Pythagoras again . . . she carried an unusual charge of erotic energy within her. He needed to see her while in Tiflis—what if she joined him on his travels? The Grand Hotel at the Mikhail Bridge . . . the Voices had spoken of a German garden where the coming event should be held, and there was such a garden on Mikhail street . . . but Mikhail was the Czar's brother, and so there were many "Mikhail" streets in Tiflis!

The German Garden . . . thus, Gurdjieff learned the name of the place, but he did not yet know the date. The Agape might take days, who could tell? Time . . . he'd better be going . . .

Maidan Square, next to the baths, was at the heart of the heart of town. It was the major marketplace, attracting goods from the East and money from the West and the North. But this was not just a place for commercial exchange—around it, you could find a Shiia Muslim mosque, Georgian Orthodox and Armenian Gregorian Chapels, and a Jewish synagogue. It was also an open market of religious exchange: a den of thieves surrounded by houses of the Lord.

It does not matter where you pray, my friend—just be a man in everything.

Gurdjieff loved marketplaces like this one—he had seen hundreds of them while traveling the globe. But Maidan Square certainly celebrated diversity like nowhere else.

Although he was still sweating after the bath, Gurdjieff felt absolutely refreshed and full of energy. Making his way among the traders and peddlers in the broad sunshine, he felt the light shining down on his head like never before. He decided to make straight for the German Garden to investigate the site of the upcoming mysterious event. Since he had to get to the left bank, he walked towards Avlabari Bridge. Suddenly, as he was passing a small *chaikhana*, a man was kicked out of it with curses and laughter, falling right at Gurdjieff's feet.

"Didn't I once say that the whole world is based on contradictory forces?! The kick I just received was the consequence of exactly this order, I swear by the most desired, most venerable Al-Mu'tasim!" said the kicked-out man as Gurdjieff helped him up.

Dressed in a threadbare jacket, ragged pants, barefoot and lacking a shirt and underwear, this man looked very much like an Iranian, though he spoke crystal-clear Georgian. Gurdjieff, acquainted with many different tongues though master of none, spoke pretty decent Georgian—or, at least his Georgian, like his Persian, was much better than his curiously broken Russian.

As the poor fellow straightened up, he looked at Gurdjieff and declared, "How good to see you, Tiger of Turkistan! Or do they still call you the Black Greek?"

His long aquiline nose was bleeding.

"Both," replied Gurdjieff, slightly nonplussed.

"My name is Sohrab, Sohrab Addin the Noble," the threadbare-jacket-ragged-pants-barefoot man introduced himself.

"I'm not sure we've met before." Gurdjieff was polite.

"Why, have we not met in Constantinople—that fabulous city of Byzantium? You came to study some Dervish practices there . . ." Sohrab Addin then began to singsong a lament: "Love's fool am I; Love's favorite am I . . . Love destroyed me and Love elevated me to see the agate curls of God, who is Love, which is All . . . its center is everywhere, and circumspection nowhere, I swear by the golden beak of our Lord Simourg!"

"Yes, it is so, but you are not a true Dervish, you just mock them," said Gurdjieff, trying to get rid of the dirty fellow and move on.

"Wait, wait, my Tiger!" Sohrab Addin clutched his hand passionately. "You don't know me, but I know your mission here and there is something I have to disclose about the Celestial Love Feast, or the Cosmic Agape!"

These last words changed Gurdjieff's mind; *the tramp could be a messenger*. He looked into Sohrab's eyes, still harboring some doubt.

"What can you disclose?"

"Buy me a drink, I need to boost those brain cells in charge of words and their connections," Sohrab Addin the Noble wheedled.

Gurdjieff smiled and then, hesitating, produced a small flask of Armagnac from his inner pocket and passed it to the mock-Dervish.

"Thank you, my Tiger! May Al-Mu'tasim open up Himself to you!" With enthusiasm, Sohrab Addin swiftly grabbed the flask and opened it as if to demonstrate what Al-Mu'tasim would do. "May you drink from His golden flasks . . ." with a substantial gulp, Sohrab devoured three quarters of the liquor. He choked and, coughing, returned the flask back to the owner, wiping his mouth with the tainted sleeve of his disgusting jacket.

"Speak up," Gurdjieff said.

"I think we'd better walk; the message that I have to pass on needs movement, after the peripatetic fashion of Aristu the Sage or Aristotle, as your ancestors named him," Sohrab said, taking the Black Greek by the hand and moving towards the bridge.

Anyone other than Gurdjieff would have swooned from the stench coming off that fellow's clothes, but he'd learned to tolerate such discomforts, having met all kinds of Dervishes in his life, even mock-ones like this one walking by his side and speaking rapidly.

"The fact of the matter, my Tiger, is that what I have to tell you will make greater sense to you than it does to me—I'm just a deliverer, *a vehicle* if you like . . . the Voices that I heard before told me that you're pretty skilled in esoteric crafts and occult knowledge, for which I've never cared a fart, to put it mildly."

"Thank you, my noble one, for being so frank in your ignorance." Gurdjieff was beginning to like the fellow.

"Shall we proceed?" asked Sohrab.

"Oh, yes," the other nodded.

"I don't have to be here dressed in these nasty clothes and with my nose broken . . . but something makes me do this, although I don't know what. Maybe the mind of some higher order, which I can't interpret? But these are only wild and whirling words. Let me tell you what I do know: I'm here to deliver a message that deals with music and this is why I have accepted this fate. Yes, the whole damned thing is about the movements and the music!"

"That's what I thought it would be," Gurdjieff said with appreciation.

"So then, let me tell you something that you know. All movements in the universe come from the interplay of contradictions, and their succession is endless, as is the endlessness of our His-Most-Endlessness. However, all these myriad contradictions come from the primordial one—the contradiction between existence and nonexistence. And it is obvious that this Primordial Contradiction encompasses all the rest as they unfold. But here comes the question—what is the mysterious essence that maintains this Primordial Contradiction? It is the sacred substance Askokin; it is Love."

At this word, Sohrab started his melodic lamentation yet again. "Love is the third of the two, of existence and nonexistence; Love holds them together as the holy meaning of the Primordial Contradiction. Yes, Love as the third out of the two is the meaning. And as all contradictions come from the primordial one, Love is the meaning of all meanings in the universe . . ."

"Calm down, my friend, I know all this," Gurdjieff said, trying to pacify him. "It brings us to, and could be subsumed under, the Law of Reciprocal Maintenance of all existence, originally discovered by Makary Kronbernkzion—'the involution of the causes and the evolution of the effects.'"

"What goes up, must go down," sang the mock-Dervish. "Methinks your Makary, who lived on the continent Atlantis thousands of years ago, himself could be subsumed under the laws of Hegel's dialectics: 'The effect of a cause must always re-enter the cause.'"

"Well, Makary has been misread by many people, regrettably, and they ended up with that ignorant distinction between good and evil."

"There is only one evil—Entropy!" the mock-Dervish interrupted him passionately. "Entropy will kill the universe if the contradictions diminish. The universe needs to remain a complex dynamic system, and Love is the meaning that keeps everything going. Love is zero entropy—the meaning is zero entropy! Behold, my Tiger, you need this meaning for your mission, and you will get it from music."

"What kind of music?"

"The one that provides maximum meaning in the least materiality."

"All music does so . . ."

"But there is one kind which provides more than maximum meaning in less than the least materiality . . . the music created by the greatest shaman of all time!" Sohrab Addin stopped in admiration.

"Who is he?" Gurdjieff asked, becoming intrigued.

"You'll learn the name later . . . now my Tiger, it's time for me to specify your task: give me one more drink." He stopped again.

Gurdjieff took out his flask and opened it. The mock-Dervish drank it bottoms up, put the flask into his pocket, and continued, "Together with the other Shamanic Individuals, you'll have to process this music through your awareness, extract Love as the sacred meaning of Primordial Confrontation out of it, and translate this into the language of the movements of thought that traverse the fields of thermodynamics and information. You know these movements—they're what you call the Sacred Dances, in which I see a mixture of corporeality and knowledge, where movement means and meaning moves. Transcribe these movements into the holy texts of Love and disseminate them!" He stopped once more.

"The holy texts of love? How do I perform this dissemination?"

"You'll disseminate the Body of Love for people to eat in the holiest of communions, and you will save the masses from the upcoming madness, in other words, you will stop the Cow from flying to the moon, as simple as that," was the answer.

"But how exactly can I disseminate the Body of Love?"

"Don't get too ambitious, my friend, remember—you are just the liaison man. A special navigation center will be set up on Saturn to arrange and manage communications through the etherograph system, and since you know the system well, you'll take charge of the network here.[13] Through the etherograms, you'll be able to attract the best shamanic minds to this city, where east meets west and north meets south! Draw in the minds that are the major nerve endings of the earth, through which planetary vibrations are received for transmission! The desired dissemination will happen through these very planetary vibrations."

"Vibrations . . . whose music do I have to process? Who is the greatest shaman of all time?"

13. I would suggest that the "etherograph system" was Beelzebub's preconception of the Internet. However, his contained a much higher degree of virtuality than what we know today. To an extent, the system was based on the exchange of ideas suspended in the air.

"His name is inscribed on my back," Sohrab the Noble said, taking off his jacket. "One of your divine individuals inscribed it there for you; he told me he originally came from some place in Central Asia."

Gurdjieff considered the inscription on the mock-Dervish's skinny back. It read: *Shaman of Haizanakh.*

"Haizanakh . . . Eisenach . . . you mean this shaman is Bach?!" Gurdjieff was slightly disappointed, as he preferred to deal with something more Pythagorean.

"Forget your Pythagoras, for God's sake; his music is too scientific for this task. On the other hand—what could be closer to the Primordial Contradiction than the counterpoints and fugues of the Haizanakh Shaman?! I specify your task as follows: you will have to engage the shamanic minds of the Orient to read and interpret the medium through which the Occidental mind spoke its utmost—Bach's music." The drunken Dervish took out the empty flask from his pocket, and, seeing that it was empty, put it back. "Don't ask me any more—I'm through. The rest is up to you and your companions. As your esteemed Hoja Nassr Eddin would say, ahem, *Ars longa, vita brevis.* There are more details of the sacred event on the poster at the gate of the German Garden. By the way, this all has something to do with the panther's skin poem—have you read it? The Voices have not been very forthcoming about this so far. But I'm sure all will clear up in time . . . I'll see you there, my Tiger!" And with the agility of Guido Cavalcanti jumping over the cemetery wall, he jumped from the bridge into the turbid waters of the river.

"I hope next time the Voices will send me a messenger more reliable than a drunken one," Gurdjieff thought, and walked straight on.

It was a long walk to the German Garden, but as Gurdjieff had to digest the jumbled advice he'd received from the mock-Dervish, walking was—*in the peripatetic fashion of Aristu*—truly apropos. The Tiger of Turkistan had never been very enthusiastic about occidental art and culture, let alone its music. The Truth was out there—but in the East. The West was meant to provide a mere material basis, mostly a financial one, to help eastern Truth to flourish and reach the people. Bach . . . "the greatest shaman of all time"? When in Switzerland on that ridiculous Dashnak mission, Gurdjieff met a musicologist—what was his name? Ah yes, his name was Kurt. The fellow was concerned about the crisis in "Romantic harmony"—what a stupid notion, "Romantic." Wagner's *Tristan und Isolde* was the beginning of the end of that "harmony," Kurt said. But he was obsessed with Bach—all those "linear counterpoints" and "melodic polyphonies" . . . well, some of his ideas regarding musical energy and movements did echo Gurdjieff's concept of the dance, but when asked for his opinion on Eastern Asian throat singing, Kurt had said that it was "too primitive." Alas, the dull and "primitive" Western ear could not catch the beauty of throat singing—the magnificence of the overtones, the stamina of the sounds . . . Eastern art was based on mathematics, while Western art drew on sheer sentiment.

To accomplish the musical task set for the Cosmic Agape, he would need people with special abilities . . . he would need the support of the Leader of the Seven: the great keeper and transmitter of the teachings of Saint Krishnatkharna. He would need the Leader's presence, direct communication with his reason and his higher-being body, that's what he would need . . . Through etherograms, he'd also have to communicate his message to the few members of the Akhaldan Brotherhood who were still alive—*the men striving to become aware of the Being of beings.* Hailing from ancient Atlantis, they were dispersed all over the earth, some of them in Europe, and known as the *philosophers of existence.* Absolutely essential to the project of channeling the sacred vibrations of Love was the virtual presence of the Chinese King Too-Toz, the inventor of an apparatus which could span seven octaves of whole tones, the total consonance of which coincided with the great World Sound, discovered by yet another ancient member of the Akhaldan. The whole arrangement of strings on that apparatus corresponded to the concise arrangement of vivifying sources between any planet and the Sun Absolute. But how could Bach, that sausage-eating burgher, have any awareness of the World Sound and the seven octaves?! It could never be found in his music, which evolved from a tainted source—all music is blessed, though. The Shaman of Haizanakh?! On the other hand, the inscription on the mock-Dervish's back must have been made by Kerbalai-Aziz-Nuaran . . . Nuaran—a true Dervish, though a watchmaker by trade. He was living near Boukhara and was friends with the marvelous musical scientist Hadji-Astvatz-Troov, the discoverer of the law of vibrations, who was studying the theories of Malmanash, Selneh-eh-Avaz, and Pythagoras. Together with Nuaran, he invented a mechanical piano to be tuned in one-eighth tones according to the ancient Chinese absolute sound "*do.*" Why had the Voices indicated Bach to Nuaran and Troov?! It didn't make sense. Some shamanic initiates said that Troov was going to engage himself in scrutinizing the question: "Why did God make the louse and the tiger?" Why does something exist and not the other way around? The Primordial Contradiction . . . Love is its sacred meaning . . . it shall be disseminated through planetary vibrations . . . through the clear and dynamic movements of thought . . . the dances . . . the Cow will fly to the moon, unless it learns to dance . . . ha-ha . . . and yes, he would have to go see that poet-highlander . . . where? Since the Voices had mentioned him, that meant the poet would show up somewhere . . . yes, but what about that panther's skin poem?

Gurdjieff stood at the gate of the German Garden on Mikhail Street, across from the Mikhail Hospital, and read the following poster:

Monday, June 4th, 1901
8 o'clock in the evening, in the hall of the German
    Garden:
Positively the grandest and
Definitely the most sensational spectacle:
The well-known traveler Gene Morris (for the
second time in town) will present
**A magic lantern show, projecting "mystical
pictures"** from the poem by the famous Shota
Rustaveli:
The Knight in the Panther's Skin
(Illustrations by the court painter, Mr. Zitch)
Followed by:
The Leipzig Orchestra and Choir, presenting
    excerpts from the
St. John Passion by the German composer **Bach**
Followed by:
Pictures of the England-Transvaal War and the
    Chinese War!
The event is sponsored by the Marcus Samuel and
Alfred Nobel companies in Batumi and Baku
Co-sponsored by the Georgian Landowners Bank
and the Georgian Literacy Society
Snacks and drinks will be served during
    intermission
Tickets without stamps are invalid.

"What has the panther's skin poem by Rustaveli got to do with
Christ's Passion according to Saint John set to music by Bach?!"
He was nonplussed. At that very moment, his brain located an
etherogram:

Oh, East is East, and West is West, and never the
twain shall meet,
Till Earth and Sky stand presently at God's great
Judgment Seat;
But there is neither East nor West, Border, nor Breed,
nor Birth,
When two strong men stand face to face, tho' they
come from the ends of the earth!

He had fourteen more days to prepare for the Cosmic
Agape.

From her very first day in Tiflis, Dagny attracted a fair amount
of attention when she showed up in public places. The attention
mostly came from Georgian males, delivering glances that were
more overtly suggestive than those of the man who'd looked at her
in the railway station buffet. She was "blonde, slender, elegant and
dressed with a refinement that well knew how to accentuate her
body's suppleness . . ." as one of her admirers from the Schwarze
Ferkel remembered.

Such women—I mean the "blonde and slender"—held a
unique position in the sexual fantasies of Georgian males, maybe
because the majority of Georgian females were brunettes. But
such a quantitative explanation is irrelevant. Blondes have always
been something special for the male sexual appetite. Besides, a
hundred years ago when my story takes place, Tiflis women were
more restricted in terms of erotic relationships than were their
"blonde and slender" European or Russian counterparts. Consider
for example the twelve hundred young Georgian intellectuals who
had to flee the country in 1726 and immigrate to Russia in order
to escape yet another Persian invasion . . . what happened to their
remarkable intellectual capabilities when they found themselves
among so many slender and inviting blondes? Well, some of them

ended up as important contributors to the fledgling Russian academe, but most were lost to scholarly activities, choosing to experiment instead with more sensuous substances. Or maybe I'm exaggerating . . .

Either way, Dagny Juel Przybyszewska must have been a remarkable addition to the Tiflis social scene. It wasn't only on account of her supple figure; everything about her seemed attractive: the way she wore her hat, the way she sipped her wine, the way she smoked her cigarette—oh yes, that angel with a cigarette in her mouth would catch the eye of every student or military officer, every hot-blooded noble, every sticky-fingered servant. Her style, a mixture of bohemian and aristocratic, stirred up many who shared her company. To her, there was nothing unusual in the way she attracted men—after all, she had been "the queen" of the Berlin and Warsaw artistic circles. But here in Tiflis, she felt more heat in the looks of those who coveted her—as if undressing her and wrapping her in the hot southern temperature. These looks were more outspoken than those she was used to in Europe. Passing men at social gatherings in Tiflis, Dagny felt like a woman—yes, a woman, and not an "object of absolute intellectual inspiration," or "the sphinx" or whatever garbage she'd hear back in Berlin. With their glances, these men delivered hot waves—sometimes squalls—of desire and excitement, and she felt them like . . . remember the superb description by D. H. Lawrence of Connie Chatterley passing a meadow on the way to her lover? Her erotic perception of the nature around her? No, this allusion is misguiding . . .

All this male attention only occasionally distracted Dagny from her real problems: Stach was not responding to her telegrams, in which she implored him to make arrangements to send passports for her and Zenon; she fiercely missed her sisters and her daughter Iwa; her future here was murky, and Emeryk seemed to be having problems too; he was jealous about everything and everybody around Dagny in Tiflis, but, poor thing, he could not speak because he was not supposed to be jealous—he was just a friend, a friend who'd assumed the responsibility of looking after her. Besides, his salt business was collapsing, and his spending was getting worse. *She should not have come here— she should not have accepted his invitation . . . how irresponsible, how frivolous of her . . .*

The same night she sat worrying, she was hosted by a certain Count Avalishvili, or Avalov.[14] Anton Keller and Wlad Emeryk were also present at the dinner Avalov gave. They sat in the restaurant of the Hotel London, right across from the hotel where she was staying. Little Zenon was back in her room with a Polish nurse, hired for such occasions.

Dagny enjoyed the Tiflis food—flavorful, spicy stuff with cilantro and walnuts in almost everything (aubergines, beans, cabbage). Then there were strange vegetables, like spinach and beets. She liked the wine too—the red Kakhetian especially.

"This morning at breakfast we were given a wonderful dish, curds mixed in with mint to taste. What do they call it, Wlad?" asked Dagny.

"It's called *matsoni*, a sort of a condensed milk—buffalo milk, to be more precise," Anton Keller explained.

"*Matsoni* is the chief dairy product in this area, especially in the highlands—a very healthy foodstuff, good for the stomach, the gall bladder, the liver, everything," Count Avalov said. "The day will come when it will conquer the dairy market all over the world!"[15]

"And it is especially good after too much Kakhetian the night before," Keller noted, kidding.

"No wonder—these people drink so much, I do not doubt

14. Several years later Count Avalov married Dagny's friend, Maya Vogt (who was also Stach's lover). In 1905, Maya Vogt settled in Tiflis with her husband and had a tombstone put up for Dagny.

15. He was right, as "matsoni" is today known globally as "yogurt."

they have a broad variety of such special breakfasts," Emeryk conceded.

"Come on Wlad, the Poles are also mad about drinking! Naturally, I love people who drink a lot," said Dagny, savoring her red wine. "This wine differs from European-style wines. It is *austere.*"

"Wine is the national pride of Georgians," Avalov cut in, picking up the topic. "We claim that this country is the cradle of viticulture and wine-making, and that the European words *wine* and *vino* come from the Georgian *ghvino.*"

"Georgian sounds are so unusual, I can't discern a single word which even slightly resembles Slavic, let alone Germanic, languages," Dagny said.

"Never try to learn it, everything is upside down here—*mama* is *papa* and *papa* is *mama*," said Keller.

"Right," Avalov said, smiling, "incidentally, in some Georgian provinces, breastfeeding mothers usually take some wine to make their babies sleep well."

"Now I see why Georgian men remain attached to their mothers so much longer than we do in Europe, and why they drink so much," Emeryk concluded, with a touch of irony.

I'm a bad mother, I've abandoned my daughter . . . Dagny thought masochistically, and had some more wine. "Tell me about Georgian women—how much freedom do they have?" she addressed Avalov.

"*En masse*, they are less free than the Europeans, but they have relatively more liberties as compared to the women of the Orient," Avalov answered. "Yes, tradition is very strongly observed here, but the traditional role of women in Georgia is not as submissive as in Asia. Historically, women in Georgia played a vital role in the life of the country. After all, we had very influential queens, like Tamar, who still dominate the popular imagination. In the Georgian highlands, due to hard living conditions, the women also have important roles when it comes to, say, conflicts . . . but I would agree that here in Georgia there is a more pronounced cult of motherhood than of womanhood."

"You mean that the young man at the table over there is worshipping the potential motherhood hidden in that beautiful girl?" asked Emeryk, pointing to a scene in the middle of the room. A man, obviously a noble, was kneeling in front of a young woman, and with a goblet in one hand, was declaiming ardent words of praise.

"That is the young prince Sidamon-Eristavi, a rather flamboyant fellow," Avalov said, narrowing his eyes. "No, that has nothing to do with motherhood; it's just an excessive display of Georgian-style courtship and theatricality."

"Let's drink to love," Dagny cried excitedly. "Love is everything!" She drank a glass of wine down to the dregs. "How warm I am, hoo . . ." she said, loosening her hair, as she would have done back in the Schwarze Ferkel.

Avalov blushed; Emeryk got slightly nervous.

"I would be more careful with the wine, Ducha," he remarked.

"You shouldn't worry about me, Wlad," said Dagny, putting her hand on his shoulder. "This wine is nothing compared to the absinthe we used to drink in Berlin!"

"We could have something stronger with dessert, say—brandy? The local brandy is rather good," Avalov suggested.

"Thank you, I prefer wine," said Dagny, and to Wlad's horror picked up another glass.

"I'm afraid this music bores me," she said, gesturing across the restaurant to where two men on violin and piano played some popular French ditties. "I miss Chopin, Grieg . . . let's drink to music. To music before everything!"

"To music!" Avalov and Keller joined the toast; Emeryk was less enthusiastic, though he said, "Ducha plays piano brilliantly. She is an excellent musician."

"I could have become one, if not for the man in my life—Stach, to whom I have devoted myself," Dagny said, with a melancholy smile.

"Oh please, Mme Przybyszewska, would you play for us? Indulge me, please," Avalov said, "I could arrange it with the musicians . . ."

"Oh no, I have never performed in public—only once back in Norway . . ."

"Do please, Mme Przybyszewska!" Keller entreated her with excitement.

"Go ahead Ducha, flaunt your talents . . ." Emeryk gave up.

"No, I'm not sure the people here are in the mood for my kind of music," Dagny maintained.

Though she had refused to play, Count Avalov stood up and approached the musicians. He whispered something in the violinist's ear and put a rouble bill into his pocket. The music stopped. Avalov gave some more notes to the pianist, and the latter announced:

"Ladies and gentlemen! It is my honor and great pleasure to invite to the stage a famous pianist much celebrated in Norway, Germany and Poland, Madame Dagny Juel Przybyszewska! *Regardez!*" and he directed the attention of the public to the table where Dagny was sitting. The restaurant hall burst into applause and shouts of excitement. Prince Sidamon-Eristavi rushed up and took out his handgun, hoping to salute her by firing into the ceiling, but thankfully his tablemates dragged him off. Several men approached Dagny, asking for permission to escort her to the stage.

"This is a trap!" Dagny said furiously. "I despise you, Count Avalov!"

But as she saw that there was no way out of the mess, she picked up her glass of wine, drank half, stood up, and made her way to the stage. Trying to ignore the audience, she sat at the piano and rushing at the keyboard began Chopin's *Étude Op. 10, No. 12,* with the turbulent passages in the left hand and the vehement chords in the right. Why Chopin? Because she admired him, and also because, back in Berlin and Warsaw, Stach would always deprive her of the chance to play Chopin. He would stop her and play it himself instead. Chopin was his property—*the property of Young Poland, not hers!*

How to describe her playing? Rather than cooking up another false description, let me accompany it, illustrate it, with Dagny's own writing instead:

> . . . the melody lifts its bleeding wings and flutters enrapt into
> space, searching, searching, and turning back with a sigh.
> And again it raises its wide wings, and light as sundust flies up
> to the stars and sits among them, itself a star.
> And now the melody lifts its broad wings and majestically sails out
> over the wide, wide sea, over high hills and mountain crests, higher,
> higher, reeling oblivious—ah, it's flying into the sun.

A nimble coda, the final chords . . . Dagny reaped huge applause and even more shouts and ovations. And yes, this time the drunk and excitable Prince Sidamon-Eristavi did fire his revolver into the ceiling, which obliged his companions to disarm him immediately. Dagny stood up, bowed to the audience, and, escorted by Avalov, made her way back to their table.

"Count, would you be so kind as to indulge my whim this time, as I indulged yours just now? Could we leave this place, please? I'm dying for fresh air."

"But of course, Mme Przybyszewska!" Avalov said, and as they approached the table he suggested to everyone that they leave for the Alexander Garden, and have dessert somewhere else.

Walking through the hotel lobby, they were followed by some people from the restaurant who were eager to introduce themselves to Mme Przybyszewska and to express their admiration for her performance. They were local Germans, Poles and Russians whom Dagny's companions knew, and also a few foreign businessmen, who had stopped in Tiflis on their way to Baku and further destinations.

"I think we should arrange a solo concert here for you, Mme Przybyszewska," Avalov suggested.

"Count, one fine day you'll go too far!" said Dagny in mock-fury.

"So then I will die a most beautiful death!" Avalov responded, with some theatricality.

"Yes, a true Cleopatra night." Emeryk's forced grimace suggested that he was suffering from another pang of jealousy.

"Well, at least my nose resembles hers." Dagny seemed agitated, the alcohol and the fresh air leapt together within her.

They were sitting on a bench in the Alexander garden, a breeze coming up from the river down below. They laughed a lot, as Keller was telling jokes. And then Dagny saw the face of the man with the piercing gaze—the man from the railway station buffet. He was approaching them.

"Hello gentlemen, madame, please, allow me to introduce myself," he said. "My name is George Georgiades. I happened to be passing by the hotel, and as the windows of the restaurant were open, I heard you playing, madame, and was extremely impressed."

"I'm flattered, Mr. Georgiades. Thank you very much. My name is Dagny Juel. Please, meet my friends—Count Avalov, Wlad Emeryk, and Anton Keller." Dagny easily smoothed over this small intrusion.

"Gentlemen, it is my pleasure," said Gurdjieff, whose real Greek family name was in fact Georgiades.

"Come, join us," Dagny invited, "we've just escaped that noisy crowd and are planning to go somewhere else for a drink."

"Oh, no, I'm afraid I cannot take advantage of your generosity," said Gurdjieff.

"What is your trade, Mr. Georgiades?" Keller asked him.

"I teach dancing," was the answer.

"What kind of dancing—European? Modern or classical?" Dagny became interested.

"None of those," said Gurdjieff. "To some extent the dances I teach are somewhat Oriental, but to be more accurate, I would say that mine are a more universal kind of dancing."

"How promising," said Emeryk and looked aside to show that he did not care a damn about this fellow. From then on, he looked as if a demon of depression had passed by and touched his brow.

"These dances are based on certain movements, which charge the human body with cosmic energy," Gurdjieff went on, though he had noticed Emeryk's forced grin of dismissal and suppressed annoyance. "One may claim that these movements comprise the basic elements of a Dervish dance."

"How interesting!" Dagny got excited. "I'd love to see it."

"Could you demonstrate some of the Dervish movements here?" Avalov asked with a polite smile.

"Oh no, not here and not now. But maybe some other time, maybe I'll come to your residence and talk more about my dances, and demonstrate some of the essential positions," Gurdjieff said.

"Oh certainly, let's do it tomorrow in the hotel where I'm staying—the Grand Hotel." Dagny did not hesitate.

"Thank you for your interest in my simple art, madame," Gurdjieff replied, and then added as if absentmindedly, "excuse me madame, but I hope you won't misunderstand me. But it struck me that the music which you played was absolutely unrefined and full of errors—a jumble of misguided, passionate illusions, which have nothing to do with objective knowledge . . . but you played with such commitment, such absorption . . . no, you did not simply play the music, *you made love to it!*"

"Ooh la la!" Dagny was almost shocked. "How dare you call Chopin unrefined? Chopin, the greatest among all the composers of Europe!"

"Sir," and here Emeryk got really cross, "I think you should take back your words about making love!"

"Yes, immediately!" demanded Avalov.

"Oh, all apologies!" Gurdjieff said with his hand on his heart. "It was just a figure of speech. I fully admit I've breeched the norms of decency."

Keller looked absolutely confused, though still he tried to smooth over the matter.

"Come on, my friends," he interrupted, "this man just wanted to express how much he admired Mme Przybyszewska's musical skills. Let us not go deeper into this."

"Moreover, gentlemen," said Dagny, "I liked the comparison and, as a matter of fact, I accept it."

"Bravo!" Avalov's mood changed.

"As for you, my dear," she said, turning to Gurdjieff, "never again dare to say what you've said about Chopin. You know nothing of his music."

"I swear, madame," said Gurdjieff solemnly, "especially as I myself cannot play a note."

"To excuse yourself for what you've said," Dagny added, smiling her tipsy smile, "tomorrow at eleven in the morning you must come to my hotel and show me what dances you teach. If I don't like them I'll order your head cut off, but if I like them—then we'll have lunch together. Wlad, would you mind?"

Of course Wlad minded, and was about to object when

suddenly they heard shouting and whistles coming from another part of the garden.

"What is that?" inquired Dagny.

"It must be fistfighting—a kind of impromptu boxing match which they occasionally hold here," Avalov told her. "Actually, boxing downtown has been banned, but . . . would you like to take a look?"

"No, thank you, such sports do not appeal to me," replied Dagny. "Besides, I want to see my son to bed. Will you walk me back, Wlad?"

"Certainly, Ducha, let's go." Emeryk offered his hand and glanced at Gurdjieff.

"Have a good night, Mr. Keller. And thank you very much for the dinner, count," Dagny said.

"The pleasure was all mine," Avalov declared, making a bow.

"But I still despise you for that nasty scheming," she said, giving his arm a light pinch.

"Thank you for the wonderful performance, on behalf of the audience and myself," the count said.

"Mr. Georgiades, I do look forward to seeing you tomorrow," Dagny said, and then she made arrangements to meet the following day.

"With pleasure, madame, but only if Mr. Emeryk does not object," said Gurdjieff cautiously.

"No, he doesn't," Dagny said casually, turning her back and walking away with Emeryk.

"Let me give you a ride, dear Anton," Avalov said to Keller, and hailed a carriage. Getting into it, they both nodded in farewell to Gurdjieff, who was still standing there, watching Dagny and Emeryk enter the Grand Hotel.

She'll make him kill her, Gurgieff thought of the couple. *And he'll do it like a scared boy would kill a large moth rushing at his lamp.*

And then he moved, as something drew him toward the noise coming from the fistfight . . . something told him that the highland poet would be there.

As it turned out, it was not an impromptu boxing match but a street fight with some features of boxing retained. In this case, two drunken Englishmen assailed a local fellow, who had a pretty eccentric look—something between a proletarian and a shepherd. When Gurdjieff approached, he saw that one of the Englishmen had been knocked down, and was crawling and spitting blood. The other was acting more like a professional boxer, and seemed to have had some training; he was skipping from side to side, ducking down, and finding the right moment to hit his adversary. As for the local fellow, he held his fists at his chin and moved like a mongoose facing a cobra gaze. His thin, unshaven, weatherbeaten face had something outlandish to it, perhaps because of his right eye, which was wide open as if in amazement—it was made of glass. He wore a black shirt under an embroidered waistcoat, as all local highlanders did.

Some bystanders wanted to interfere and stop the fight, but the others wouldn't let them. "He'll do them both! He'll do them!" the enthused ones shouted.

"Who is this man?" Gurdjieff asked a fidgety teenage boy, standing by.

"That is Vazha-Pshavela, our famous poet!" the boy answered. "I've never seen him fistfighting before—he's tough, really tough!"

"What is the fuss about?"

"Those two foreigners made fun of his glass eye," the boy explained.

Pshavela was truly tough: he waited for the right moment, made a left hook, and was about to finish the Englishman with an uppercut when a police whistle sounded and the crowd dispersed.

The shepherd-proletarian picked up his hat and saddlebag and rushed deep into the garden. Gurdjieff followed, catching up with him when he stopped at a bench to tidy himself up. His hand was injured, probably by the last hook, which had caught on the teeth of his rival. Pshavela took out a napkin and sat down on the bench, wrapping up his fist.

"I've been looking for you," Gurdjieff said, sitting down by his side.

"I don't know you." The highlander was abrupt.

"Some call me the Black Greek, others, the Tiger of Turkistan."

"The Tiger?" Pshavela's only eye looked skeptical.

"No matter what they call me, I came here for the Cosmic Agape." Gurdjieff came straight out with it, and glimpsed a sparkle in the other's eye.

"The Love Feast," Pshavela said, stretching. "Yes, I'm hungry."

"May I buy you dinner, then?" Gurdjieff suggested in exchange.

"No, let *me* buy it," Pshavela grinned. "Come on."

They made straight for a nearby tavern run by local Persians. On the way, they bumped into the very same Englishmen. The soberer one was having a heated argument with a police warden; the knocked-down one was slouching around. The sober one put a rouble bill into the warden's pocket—a rather common gesture in the Russian empire—and the case was dismissed.

Gurdjieff and Pshavela had lamb stew with soft cheese and *lavash*, drinking and talking. . .

First, they talked of women.

The highlander spoke of the girls nourished on the breasts of violets and roses, and that some parts of the highlands resemble the parts of a female body in their enchanting beauty, and how he would share his bed with flowers. He recalled an episode he'd had in St. Petersburg, when he was following a woman who attracted him—mesmerized him—and so he tracked her as he would have tracked the shape-shifting goddess of the hunt. The Black Greek, on his part, spoke of Rabia of Basra—the prostitute and refined, mystical poet of the Sufi tradition, whom God had taught Love by putting her in a brothel for many years. Yes, and Beauty was also her teacher, helping her to know that God cared about her. He talked of Mirabai, the woman poet-saint of India, who felt she was married to Krishna and who would rush out naked into the streets, as she knew that Love would bring all the madness one needs to unfurl oneself across the universe. He spoke of drunken beauties who were like the moon, who knew that God had practiced His love in the hearts of animals before he created humans; He taught His songs to the birds first, and the planets speak at nights and tell secrets about Him . . .

Next, they talked of Nature:

"We dwell in Nature, as Nature dwells in us," Pshavela said. "It is the master and its own slave. The lowlands serve the highlands, the highlands serve the lowlands, the waters serve the forests, the forests serve the waters, the flowers serve the earth, the earth serves the flowers, and man serves them all by the sweat on his face."

"Reciprocal Maintenance, this is what it's called." Gurdjieff picked up the theme. "And this is why energy from active inner work is immediately transformed into new energy, while energy from passive work is lost forever.

"You got that thought from Rustaveli's *Vepkhistqaosani*, the panther's skin poem, which says that 'What thou givest away is thine; what thou keepest is lost,'" Pshavela suggested.

"I should think so," admitted Gurdjieff, and then said, "what I call 'inner work' is love; he who can love can *be*; the rest is death. This is the ratio of Primordial Contradiction: Love is the transubstantiation of nonexistence into existence and this is the idea carried through in your panther's skin poem, as far as I know."

"Death," Pshavela said. "You know, sometimes I see a hoopoe bird with a golden crest sitting on my tombstone, when I'm dead and buried . . . and my feelings are mixed with the grave's cold earth and the frenzied maggots eating my heart. The flowers that I share my bed with are afire in the rays of the afternoon sun."

Gurdjieff tried to clarify this point but he noticed that the highlander was distracted; Pshavela had gone suddenly pale, sitting and staring terrified into the bowl of stew in front of him. Then the terror turned into disgust.

"What is it?" Gurdjieff became worried.

Pshavela sat looking nowhere, his mouth open. Then he came back.

"Excuse me this . . . I'm stupid . . . I had something of a hallucination. It occurred to me that this stew is made of human flesh. Yes, I saw human fingers cut into it . . . Something must be wrong with my brain. I've been talking too much to plants and rainstorms. This April was cruel, the cruelest. In my tears I boiled the porridge of my desires. Mushrooms, mushrooms can talk you into the craziest things . . . On the other hand, I'm having fits of anxiety—what if one day I lose my magic powers?"

"There is only one kind of magic and this is *doing*," Gurdjieff said. "The highest magic a man can attain is to be able to *do*."

"It follows that the highest 'doing' is suffering," surmised Pshavela.

"Yes, deliberate suffering . . . in conscious life this is of great value." Gurdjieff looked keen to elaborate. "In the river of life, suffering is not intentional; people suffer like machines, trapped in various mechanic interactions; while, unfortunately, the conscience is covered up by a kind of crust, which can be pierced only by intense suffering, which one attempts as a critical experiment—"

"Yes, self-sacrifice is a science," Pshavela inserted, almost positivistic, almost alluding to Herbert Spencer, whose writings he read through his own shamanic eye.

And they talked Suffering and Sacrifice as a science—the avant-garde science of exaggeration, the science of stepping beyond yourself—to stretch your space into pure time, like a string is stretched to an extreme, transforming the frequency of its vibrations into the volume of a sound; the art of the sublime, of fracturing yourself from a social group to face the gaze of Infinity in the animal eyes of Nature, the gaze which disperses you like light is dispersed by a prism, arraigning your parts in the order of their wavelengths.

Gurdjieff was well aware that Pshavela's unique ability to communicate Nature's message was extremely significant in terms of the success of the intended Cosmic Agape. He knew deliberate suffering was something totally unknown to Nature; vegetal growth and animal instincts carried no intentionality in them. But Nature was the deliverer of the charge that combatted the unconscious mechanics of human suffering—the clockwork psychoses which would eventually end in mass madness. The end of the nineteenth century heralded spectacular developments in engineering, which, in turn, made human passions even more mechanical. These developments were prompted and propelled very much by the infection of politico-economic viruses in the human brain, which caused a dramatic estrangement between humans and organic life, although the latter had an extremely important cosmic function.

Gurdjieff espoused the philosophical idea that organic life on Earth constituted an indispensable link in the chain of worlds, neither of which could exist without the other. His point was that there is a flow of vibrations, of influences coming from the planets, and to ensure the fluent passage of these influences through Earth, organic life was created as a receiving and transmitting mechanism. Thus, by estranging themselves from organic life, humans became estranged from the very planetary vibrations which were the vibrations of the megalocosmic music of love—between existence and nonexistence—the very meaning of Primordial Contradiction mentioned above; they became estranged from the force which maintained the difference and diversity of Being against the totality of non-Being. To impede this estrangement, humans needed a special language—the *parole* which would verbalize the flow of the planetary vibrations and influences through organic life and thus pass the message to the mechanized masses. Therefore, Gurdjieff's interest in Pshavela was very well motivated: the highland poet was one of the few shamanic-Pardimemes of his age who could come up with such a language. Moreover, Pshavela knew how to distill poetic substance from organic life—a substance which made up the human soul, and which was indispensable for the Agape, as it was specifically this poetic substance which would help transform the *parole* into "flesh" and "bread." Remember the two disciples at Emmaus? They could not recognize the Word of God when He walked among them, but when they broke the bread with Him, they recognized It. One of the intended effects of the Cosmic Agape was that it would make people feel what they think, and think what they feel . . .

There came a song from the musicians in the corner of the tavern—their leader, the *sazandar*, was strumming an elegant string instrument called the *saz*, on which he played a story about his "feelings that could not be comprehended by his thoughts." And then he reproduced something from Jalal Ad-Din Rumi, something like: "With passion make love / With passion eat and drink and dance and play."

Gurdjieff enjoyed it, recalling his encounters with the Whirling

Dervishes in Boukhara. Pshavela seemed less impressed—he must not have been very keen on that kind of music, preferring highland ditties full of humor and eroticism, sung on the *pandouri*, a three-stringed instrument, and the *salamuri* pipe.

"I need a woman," Pshavela said suddenly, yet again staring nowhere with his dead eye, the live one shut.

"I'm afraid they don't provide such services here," said Gurdjieff, slightly nonplussed by such a statement.

"I don't need a mere prostitute," the highlander said, "I need a woman who has loved much."

Gurdjieff quoted a verse by Mirabai: "God has / a special interest in women / For they can lift this world to their breast / And help Him / Comfort."

Quintessentially, the complex symbolism of the Celestial Agape was about the collective eating of the Body of Love, through which rite the Body would reach the human brain, which was entangled in mechanistic suffering, crusted and numb. To make the Body effective upon such numbness, a receptacle was needed, within which the Body would materialize, assuming a certain density and form, mingled with both the poetic substance extracted from Nature and the meaning extracted from compound musical clusters. To some extent they needed something roughly analogous to, and in this respect significantly though indeterminately distinct from, an alchemical vessel, containing a pure erotic element and a supple female sensibility—*a woman who had loved much.*

Gurdjieff was lost in these ruminations and the song coming from the *saz*, when suddenly he felt somebody's hand touching his shoulder.

"*Cherchez la femme!*" it was the mock-Dervish, Sohrab Addin, dressed in rather decent Persian garments, holding a pack of printed cards in his hand, and drunk as usual. Grabbing a chair from the table next to theirs, he said, "and what is better than wisdom? A woman is better. And what is better than a good woman? Nothing."

"Who is this man?" Pshavela was not very pleased by such an intrusion.

"Geoffrey Chaucer," the Dervish said.

"Who?" inquired the highlander, with a touch of irritation in his voice.

"I mean, the quote I paraphrased just now was Geoffrey Chaucer—the father of English poetry," the mock-Dervish clarified, adding, "and I am most honored to meet here the father of the new Georgian poetry."

Pshavela seemed flattered but still maintained a gloomy gaze in the stranger's direction.

"Another joke like that about my writing and I'll drag you out and throw you into the river," was his reply.

"He's a good diver, this man. Take it easy," Gurdjieff said. "The other day I saw him jumping from the Avlabari Bridge and now he seems fine."

"Oh no, I'm not a diver, just a swimmer," the Dervish said. "I usually don't go deep into matters; I just glide upon the surface."

"So you have met before, haven't you?" Pshavela asked Gurdjieff.

"Yes, and the pleasure was mine, since he knows more about the Cosmic Agape than I do," answered Gurdjieff. "Consider him a liasons man, like me."

Hearing this, the highlander relaxed, sat back, and said, "welcome."

"It is my great honor to be part of this remarkable company," the mock-Dervish said, "Vazha-Pshavela, you are the—"

"Enough!" the highlander interrupted, foiling yet another attempt to determine his place in modern Georgian literature.

"All apologies!" Sohrab Addin had got the message.

"Any tidings since we last met, my dear friend?" Gurdjieff asked the mock-Dervish.

"No, no . . . no Voices, no instructions so far . . . just relaxing . . . drinking . . ." Sohrab Addin spoke with his head down as if falling asleep, and then, as if waking up, continued. "By the way, I've just had a couple bottles with a very nice guy, a local painter—he paints walls, you know, in the taverns and shops. What's his name? Damn . . . it's something to do with fireworks, yes, pyrotechnics . . . yes, Pirosmani, Nikala. We had some drinks close by. He's a painter and I saw his works, very nice, very nice images of mere Being . . ." He seemed to speak to himself, muttering and grumbling. "Mere Being . . . beyond the the finality of thought, rising in the bronze décor . . . giraffes, panthers, roe deer, people feasting, a boy on a donkey, moving in the darkness, all before the first thought . . ."

Pshavela and Gurdjieff sat grinning at this drunken stream of consciousness.

"Wake up, my friend!" the highlander lightly punched the Dervish who, as a matter of fact, lost his balance and would have fallen off his chair had Gurdjieff and his companion not been holding him onto it. The sobering effect of this incident was augmented by a loud introductory chord made by the musicians, who were starting a new song.

"Oh, Sayat-Nova!" Gurdjieff said, recognizing the first line.

"Sure, Sayat-Nova!" The drunken Dervish had picked up on it too. "An Armenian serving as a court poet to the Georgian King Irakli the Second, and writing his songs in Azeri . . . what a diversified ethnic identity, what a happy marriage of cultural affiliations! Let me tell you something that I know—the Voices from above predict Irakli's reincarnation,"—he switched to *sotto vocce*—"in a couple of decades he'll come back as a *motion picture* maker and a visual artist . . . yes, again as an Armenian, living in Tiflis, and encorporating Azeri motifs into his remarkable works."[16]

"Motion pictures . . ." Pshavela mused. "You talk of future artistic forms, although, as far I can see, the art you've mastered best of all is the art of drinking, my friend." And he winked at Gurdjieff.

"What are those prints you have?" Gurdjieff asked.

"Ah!" Sohrab Addin cheered up. "This is something that Nikala the painter left behind. He got so hot-boiled and soused—venting, sobbing, telling me he was in love with a cabaret woman named Margo, then lamenting about his poor, primitive paintings. He has such a low opinion of himself, maintaining that he has no skill, no craft . . . and then he produced this pack of printed cards, which he'd borrowed from another fellow. The prints featured the work of new European artists . . ." and the mock-Dervish spread some of them right upon the table, making quite a mess.

"Easy, easy!" Pshavela, who could tolerate hordes of drunken highlanders back at home, nonetheless became very displeased with the fact that this fellow had splattered wine on his pants. *Should he throw the ugly freak into the river after all?*

Gurdjieff carefully picked up some of the prints and considered them. Pshavela, having dried the stain with a napkin, glared at the Dervish with his only eye, but then cast a half-glance at the pictures spread in front of him too.

The prints represented paintings by modern German, Austrian, and Scandinavian artists: Gustav Klimt, Oskar Kokoshka, and others. Gurdjieff read in them echoes of Decadence, Nietzsche's *Twilight of the Idols*, some sort of uniform deformity enveloping all forms, things falling apart, the Occident rejecting itself . . . Then

16. The mock-Dervish must be referring to Sergei Paradjanov, an Armenian filmmaker, who spent most of his creative life in Tbilisi. His last movie, *Ashik Kerib*, is based on an Azeri legend about a wandering poet in love. Paradjanov died in 1990; the bloody Armenian-Azeri war in Nagorno-Karabakh was to come soon after.

came Edvard Munch's figure standing on the Mikhail bridge and screaming; his tortured gaze captivated the viewer, and seemed to pass along some sort of a message—could it be yet another hint of the Pardimeme Premonition? Yes, absolutely; Munch had seen the coming madness . . . he had broken through to something formidable, foreseen the ruthless beauty of political terror. Then Gurdjieff shifted to another painting by Munch entitled *Madonna.* In this one, a woman flaunted her nakedness, wearing a strange grin, almost whorish; there was a tiny, dead fetus in the corner—Our Lady of Death. But why Death?! How morbid this vision was, how childish its aversion to the incontrovertible reality of life, when compared to the impersonal and precise iconography practiced in the Orient, which embraced the reciprocity of life and death. However, the woman in the painting was fascinating. She seemed oddly familiar, too . . . Gurdjieff suddenly realized that her features reminded him of the "Chopin lady" he'd met earlier—*Mme Przybyszewska*! Didn't she say she'd come from Norway?! And Munch was Norwegian too . . . The next one, *Sphinx,* was also by Munch: a woman, totally naked, with her hands behind her head as if stretching, yet again flaunted the beauty and mystery of her femininity, behind her a backdrop of dark, writhing bodies . . . yes, this was truly Dagny Juel—Munch's inspiration came from her. And Gurdjieff's too: death should not have dominion! This woman would become Our Lady of the Love Feast! The Blessed Vessel of Love's Alchemy!

"I think I know the woman we need," he said passing the *Madonna* and the *Sphinx* prints to Pshavela.

"The one who can lift up the world to her breast . . ." the mock-Dervish sang, his voice soaked in alcohol.

"The one who has loved much?!" Pshavela said, picking up the prints and looking at them. He considered the pictured forms closely, but his face betrayed no excitement. And yet, Gurdjieff noticed how his artificial eye started to flicker, suggesting a certain intense, erotic current running along the highlander's spinal column and reaching his head.

"Why was I born a man? I should have come as rain instead, so I could pour on nude bodies like this!" uttered the shamanic poet.

"Enjoying bourgeois art?! Master Pshavela, I thought you identified with the proletariat!" This came from a short young man who'd approached the highlander from behind. His hair was dark, while a thin beard and mustache covered the traces of smallpox on his cheeks. The crude cunning of a jaybird flashed in his eyes.

"Who are you, then? What makes you call me *master*?"

Ladies and gentlemen, it is my pleasure to introduce here the "strongest" of the twentieth century's strongmen and the greatest of the false shamans—Premier Joseph Stalin!

That spring, when Dagny arrived in Tiflis, he was neither "Premier" nor even "Stalin," but a young man of twenty-one named Ioseb Jughashvili. An enthusiastic revolutionary and a superlative conspirator, he was the reigning prince of the Tiflis political underground, occasionally emerging at worker rallies with manifestos and speeches, calling to prepare the way for the future. Expelled from the Tiflis Religious Seminary for atheistic inclinations (though some historians suggest it was because his widowed mother couldn't afford the tuition), he was then known as *Koba*, a name he took from *The Parricide*, a novel by Georgian nationalist author Alexander Kazbegi, who inspired many youngsters.

As a teenager, Ioseb Jughashvili was called *Soso* or *Soselo*. A quick learner at school, he showed signs of being a future leader; he was vengeful, self-confident, and ambitious. His father, a shoemaker and heavy drinker from the small town of Gori, was killed in a drunken fight when Ioseb was ten. His mother,

Ekaterine (known as *Keke*), was a seamstress. A modest and loving person, she dreamed of her son becoming a priest. As a matter of fact, he did become one—the high priest of a diabolical congregation called the Socialist Party, which oversaw a huge parish that extended from the Far East to Central Europe, with hundreds of millions of believers worshipping its dictator-deity.

In some respects, Stalin's is yet another Cinderella story: from dire provincial poverty, he rose to absolute and total power. Some people project the trajectory of this story onto the whole of Russia. An oft-repeated quote about Stalin is that "he found Russia working with wooden ploughs and left it equipped with atomic piles." Yes, he was Russia's final Tsar—Ioseb the First (and the Last).

However, was not Stalin in the spirit of his age? An age which also produced other terrifying "Cinderellas?" Modern politics was like modernist poetry as defined by Anna Akhmatova: ". . . poems grow like flowers shamelessly out of garbage." Little Soselo once wrote poetry too, as any proud Georgian is supposed to do. He wrote short, patriotic poems, which were applauded and published by Ilia Chavchavadze himself—the premiere public intellectual of the time. Known as the father of the nation, he was sadly assassinated by representatives of that very nation in 1907. ("Don't shoot me!" he cried to the assassins, "I'm Ilia!" "That's exactly why I'm going to shoot you!" one of the assassins shouted back, and fired his gun.)

I would love to include a tiny poem of Soselo's here, but I'm afraid my translation would deprive it of whatever poetic value it might contain. It's a nice piece, written by a little boy from Gori after all, and not totally devoid of literary skill. Everyone in Georgia knows this poem; it is about a rosebud in bloom embracing a violet, a lily waking up and bowing to the breeze, a lark tinkle-tinkling its song high in the clouds, and an excited nightingale saying in a soft voice, "may thee rejoice, sweet country, may thee flourish, land of the Iberians, and may thee, little boy, be good at your studies, and make your motherland happy." Pathetic fallacy? Yes. Patriotism mixed with pastoralism? Yes. But why not?! Even mature poets in late nineteenth-century Georgia came up with the same kind of vision, linking nature to the motherland—with the exception of Pshavela of course, of whom we've already spoken.

It was chiefly because of Stalin's vestigial poetic ambitions that he addressed Pshavela as "master" that night in the Persian restaurant. But as his comments show, his admiration for the great highlander was tinged with apparent irony. At twenty-one, Stalin already felt that he'd outgrown Georgia and its poetry. However, old habits die hard—as Mick Jagger (another pop culture shamanic person) once sang. Even when he occupied the highest position in the Bolshevik hierarchy, Stalin tried to pay Pshavela his due as a master; in 1934 he decreed Vazha-Pshavela's work among the classics, alongside Ilia Chavchavadze's, (at the time, the latter was not much celebrated in Georgia, let alone in the other nations of the Soviet Union). That Stalin edited the Russian translation of Rustaveli's *The Knight in the Panther's Skin* indicates that poetry had not yet deserted him completely; or, at the very least, he was willing to give it a seat on one of the back benches in his Supreme Council.

What transformed this tender boy, Soselo, into a vengeful and cold-blooded activist of the Bolshevik underground? That is the question. How was his nascent creative imagination channeled into revolutionary conspiracies, ending in the ruthlessly pragmatic abuse of the technology of power? Remember, Walter Benjamin described Stalin as the leader who "politicized aesthetics," whereas Hitler "aestheticized politics." Regardless, both of them misappropriated their shamanic gifts for the sake of pursuing political power, and that's why love shunned them in their lives. Both Stalin's wives died young, while Hitler suffered from sexual impotence. They were certainly loved by crowds, and they made love to those crowds too, but there's a catch to making love to shapeless masses—it's like making love to the decomposing corpse of an elephant.

But here comes yet another question, this time a more complicated one: why does young Koba—Ioseb Jughashvili—show up in this story of Dagny and the Love Feast?

Let me attempt an answer.

Earlier that March, the police had searched Stalin's lodgings in the Tiflis Physical Observatory, where, according to his biography, he had been staying since December 1899. Though he was working as a janitor, he still had access to observatory equipment, and would take the occasional opportunity to observe the movements of celestial bodies. What a theme for a painting: *Young Stalin Observing the Starlit Sky Above Him, and Defining the Moral Law Within Himself* . . . But joking aside, it must have been that, endowed with some shamanic traits, Ioseb Jughashvili, to put it in modern terminology, "hacked into" the Pardimeme network, managing to intercept some fragments of the Pardimeme Premonition. Luckily, the message was encrypted and Stalin could only make out a small part of it; besides, at that time his mind was totally captivated by the writings of Vladimir Lenin, which imposed on him a certain interpretative rigidity and bias. Consequently, while he did discover the prophecy about "the Cow flying to the moon," his particular ideological preoccupations led him to render it as "the imminent victory of the proletariat in the revolutionary class fight." However, he was also able to extract bits of information about upcoming, quasi-religious activities in Tiflis, featuring a highland poet and a bunch of dubious visionaries. Nevertheless, the whole thing sounded so foolish to him that he dismissed it as irrelevant. *Objective historical processes are a far more serious matter than quasi-religious trifling*, he concluded.

"Violence is the midwife of revolution!" he would say later, and yes, this strongman attended the birth of History. He began early on to fashion himself the future minister of creative violence. Could his mother Keke have appreciated that? Why couldn't he become a shoemaker like his father Bessarion, the crude drunkard? Yes, *a totalitarian shoemaker*, using human lives as leather for History's boots . . .

Koba was not supposed to show up that night in the Persian restaurant; it was against the basic rules of the political underground. Alas, his fascination with Pshavela made him do it. Besides, the city police at that time looked out for him in working-class neighborhoods, rather than in expensive dining rooms downtown.

Koba had been heading back from a meeting with some young conspiratorial revolutionaries when he saw Pshavela fist-fighting in the garden.[17] He stopped to watch, and then followed Pshavela to the restaurant, where he spied on the highlander and his companions from behind a curtain. He could catch some portions of the conversation though the *sazandar*'s music, although it seemed to churn up the words, making it difficult to hear.

What made him betray himself and speak to the "master"? Moreover, to do so with a touch of irony? It was his arrogance and ambition. Besides, he had irony in the very fiber of his being. Sure, when he became the absolute ruler of almost half the globe—the "Chief of All Peoples," as he was known in the Soviet Union—his irony receded, giving way to dark humor. In the late '40s, a Georgian actor named Mikheil Gelovani, who usually played Stalin in Soviet films, asked for permission to spend a couple days at the Chief's dacha near Moscow, to "get a better sense of the character of the Great Leader, to apprehend his routine, his

17. One of those young revolutionaries was my wife's grandfather, who committed suicide in 1936, during the Great Purge.

paraphernalia . . ." etc. When this earnest request was reported to
Stalin, he replied: "If comrade Gelovani intends to get a better
sense of my character and to more deeply appreciate my routine,
why shouldn't he go to the labor camp in Touroukhan, Siberia,
where I served my time as a proletarian revolutionary?" Not bad,
is it?

And so it happened that *round about midnight*—as the jazz
piano shaman Thelonious Monk had it—that young Joseph
Stalin faced Vazha-Pshavela, who, distracted from the pictures he
was scrutinizing, and displeased by the rude intrusion, turned his
one eye upon the "kid."

My friends, there is a popular legend in Georgia that once,
though nobody knows where or why, Pshavela beat up young
Stalin, hitting him in the jaw. Could it be that this happened late
one night in a Persian restaurant? It could . . . but far be it from
me to fatten my story with such unverified tales and legends!
Therefore, let's abandon that prospect and get back to our sheep,
more specifically, the "dark" one—Mme Przybyszewska, or Dagny
Juel.

I next see her riding westward from Tiflis to the Black Sea. The
train runs slowly, although according to the timetable at the
railway station it was supposed to be a fast train. She is there
with Zenon and Wlad Emeryk, who is going to see his partner
in Poti or Batumi, or some such place . . . *westward, as the sun goes
down . . .*

The Black Sea—the name fascinates her. A black velvet abyss
with gigantic flowers blooming on the bottom, her soul roaming
among them . . . this train will take her back to herself, to the
darkest recesses of her fantasies. *When the Sun Goes Down* was the
title of one of her plays, one of her expressionist experiments with
love triangles . . . her extreme geometry . . . "Oh, how you long to
feel my foot on your neck again," one of her male characters says

to his beloved, who abandoned her husband with the knowledge that it would crush him.

All of Dagny's plays are about the killing of innocence: you must murder your innocence to discover your real self, which then destroys you out of vengeance—such are the wicked dialectics of erotic love. Or perhaps just the petty drama of an emancipated, bourgeois woman?! When she commits adultery, she sins against the Holy Ghost . . . but her plays are not only about adultery; one describes the death of someone who happened to be in the way— *"She had to die. It was our happiness that she walked into the sea . . . Now she is out of the play . . ."* Well, does not the whole world rest upon that same destruction, the act of self-sacrifice, the suicide of innocence?! Christ in agony, dying on the cross—didn't God commit suicide for the salvation of man? Innocent victims must be sacrificed in order to reenact the creation of the world and to keep it going, because the world was created via the dismemberment of God. Kill the angel in the house, *it's too hard for you to be good, it tires you, it feels like an unbearable yoke to you . . . I know your poor, evil soul, and I love it . . .*

Zenon is sleeping, his head in her lap. She's caressing him, but a dead child sings in her soul, eaten by maggots, promising her destruction, coming from beyond . . . she wanders deep into the labyrinth, towards her true self . . . the Minotaur . . . no, she is Pasiphae, the voluptuous zoophilic queen, who desired the bull and conceived a monster . . . But is sexuality so simple— mere submission to overwhelming compulsions and obscene instincts?! Are those instincts really that obscene? What does a woman want—*a woman who has loved much*? What made her *love much*? What are these blasts of desire which can push you beyond social norms, beyond human nature? No, I am not speaking of female eroticism, of the longing for a man, through whom a woman might obtain an identity. There are women who long for more—for the touch of God, for *when He will insert his pulsating mass into her forest, and rain there.* It is about making tangible that which goes beyond perception, and the name for this feeling is *joy. Yes, he knows my poor, evil soul . . . and he loves it . . .* Emeryk, who is sitting in front, asks her something. She does not respond to him. *Kill the angel in your room, kill the false innocence . . .* It *is* false, since it exists only to lubricate social mechanisms. Emeryk is just a detail . . . No, she is the one that's *just a whore*, as the innocent would say of her. No, she is not a whore! She is a temple prostitute, making love to strangers and thus introducing them to unknown gods. But alas, Wlad Emeryk is not a stranger—he's just a detail, though mad about her, yes, *a mad detail . . .* and he does not know what *joy* is. Was it the temple prostitute in her that made her flirt with that man—George Georgiades, whom she invited over the other day, to talk about his "Sacred Dances"? The Black Greek, he called himself—a swarthy, short man with a robust, piercing gaze. Well, *he* was a stranger, a mysterious traveler, to whom she could open up the beauty of her womanhood at the altar of the unknown god . . . no, she imagined herself making love to him in a rolling carriage, à la Mme Bovary . . . how emancipated of her! And how innocently bourgeois. The Black Greek . . . the dances he showed her were unusual; *The Camel Dervish Dance*, for instance, in which human and animal inhabit and support each other; they speak one language—the language of Being. Then there was *Sema*, the dance of Sufi Dervishes when they whirl and whirl in ecstasy, revolving, like everything in this world revolves, from atoms to planets. "Their long conic headdress is their ego's tombstone," Georgiades had explained, "and their white skirt is their ego's shroud . . . they die to be reborn in dance unto Perfection." Yes, they also killed false innocence, which is obscured by the distinction between good and evil . . . a delusional distinction, which curses the Western mind; more lessons should be taken from the East; to learn the joy of spiritual dance breaks up this delusion. He'd spoken of joy and of deliberate suffering: the suffering *that is aware*, the suffering *that knows* . . . and, yes, he also spoke of Love as the "inner work," as the authentic fullness of Being. She was fascinated by the oriental texts he referred to, dedicated to the art of loving, transforming ordinary sexual intercourse into a metaphysical harmony of body and soul; in Love you serve the other in his/her endless otherness, and erotic knowledge paves the way to higher such. After that, he invited her to a special kind of "Feast," which was supposed to be held in the German Garden early in June. He then spoke of Bach as a "shaman"—her music professor back in Berlin would've had a stroke. In fact, he was not very clear about the nature of the "Feast"; he had called it a "Cosmic Agape," and a "Celestial Love Feast." Was he just trying to get her in bed with him, watching the stars and performing the sexual equivalent of the *Art of Fugue*?! At least not in a rolling carriage, though, certainly not . . . he must've had healer's skills, that Black Greek—holding his hands over her head, he'd stopped her headache and enveloped her in the sort of calmness she had felt only as a girl during occasional hikes with her sisters through foggy groves, or by the sea shore . . . *the Black Sea* . . . she was on her way back to herself.

The train stops. Their destination is Kutaisi, the second largest city in the country, and they're halfway there. They have an hour to refresh themselves, stretch their legs, drink and eat. Zenon is happy.

In the train station buffet, they bump into an Englishman named Oliver Wardrop. He introduces himself as a diplomat— Her Majesty's vice-consul in Kerch, Crimea. What brings him to Georgia? Well, a fascination, if you will, with the country and its people. Yes, Georgia's chief attraction lies in its people; the Georgians are not only fair to look upon, but they are essentially a loveable people . . . to live among such gay, openhearted, openhanded, honest, innocent folk is the best cure for melancholia and misanthropy that could possibly be imagined. That's exactly what Wardrop wrote in his travelogue, published to pretty good reviews in 1888. He's been coming to Georgia for more than thirteen years, and has made friends with local intellectuals and writers, whose works he and his sister Marjory have translated into English. Prince Ilia Chavchavadze, and Vazha-Pshavela, for instance—the latter an extraordinary poet, a highlander, who makes animals and plants speak. Dagny says that she heard of him from another extraordinary man, who she met a couple days ago, and who actually cured her of a dreadful headache. She would have loved for him to have something done for her friend's melancholia too, she adds, referring to Emeryk. Poor man, he is getting more and more misanthropic too . . . but of course not, she's only teasing, and fondly touches Emeryk's cheek . . . avoiding this mock-caress, Emeryk turns to Her Majesty's vice-consul and asks what his present trip to Georgia is about. Wardrop says that he is on a sort of fundraising mission, which involves meeting with oil magnates from Baku and Batumi and encouraging them to sponsor cultural events. Cultural? Yes, there are a couple events already scheduled in early June; for example, a British artist will be doing a magic lantern projection of mystical pictures from a medieval Georgian poem, with illustrations by an Austro-Hungarian artist. The poem is called *The Knight in the Panther's Skin*, by Shota Rustaveli. Wardrop's sister Marjory has been translating it into English. Dagny asks what sort of a poem it is. Wardrop quotes from the introduction to the poem, which almost every Georgian knows by heart; it's about the "highest Love-Divine, which is difficult to discourse thereon, ill to tell forth with tongues. It is heavenly, upraising the soul on pinions . . ." the poem also speaks of the lower frenzies which befall human beings, but these just imitate the higher, the *divine frenzy* . . . It is about wandering and solitude, rapture and affliction; it is about *passion*. As it happens, Wardrop added, the picture-show will be followed by a performance of the *St. John Passion*, by Bach. Musicians from Leipzig have been hired especially for this event.

Thoughts of the Love Feast stir in Dagny's mind yet again . . . the *Agape* of which the Black Greek spoke . . .

"How fascinating," she says, "what an unusual marriage of oriental mysticism and European Lutheran music."

"It is," the diplomat agrees. "This country is itself a marriage of East and West. In the past, it was occupied by the great Oriental powers such as Iran and the Ottoman Empire. Today, Georgians have a sense of being rediscovered by the Europeans."

Talk switches to current political and economic issues, which interests Emeryk more; he gladly proceeds to discuss the oil and manganese business, cargo transit, the Marcus Samuel tanker the SS Murex—5,010 tons and launched in 1890—growing prospects of transport communication between Turkistan and Europe via the Caucasus, the lamentable state of Georgian railroads, and the like . . .

Dagny sits distracted, not listening to Emeryk's empty talk. Words come to her mind, but droop like the feathers of a bird in an iron cage. She moves upon the surface of mere things . . . no, she's stuck really, breathless and motionless. She feels like a painted dryad in a painted forest. Then, suddenly, she feels someone craving to enter her, as if somebody is scrutinizing this painted picture, and, in a fit of madness, imagines himself entering her naked, glistening body. She feels a presence around her, rather like a light wind ruffling her hair. A strange fullness penetrates her . . . the iron cage of words . . . the rational world disrupted by some ineffable meaning coming from beyond and speaking to her senses with lusty breaths, swelling her with a sweet and subtle pain . . . and then she collapses.[18]

18. The last chapter of J. M. Coetzee's book *Elizabeth Costello* is a fictional 1603 letter from Lady Chandos to Francis Bacon. In this letter, Lady Chandos speaks of "extreme souls" not yet born who would speak the ineffable, "where words give way beneath your feet like rotting boards." Could Dagny be one of these? I can't tell. However, I would claim that the crazy masters of avant-garde art and poetry, coming three hundred years after Lady Chandos, proved to be

Back on the train with Zenon, Emeryk and the English diplomat by her side, all worried about her health, she recovers. She is on the way to the Black Sea again—heading westward as the sun goes down. "I must go back to Tiflis," she says in a faint voice.

It was Gurdjieff, the Tiger of Turkistan, who, in contemplating the painting by Munch—meticulously, just like a dermatologist would study his patient's skin—tried to enter Dagny's body.

I see a table set out in the Ortachala Garden—the most leisurely place in Tiflis. Gurdjieff, Pshavela, and Pirosmani are having tea there. Pirosmani is sitting between the other two, fast asleep, and so Gurdjieff and Pshavela use him as a cushion, resting their elbows on him and occasionally talking over his head. They are having tea in small slim-waisted glasses like those used in Turkey or Persia; one should note in passing, however, that in Tiflis, people often drink red wine from such glasses.

"Why is Love as strong as Death?" asks Gurdjieff, sounding like the Mad Hatter when he inquired: *Why is a raven like a writing desk?* "God asks this question through me, because only when it comes to Man is God so lost that he asks questions."

"The Song of Songs!" Pshavela says. "I like songs . . . and the Question of Questions—I like questions . . ."

"If death is what makes nothing out of everything, then Love is what makes everything out of nothing," Gurdjieff continues. "In both cases energy is released, binding existence and nonexistence together. This is the meaning of the word *strength*. This very energy is spent to counteract the evil of the entropy that comes with human order, imposed upon entities and non-entities by human reason. The advent of the entropic evil of human order

---

"extreme souls." In line with this, I see Dagny as a *decadent* Mary Magdalene, washing the feet of the Christ of Modernism with her tears and then wiping them dry with her own hair.

can be resisted only by the intervention of Divine Disorder, and Love is the Divine Disorder in our minds."

Pausing, Gurdjieff asks his companions if they understand. They make no answer.

"Death is human, all too human," Gurdjieff proceeds. "Only humans die; animals and plants do not—they just return to their origins. Thus it follows that death is order. Look at graveyards, cemeteries—what regularity, what uniformity—how measured everything is there! Now look at the resting place of Love— what a disorder of sheets, cushions, blankets, thighs, legs, hands, panting, yearning, throbbing . . . is what I say clear?"

"As clear as the roe deer fawn's urine pouring on the lovely violet's reclining head," Pshavela commented, digging in his nose with a handkerchief-wrapped finger.

"Very well, I'll put it to you once more," Gurdjieff persists. "If death is our little sister, as the Dervish of Assisi had it, then what is Love to us?"

"We have a little sister, and she has no breasts: what will she do for us in the day when . . . a-dying shall we goooo, a-dying shall we gooo . . ." Pshavela sings.

"The answer is in the bottle," says Gurdjieff, taking the bottle of wine off the table and putting it on his head. He begins a traditional Tiflis dance, keeping the bottle upright. Pshavela claps his hands to mark the rhythm.

"How old do you think existence is?" Pirosmani murmurs in his sleep, much like Saint Teresa of Avila.

"And how *young* do you think nonexistence is?" Gurdjieff asks in response.

"God multiplies men to multiply questions, and He is too much in love to come up with answers . . ." concludes Pshavela.

"God said: 'I am made whole by your life. Each soul, each soul completes me,'" the dancing Gurdjieff declares, quoting Hafiz. "That's why He multiplies questions."

"No, that's why the true sacrifice is human sacrifice!" Pshavela says, and then sneezes.

"May God tickle you, brother," Pirosmani murmurs. "Tickle, tickle, tickle—"

To stop him, Pshavela stuffs a piece of bread into his mouth. "When she kissed me, with the kisses of her mouth I became invisible," Pirosmani says, spitting out the crumbs of bread. "That's why I make things visible . . . giraffe, a fisherman, a woman."

From a small gate behind the table, Dagny Juel enters the garden. She is stark naked, wearing only high-heeled shoes, gold earrings, and bracelets. She approaches the company and sits down in a large armchair at one end of the table.

Gurdjieff comes dancing over to her, while Pshavela stands up, approaches her, and kneels in front of her, kissing her feet and saying in a trembling voice, "how beautiful art thy feet within thy shoes, O prince's daughter! The joints of thy thighs are like jewels, the work of the hands of a cunning workman. Thy two breasts are like two young roes that are twins."

"How do we make love to God?" asks Dagny, as if in a trance.

Gurdjieff, still dancing, replies, "first you kiss His feet, then His hands, then His lips . . . then your Beloved will put his hand into the hole of the door, and your bowels shall be moved for him. Thus, the higher blends with the lower, actualizing the middle."

"The sperm merges with the ovum to create the embryo," clarifies Pshavela.

"This is the Law of the Three," Gurdjieff says, "the interrelation of the three forces which run the whole universe. The *first* is Holy Affirmation, which is active, the *second* is Holy Denial which is passive, and the *third* is Holy Reconciliation which is neutralizing. So what? They are all active, and only in relation to one another do they become different—"

"It is like eating yourself," Pshavela interrupts. "By eating yourself you maintain yourself."

"How do you make love to Love? That's the trick," Pirosmani adds.

"There is no trick, and Saint Teresa knew this," says Dagny. "*He* simply comes to the shore of our souls, takes off His clothes, and dives into us."

"Either way, you'd have to pass through the discontinuity of vibrations coming from Him . . . You are as close to your Beloved as one cosmos is to another, a relation that is permanent and always the same. That is to say, you make love to God as zero to Infinity; His infinity penetrates your zero, like His solid mass penetrates your forest and rains there," Gurdjieff explains.

Pshavela sneezes again.

"May Love tickle you twice, brother," Pirosmani says.

Pshavela laughs. Dagny and Pirosmani start laughing too. Gurdjieff stops dancing.

"Our Endlessness-Almighty-Omni-Loving-Common-Father-Uni-Being-Creator tickles us, yes, as It tickles the Megalocosmos and keeps it going," says Gurdjieff, beginning to choke in a fit of laughter. The bottle falls from his head onto the table and shatters; red wine colors the white tablecloth.

"How much better is thy love than wine!" Pshavela says to Dagny.

"And how much better is wine than tea!" Pirosmani says, grabbing a glass and drinking, though still asleep.

"When a bottle breaks, its contents spill out, it's as simple as that!" Gurdjieff puts it categorically. "The bottle, which is active, fell upon the table, which is passive, and produced the answer, which is somewhere in the middle—neutralizing. Yes, the included middle, the third of the contradictory two . . . yes, the law of Love is the Law of the Three: the effects of a cause must always reenter the cause, producing another cause, which produces other effects, and so on, *ad infinitum*, down the rabbit hole. Now, let me see . . ."

He takes a piece of broken glass, cuts his hand, and lets some drops of blood fall into the spilled wine.

"What is this?" he asks.

"When you cut your hand it bleeds," Pshavela says, and sneezes yet again.

"No, this is deliberate suffering, which turns wine into blood!" states Gurdjieff. "Good. Now, let's have some bars of what I call the *megalocosmic solfeggio!*"

Picking up a spoon, he strikes notes of the tableware: *do, re, mi, fa, sol, la, ti, do.* "Can you hear the octave, produced by mere utensils designed for serving tea? It replicates the Grand Octave which spans the great universe!" Gurdjieff declares. "It also introduces the Law of Seven, which covers all development, no matter the scope—infinitely big or infinitely small, ascending or descending. Every complete process must, without exception, have seven discrete phases, as decreed in the Seven Last Words, or sayings, of the dying God. Take for example, 'Father, into your hands I commend my spirit.' See how the effect (*Son*) reenters its cause (*Father*)? In this case too we witness the Law of the Three in action."

"Let's drink to mere Being . . ." Pirosmani says in his sleep, sipping wine from his tea glass.

Pshavela keeps kissing parts of Dagny's body; she sits mesmerized, looking somewhere beyond the present scene.

"Listen," Gurdjieff says persistently, "*do, re, me*—the full tones . . . *fa*—the semi-tone . . . *sol, la, ti*—the full tones again . . . *do*—the semi-tone . . . I call this the Law of the *Doremifasollasimus.*"

"No, you'd better call it *Silasolfamiredomination,*" Dagny suggests.

"Your hair needs cutting!" a displeased Gurdjieff says. "It is not polite to make idiotic remarks!"

"No," Pshavela interrupts, "her head should be shaved bare like yours, Tiger of Turkistan."

"Yes, as a token," agrees Gurdjieff. "As a clear sign that the zero of her mind is open to the infinity of Our Endlessness-Almighty-Omni-Loving-Common-Father-Uni-Being-Creator. And then to the nunnery go!"

"The human mind is not zero," Dagny counters.

"It is," maintains Gurdjieff. "It is zero, until it is penetrated by infinity! As soon as it is penetrated, the zero turns into 1, 2, 3, 4, 5, 6, 7, 8, 9, 12, 13, 666, 999, 30,000, a million, a billion, a trillion, etc., *ad infinitum*, like up the Mount of Olives!"

With these words, he picks up a guitar from behind his chair and produces some loud, atonal chords.

"Let's drink to music, my friends," Pirosmani murmurs.

"Vibrations, vibrations!" repeats Gurdjieff, playing a Middle Eastern tune on only one string. "The Megalocosmic Octave is made up of vibrations, and the frequency of these very vibrations comes irregularly, very irregularly, with two predictable deviations, exactly where semi-tones are missing, between *mi-fa* and *ti-do*. This very irregularity is the Omni-Creative Irregularity of Love, which the Shaman of Haizanakh did discover, did cherish, did elaborate and did refine into the mystery of self-realization and self-knowledge—the ascension by descending semi-tones: *b-a*, *c-b*—he discovered it upon departing this world via the shamanic art of fugue . . . it is what I call the *evolving involution of love*, and I swear to it by the rudiments of my Kundabuffer!"

"Kundabuffer?" Dagny wakes up and pushes Pshavela away. "What does Kundabuffer mean?"

"It is a tale told by an idiot," Pshavela says.

"Yes, it is the tail with which humans are born, facilitating the telling of idiotic tales," Gurdjieff explains. "When humans lost their natural tails, they developed unnatural ones, which they used to tie themselves to the moon and perpetuate the idiotic tales they told of themselves, to themselves and to each other."

"When Nature is suppressed, Cows start flying to the moon," Pshavela adds, and then elaborates: "the problem is, my dear, that since the Ur-Leopard Unity was disrupted, humans can see only what they eat instead of eating what they see. Alas, it is true . . . because of this, humans can see only a meager, underdeveloped part of the entire Being—as little as a loaf of bread, a hunk of meat, some vegetables, or some nuts and berries . . ."

"And they drink some wine, too," says Pirosmani, taking another sip.

"Thus, thanks to that very insidious organ, the Kundabuffer, humans cannot perceive the other edible parts of the Megalocosmos," Gurdjieff says, and then exclaims, "my God, but there are so many delicious things to eat—such an abundance of extraordinary tastes and endlessly nutritious varieties! But nothing, *nothing* compares to the taste of the Word of God, which is Love! It tastes better, much better, enormously better, *divinely* better than honey and milk, or a woman's breasts, which are better than wine . . ."

"Your Honor, I protest!" Pirosmani mutters. "Only wine could taste better than wine."

Gurdjieff starts singing, frenziedly stroking the guitar strings:

> You are what you eat,
> You eat what you are . . .
> You are what you love,
> You love what you are not.
> Eat God, who is Love,
> Eat Love, which is God . . .
> Eat yourself, to maintain yourself for Eternity . . .

Pshavela joins him, singing:

> Let the forests be
> To let your children be

Let beings be
Just let beings be ...

For his part, Pirosmani sings a refrain:

Trink, trink, trink, trink ...
Trink, trink, trink, trink ...

In a somnambular voice, Dagny intones:

I laid my body down to be cooked
by the heat of the kisses of thy mouth
for the feast of love yes
come yes come my beloved one
I'm the deer you are the panther
yes your love is like the panther's claw yes
come with me from Lebanon my spouse
from the lions' dens from the mountains of the
    leopards
your love is like their teeth
eat me eat my thighs and the flesh on my ribs
my hands my neck you are like the tower of David
    penetrating me
where art thou my love in me burning bright in the
    middle
make me your channel to pour your waters upon the
    dead earth
mixing desire and affection
you are my spring opened and my fountain unsealed
come yes come in me into my garden
and eat my pleasant fruits
yes my breasts are your pleasant fruits
and my womb is your orchard of pomegranates

eat them bursting yes bursting drink the sweet juice
devour me with your love so that I'm in you while
    you're in me
I'm black but comely I'm sinful but innocent
come not like watchman to find me and smote me
    and wound me
but come in me with your hot seed
and I will conceive your thoughts your passion
yes your passion goes through me through my body
which I laid down for the feast of love
which is your love which is my love
which is more than itself yes only love is better than
    love
only love is stronger than love than death when you
    come in me
like an army with banners in death's battlefield
for yes love is stronger than love
which is your love which is my love
yes my body is your love which you eat
and I am what I love and I love what I'm not
yes I am what I love and I love what I'm not
I'm not I'm not I'm not I'm naught I'm naught
naught naught naught naught . . .

Suddenly, up above the entire scene, a huge face looms like
the face of the Cheshire Cat upon the queen's playground. It is
the face of Koba, the young Joseph Stalin. He is looking down at
them from above with his eyes crossed, grinning at them as they
revel in the garden. His grin is getting bigger and wider, bigger
and wider, until only the grin remains—only the grin, and no
Stalin . . .

At last, the grin evaporates too, vanishing in the air, and the
scene changes into Edouard Manet's *Luncheon on the Grass*. The

nude woman sitting at the forefront is Dagny, with a tiny sparkle of surprise in her bright and tranquil look; she's looking at *you*.

Sohrab Addin woke up from a weird dream, fragments of it still pulsating in his foggy mind; three nutty fellows and an enchanted woman had talked about love and drank tea that turned into wine—a mock-Agape as dreamed by a mock-Dervish. He'd slept all night on a bench in the Ortachala Garden. He had a good sleep, the kind of sleep that repairs the ragged sleeve of worry; though, alas, the sleeves of his dirty jacket still remained as ragged as they'd ever been. Taking a deep breath of the fresh garden air and washing his sleepy face in the golden mist of the rising sun, Sohrab cleared his mind and attuned it to the singing of the birds in the trees around him; their music was spellbinding . . .

PART TWO

Gornahoor Harkharkh IV, great-grandson to the first Gornahoor Harkharkh, was sitting in his research nest on planet Saturn, listening to music which was coming from Earth. More precisely, it was coming from the city of Strasbourg in the middle of the European continent, in particular from the chapel of Saint Nicolas. The music was performed by the young cantor of the chapel, a certain Albert Schweitzer, a scholar of Jesus of Nazareth and of Bach. Actually, at that very moment it was a piece by Bach that Schweitzer played—a choral prelude entitled: "O Mensch, bewein dein Sünde groß."

Like his great-grandfather, Gornahoor Harkharkh IV was a scientist, and like all the beings on his planet he had the bodily form of a raven. From his famous ancestor, he'd inherited special skills for inventing all kinds of instruments and apparatuses. Thanks to his heritage, he also harbored an ardent scholarly enthusiasm for something called *Okidanokh*: a uniquely active element, the particularities of which are the chief cause of everything existing in the universe. It is governed by the principle of the included middle, in which two contradictory terms, by including a third, lose their individual values. This is exactly how quantum physics describes the state in which quantum particles are waves and corpuscles simultaneously. The conjunction of these three produces a fourth element, the *Etherokrilno*, which confers on the Okidanokh the character of a substance.[19] Gornahoor's experiments mainly focused on this substance.

To some extent, Gornahoor's enthusiasm was perilous, because his great-grandfather had fallen into disgrace throughout

19. *Okidanokh* and *Etherokrilno* are terms which first appear in Gurdjieff's *Beelzebub's Tales to His Grandson*. Gornahoor Harkharkh was also his invention.

the universe for experimenting with that very same Okidanokh, as with the sacred mystery of substances. Old Gornahoor was crazy enough to suggest the possibility of artificial manipulations, through the separation and reconstitution of the Okidanokh's three elements.

However, the young Gornahoor proved more down to earth (sorry, "down to Saturn," I should have said); he focused on Etherokrilno, which, in its relation to Okidanokh, is a hodgepodge of movements, transformations and energy transmissions. It is full of ineffable meanings vibrating from the Okidanokh, produced by the Music of the Spheres within and beyond the solar system. In order to transform those meanings into visual and acoustic entities that might be understood, he invented a multi-dimensional, semiotic-space-time apparatus called the the *lingvo-chronotopos accelerator*; through this apparatus, he was able to audio-visually render any clusters of meanings emanating from the various parts of the universe, decipher them syntactically, and reply to those messages, rearranging them into etherograms. The scope of his exchange grew to tremendous proportions; he even managed to hold a dialogue with the remotest of galaxies. The old Gornahoor would have been proud of his descendant!

Because of this invention, the Voices contacted Gornahoor Harharkh IV and commissioned him to look after the (verbatim) "acceleration-and-increase-of-vibrations-filling-up-the-obligatory-gap-aspect-of-the-unbroken-flowing-of-the-whole, as transmitted by some creative-featherless-bipeds, who were planning to discharge these vibrations in a ritual involving the extraction of maximum meaning from the least materiality, which would take the form of an Agape, which was pending in a small urban area between two seas on the planet Earth."

Due to the vastness of his galactic survey, it cost Gornahoor some effort to locate this minute project. For the last two hundred and fifty years (our time), he had been listening to the unusually pleasing combination of sounds coming from the European part of Earth; remarkably creative featherless bipeds made the sounds by playing various instruments, involving keyboards, strings, woodwinds, brass . . . the first one hundred years of his listening encompassed such a complex juxtaposition of diverse melodic sequences, that even Gornahoor had to wonder at the acuteness, versatility, and skill of those bipeds. For Gornahoor, the fugue represented the acme of that music. Made up of three different themes, each developed separately before combining in an overwhelming simultaneity, and culminating in the ascending descent of the semitones B-A-C-H, and then finally collapsing. From that point on, the music coming from that area of Earth became less sophisticated, though by no means less fascinating; sonatas, concertos and symphonies would swirl in Gornahoor's apparatus like huge schools of fish in a fisherman's net. Eventually, he fine-tuned the time-space dial to the terrestrial year of 1901, and that's how he ended up focused on the chapel of Saint Nicolas in Strasbourg, with the young cantor Schweitzer at the organ.

Gornahoor concentrated on what the featherless bipeds call the "cantus firmus" of the choral prelude, as rendered by the cantor; alongside the sustained melody of the cantus firmus, a separate voice sang in the counterpointal fashion, marked by a non-continuous freedom. This melodic combination produced not only acoustic feedback, but also clear-cut visual images in Gornahoor's apparatus—namely, a gigantic index finger hanging above a kneeling featherless biped; one could even hear the words, "O man, lament thy great sin!" Gornahoor Harharkh IV very much enjoyed the synthesis of music, visual imagery and verbal meaning in that piece.

I can't tell what made Gornahoor focus on the cantor Schweitzer; I don't know whether it was random selection, as our statisticians put it, or a meaningful target earmarked by the Voices that had spoken to the Saturnal raven. One thing I can tell, however, is that Gornahoor's project underscored the vital exchange of ideas between the Orient and the Occident on planet Earth—a mutually enriching brain drain, so to speak; a fusion of diverse signifying systems which would bring together creative featherless bipeds from the terrestrial East and the terrestrial West. Such an entwinement of all the energies on that small planet was exactly what was needed in order to secure the smooth, comprehensive discharge of the cosmic vibrations—the sacred substance Askokin—during the aforementioned Agape, also called the Celestial Love Feast . . . But first, let me get back to our "cantor firmus."

Albert Schweitzer had his first glimpse of the Pardimeme Premonition in Paris in the late 1890s, when, glancing into the carriage next to his, he accidentally caught sight of a false shaman—Georges "The Tiger" Clemenceau, who was the future prime minister of France and the mastermind behind the Versailles Treaty, which would eventually lead to World War II. Looking at Clemenceau's face, which was framed by a glossy top hat, Schweitzer experienced mixed feelings of disgust and sorrow: the face of that strongman was totally devoid of any hint of spirituality. Moreover, it seemed to imply an aversion to spiritual topics, reflecting uncivilized, uncultured human nature and unreasoned, ruthless will. Such were the "men of progress" then prominent in European politics, infected with the power-hungry desire to manipulate the mad Cowmeme masses. That year, Schweitzer put down his impressions and ideas into a book about the decline of world culture: humans just consumed what was created before, they were mere epigones! The modern age was overwhelmed by the fad of organizations, thus clustering men into mechanistic groups of consumption—that was the message carried by the book.

However, it was not simply his insight into the Pardimeme Premonition that turned Schweitzer into an eligible agent of

Gornahoor's task. As mentioned above, Schweitzer in and of himself combined the experience and knowledge of the two spiritual territories which made up the major dimensions of the Agape: Bach's music on the one hand, and the life of Jesus on the other: more precisely, the reality of His Passions. In 1901, Schweitzer wrote two books, which I render as *The Problem of the Last Supper: An Analysis Based on Historical Accounts and the Scientific Discoveries of the Nineteenth Century* and *The Mystery of Messiahdom and the Passions*, and which were followed in 1906 by his seminal study *The Quest of the Historical Jesus*. In these works, he detailed the profundity of Jesus's perceptions, and through his meditative endeavors and shamanic ecstasies, Schweitzer managed to overcome the false limits of time and encounter the real Christ, engaged in His eschatological mission.

Given that the Agape was meant to center upon the collective mental processing of Bach's *St. John Passion*, the Voices could have hardly found a better agent than the young cantor from Strasbourg; he understood that the Last Supper was comparable to the extreme materialization of an Agape, and that the Eschatological force of Christ's Passion related to the comprehensive vision of structure and spirit evident in Bach's cantatas and his *Passions*; this latter point Schweitzer demonstrated in his magnificent book on the Great Shaman of Eisenach's unsurpassable art.[20]

Schweitzer's theology was an enigmatic mixture of agnosticism and animistic pantheism, which he himself labeled "ethical mysticism." Such a mindset prepared him for the radical decision he made later: at the age of thirty, frustrated by European cultural decline, he abandoned theology and music in favor of medicine, going on to spend several decades of his life in Gabon, where he refined his shamanic skills among African wizards and treated

20. It should be noted here that Schweitzer always emphasized the difference and the exquisite significance of the fourth gospel (i.e., the one by St. John), as it carried mystical information of particular importance lacking in the other three.

the illnesses of the poor. In 1954, he was awarded the Nobel Peace Prize.

The choral prelude came to its decisive end. "*Bene!*" said Gornahoor in Latin, which he spoke pretty well, having scrutinized some seventeenth-century religious music—Gregorian chants, masses, and the like. The next step towards accomplishing his task was as follows: via the lingvo-chronotopos accelerator, he would have to physically *transfer* Schweitzer to the site of the pending event in the "small urban area between two seas." Based on the Law of Discontinuity, such a transfer seemed actually possible; put in the language of terrestrial physics, it would involve an elementary "quantum of action" (as defined in 1900 by a certain featherless biped named Max Planck). "Action" is a physical quantity, which corresponds to "energy" multiplied by "time." The Law of Discontinuity makes all kinds of action possible—take, for example, a bird flitting from one branch to another without encountering an intermediary point; it exists on one branch, then suddenly materializes on another. Being a quasi-bird himself (a Saturnal raven), Gornahoor knew how to perform such transfers; besides, what for the featherless bipeds only existed in the hypothetical realm of mathematical theory was physically possible on the planet Saturn.

Given that the Voices had also indicated that the Agape would deal with a special kind of poetic fabric (which was where the *Panther's Skin* came in), Gornahoor's next "etude" (as he labeled his pilot models for the discontinuous transfers) should feature some featherless bipeds of poetry, who would be able to square singing with Being. Despite such nebulous criteria, he managed to select someone called Rilke, whose poetic discourse was highly prized by the rest of the versifying bipeds.

Thus embarking upon his task, *transfers* and *discontinuities* swirling in his mind, Gornahoor Harharkh IV suddenly heard an awful cracking sound coming from the space sub-block of his lingvo-chronotopos accelerator.

"Space is out of joint!" exclaimed Gornahoor, checking the sub-block. "Despite everything . . . I'll need some time to set it right."

By these words, Gornahoor meant that he would need to transform some extracts of time into pure space, which he could then use to mend the quantum discontinuity fracture that had occurred. Such transformations were only possible through *objective music*—which Gornahoor knew how to manipulate.

"It might trigger some minor lingvo-chronotopos confusion on the ground down there . . ." the Saturnal raven thought. "But I'll see how it goes; sometimes spatial cracks prove epochal, prompting new developments and important changes; perhaps the featherless bipeds will completely modify their perception of space! Yes . . . epochal—almost *epochaliptic!*" Cracking puns like this, Gornahoor bent over the spacial crack and uttered the words "*kin dza-dza!*"—which is the Saturnian for "shit happens."

Yes, my friends, *quantum discontinuity*—or put differently, the fact that shit happens—this is what makes our world go round, and what propels my narrative, too.

Some of you must have read Milan Kundera's novel *The Unbearable Lightness of Being*. Among other curious observations, this remarkable book puts forth a very interesting definition of "kitsch." I'm not sure about the exact wording, but the gist is as follows: *kitsch appears when people try to ignore that shit exists*. And this is truly the case.

Therefore, to prove that there is nothing kitsch about my story, I would like to introduce another remarkable man: Simon Arshakovitch Ter-Petrosiann, known to Soviet history by his nickname, *Camo*. An ardent revolutionary, Camo was involved in the the Party's "fundraising" efforts: bank robberies and minor acts of terrorism were his major fields of achievement. He was also Stalin's childhood friend—they grew up together in the small, Georgian town of Gori; Koba looked after the Armenian boy as if he were his brother. Koba's mother, "Aunt Keke," was also very fond of him. It's also worth noting that even Lenin treated Camo benevolently, marking him out as a special favorite from among the other Party activists.

Camo joined the Party in 1901—Stalin recommended him—and remained a devoted member until he left this world in 1922, right after Soviet Russia's invasion of Georgia; one fine evening in Tiflis, he was riding a bicycle—his favorite form of transport—when he was hit on a hill by a truck. An accident, you could say—except for the fact that back then, there were only two or three trucks in the whole of Tiflis, let alone any other motor vehicles, so the probability of a car "accident" was pretty low. Such accidents rarely happened without the permission of a very high-ranking Party leader: could it have been Koba's? Who knows? Anyway, "the revolution always eats its children," as the saying goes. Alas, Camo was "eaten by the revolution," just like its much bigger children were—Bukharin, Trotsky, and many others . . .

Camo was buried in the central square of Tiflis, now called Liberty Square, next to a tiny garden featuring a bust of Pushkin—the first monument in the whole of the Empire to commemorate the "father of Russian literature."

As it happens, *eating* from an anthropological perspective acquires special significance with our friend Camo, who pushed the limits of the edible to extremes; the fact is, he once ate his own shit (although, some maintain that this happened on several occasions; in this case, determining quantity is not essential.) This happened in 1907, in Berlin, where Camo was arrested by the police and accused of terrorist activity. In order to prove that he was not a terrorist or a member of the Bolshevik Party, he simulated madness by eating his own excrement. His was a sinister genius.

The Bolshevik mentality inherited a lot from the Russian revolutionary anarchists of the 1870s—Nihilist ideology, for instance, and the rejection of all traditional values and attitudes. Without delving into the epistemological intricacies of such a mindset, I would like to assert here that Camo managed to creatively develop the legacy of his predecessors in a very special way, because *eating your own shit is the ultimate form of Nihilism!* Moreover, he was a creationist-revolutionary, believing in the creation of Something out of Nothing; again from an anthropological perspective, shit is that very Nothing out of which the world comes forth. Thus, Camo's scatological act (or rather, his deconstructionalist act, as the shaman of writing, the Dervish of difference, the tiger of post-structuralism—Jacques Derrida—would put it) acquires mythological dimensions. To an extent, popular memory did mythologize Camo in songs and rhymes, turning him into the revolutionary hero of collective anal fantasy . . .

It would be worthwhile to compare, very briefly, Camo's scatophagy with that of the Marquis de Sade and Pier Paolo Pasolini, respectively. In de Sade's case, eating excrement is an act of total freedom, a sort of a libertine breakthrough, representing triumph over societal mores and norms, whereas for Pasolini, who was more engaged politically, scatophagy symbolizes the suppression of individual rights and liberties, in which fascism and totalitarianism are equated to the communal consumption of communal excrement.

Having had enough of shit, let's get back to our story.

One morning, in late May of 1901, Koba and Camo were sitting in their underground headquarters in the Avlabari district of Tiflis, having a simple proletarian breakfast and talking.

"Koba-jan, I'm still thinking about that book which you read to me the other day," said Camo, "It was powerful, very powerful . . ."

"Which book?"

"The one by that Fyodor Dostoyevsky, *The Devils* . . . it is so instructive, we can learn plenty from it."

"Yes," Koba said, sipping his tea, "we will learn from it, and then, when we come to power, we will ban it.[21] It is about creative individuals like you and me, who desperately seek ways of making people equal and happy . . . Pah, this lukewarm tea tastes like urine. A good tea should be like the kiss of a beautiful woman— hot and strong."

"Very good observation, Koba-jan," Camo said laughing, "strong and hot . . . hot and strong."

"I'd better put in some cherry preserve to improve the taste."

"Aunt Keke's cherry preserves are truly the best. How is she? Have you heard from her lately?" Camo inquired, nostalgic for his boyhood days in Gori.

"No, Camo-jan, we've no time for that," Koba replied. "The revolution makes the same demands on a man as those Christ put to the true believer: give up your parents, your wife, your children, your brothers, and your sisters, and take up your cross and follow me! Desperate, creative individuals—remember Shigalev, that ingenious theorist of political reform, painstakingly trying to solve the perennial question of social equality? He was the best character Dostoyevsky ever created."

"Yes Koba-jan, that's what I had in mind when I mentioned Dostoyevsky's book," Camo said, becoming animated. "The revolution should be as strong as religion—hot and strong!"

"Equality, Camo-jan, *equality*—when each belongs to all and

21. And so they did. Actually, it was Lenin who denounced Dostoyevsky for his ultra-reactionary attitudes and his religious obscurities (*mrakobesiye*). Instead, he championed Tolstoy as the "mirror of the Russian Revolution." Later, in the 1930s or so, some people suggested setting up a monument to Dostoyevsky in Moscow; discussions took place about what to inscribe on it. One of the writers came up with the following line: "To dearest Fyodor Mikhailovich Dostoyevsky, from the grateful Devils."

all belongs to each—this will be our religion. From absolute freedom to absolute serfdom, and from absolute serfdom to absolute freedom."

"Yes Koba-jan, how poetically you speak! Very much like the chief "devil," Verkhovensky, who exclaims in Dostoevsky's book, 'I am a nihilist, but I love beauty.'"

"Revolution is not about beauty, it is about mystery, Camo-jan," said Koba. "He that possesses mystery possesses the Truth, and he that possesses the Truth possesses the freedom of the people."

"That sounds murky to me, but I agree with you in spirit, Koba-jan. I would put it more simply, however, so that the people might understand: take from the wealthy and give to the poor and hardworking."

"But what are you going to give to the people after the resources of the wealthy are exhausted, my friend?! Have you ever thought of that?" Koba asked, speaking as an adult would to a little boy.

"I don't know, Koba-jan," Camo mused. "To me, the redistribution of bourgeoisie wealth amongst the poor seems enough to provide the bare necessities currently lacking."

"Right, bare necessities . . . and what is man's major necessity?"

"I don't know, Koba-jan, what?"

"Mystery, you have to give them the truth of mystery," stated Koba. "The mystery of communal labor. Only communal labor can liberate the masses. We will make the people build huge plants and dams, and then they will congregate in these plants as if in temples or cathedrals, uttering the prayers we write for them—we, the supreme clergy of the permanent revolution."

"What is permanent revolution, Koba-jan?" inquired Camo.

"It is permanent transformation."

"The transformation of what?"

"The transformation of love into power, Camo-jan, and

the transformation of power into love!" Koba was inspired by his own thought. "I would put it as follows: the working class generates love, which we—the members of the order of creative individuals— transform into the power necessary to begin the revolution. It also works the other way around; we, the creative individuals, generate power, which the laboring masses transform into love, which we, yet again, transform into power. This would then go on endlessly."

"Koba my brother, what can I contribute to the permanent revolution?" Camo asked, visibly thrilled.

"Spill blood."

"Blood?"

"What is the fundamental substance of all religions?"

"I don't know, Koba-jan, I didn't go to seminary, you did."

"The substance is Blood," said Koba pensively. "When I saw my father after they'd carried him home, after he was beaten to death—his face covered with blood—I got scared. I was a little boy . . ."

"Oh, I remember that black day, Koba-jan, poor Uncle Beso!" Camo said sorrowfully. "Aunt Keke weeping . . . you standing in the corner, pale and quivering . . . but why are you thinking about it now, Koba-jan? You sound strange."

"Quivering, yes . . . but then, slowly, my fear turned into shame and disgrace." Koba's voice remained pensive. "I used to hate my father—a rude, meaningless drunkard. But then, observing his bleeding wounds and smelling his bloodstains on my hand, mixed feelings suddenly arose in me—of guilt and sorrow, both mingled with love."

"Fear creates Love, Koba-jan, as the great Rustaveli wrote," Camo said, quoting from the national epic.

Throughout his future political career, Joseph Stalin would pervert this phrase in order to justify his abuse of power, declaring, "It is safer to be feared than loved." The young

Stalin, however, still mixed revolutionary idealism with murky religious dogma. The ruthless "Man of Steel" came later, after Stalin suffered the death of his first wife; according to some biographers, this tragedy played a crucial role in the coarsening of his personality.

"Yes, this is true," Koba agreed, "but here I speak of blood, which as a substance is more mysterious than our Rustaveli, with his ideas of love, friendship and chivalry, ever dreamed of. Blood is intoxicating; that's why the founders of Christianity put it at the center of their religious rituals. Look at the peasants of this country, unthinking believers—they slaughter their sacrificial cattle for one reason only: to spill blood. They do not even understand the purpose of the damn rites! Spilt blood is the Word spoken by violence, and, my brother, through violence the future speaks. Yes, violence brings the future's good news closer, and we, as revolutionaries, are champions of the future; through violence, we will make the future our reality—the great future of the liberation of man!"

"Vah, Koba-jan!" Camo exclaimed. "Your speech makes this lukewarm tea with cherry preserve in it taste like good old red Kakhetian!"

"Camo, my brother," Koba continued, "we need to come up with new forms of violence. She's our little sister, and we need to teach her how to walk. We need small acts of terror. We need explosions. Yes, as Verkhovensky had it, we must begin with rebellion; we need at least some minor bloodshed, just a bit of it—to inflame the minds of the people . . . yes, there is too much drowsiness among us now—it's boring, *boring!*" Having stressed the point, it was clear he might as well have added these words from Shakespeare's *Richard III*: "And therefore, since I cannot prove a lover / to entertain these fair well-spoken days, / I am determined to prove a villain."[22]

22. Shakespeare's major plays were translated into Russian by Prince Ivane

"Recipes for anarchism!" exclaimed Camo, "that's what I must read now . . . hand grenades, minor explosives . . . I love fireworks!"

"Men like you will make up the new order of Ishmaelites— the new Hashashins—destroying and tearing up the bourgeois fabric of society. First plant tiny seeds of terror, and then later we'll harvest the wheat of change."

Camo was flattered—the fledgling revolutionary in him has received a big confidence boost; inspired, he began fantasizing about explosions and the "seeds of terror" he would plant.

"An event is being planned in the German Garden very soon, Koba-jan," he said as Koba listened gloomily, touching his jaw and grimacing slightly from the pain. "I saw a poster advertising 'mystical pictures.' You remember David and Alexandre Dighmelow—they put on a magic lantern show of *Vepkhistqaosani* last year.[23] They traveled all around Georgia—by "official decree of the Governor of Transcaucasia." They showed it in villages and to military regiments."

"Is it similar to the works of the physicist Doctor Dering in the Nikitin Brothers' Circus? That had lamps, multiplying glasses, and photo-projectors. A "magic lantern show" in the German Garden, you say . . ."

"What if we . . . *perform* there?"

"Why not?! It's exactly the place where the aristocracy and the bourgeois elite congregate," said Koba. "But be careful . . . don't go too far."

"You have my word, Koba-jan!" Camo was full of determination.

Machabeli more than a decade earlier, so it's possible that Stalin read them. Although Prince Machabeli was not a natural-born Pardimeme, through his translation of Shakespeare he attained certain shamanic heights. In June of 1898, he left this world in a very mysterious way—he simply disappeared and his body was never found.

23. Alexandre Dighmelow is also known for making the first Georgian silent movie in 1912.

"If I fail—if I let you down—may I eat my own mama's shit!"[24]

According to newspapers published in Tiflis in 1901, the end of May was extremely hot, and the Moushthaid Garden was one of the best places in town to relax and cool down. Count Avalov explained its history to Dagny: "This beautiful garden was founded in the 1830s by a man called Mir-Fatah-Agha Said, a Shiia leader from the city of Tabriz (Moushthaid is a religious title) who fled Persia in 1828 after the Russian-Persian war, having masterminded a plot against the Shah. Although the plot failed, the grateful Russian authorities granted him generous asylum— a fifty acre lot in Tiflis that he turned into a garden. In 1845, the Shah pardoned Moushthaid and permitted him to return to his homeland."

Dagny and the count were playing billiards in the hall adjoining the restaurant of the Moushthaid Garden. A woman playing billiards?! With a man?! That would be reprehensible even in the heart of Europe, let alone in a semi-Asian Eastern Orthodox country like Georgia. Dagny had learned to play the game in Warsaw from a circle of local bohemians—specifically, Tadeusz Boy-Żeleński, a good friend of her and Stach's (although maybe he was more than just a friend).

For the rigidly conservative public of the early twentieth century, the worry was that female players would turn billiards into a sexually charged game. Just picture it: an attractive woman in a light summer dress bends over the billiards table, pushes ivory balls into pockets with a long cue stick, and allures male bystanders with the spectacular "pocket" of cleavage between the "balls" of her breasts. That's the image of her if you looked from the front—but if a man looked at her from the back, just as she

24. "To eat your mamma's shit" is old Tbilisi slang, meaning "to do a very wrong thing," "to make a big mistake," or "to play a nasty trick." It has obvious Oedipal undertones.

was bending over, the sight might inspire sexual fantasies. Such was the historical period we are currently dealing with. As banal as that!

However, male sexuality back then was not that banal—it was pretty complex as a matter of fact, caught between conflicting attitudes. Earlier we touched upon experiments in "free love" practiced in the good old European capitals, as a way to assert individual freedom via promiscuous sexual relations. But freedom proved a pretty heavy weight to bear—especially sexual freedom; at the worst, it lead to suicide, and at best, merely alcoholism. Polygamous promiscuity might have been common in earlier cultures, but none of these charged it with such profound "existential" significance—equating it to the achievement of individual liberty—as did the males of the late nineteenth century. What has individual freedom to do with the quantity or diversity of sexual experiences?

On the contrary, in those very males we witness what Stach Przybyszewski described as "the inferior man's tragedy under the matriarchy's oppressive yoke, that has never been more powerful than perhaps precisely in our age." Moreover, to men like Stach, women like Dagny were "an exotic disease infecting the creative genius of her artist-husband." In one of his novels, Stach compares such women to malaria, and makes overt references to his wife. Poor Dagny—upon reading the book, she sat motionless "and whimpered softly like a sick animal," as she later wrote in a letter to him. Misogynous sentiments such as these arose from a view of women as carriers of suppressive power, which they exercised upon "inferior men." The act of killing a woman, either in real life or symbolically, became another way for a man to achieve "liberation."

Thus, the paradox of the masculine psyche at the turn of the century was that women represented both liberation and imprisonment. I call it a "quasi-Manichean sensibility." In fact, it all boils down to the male proclivity to mythologize women: men like to attribute godly or demonic features to their sexual partners, and get off on it. The iconography of the late nineteenth century abounds with images of women as double-natured creatures—simultaneously angels and demons, nuns and whores. Love is as strong as Death, which is to say that killing a woman is as liberating as loving her.

Bullshit!

Yes, bullshit! I came up with this bullshit for the sole purpose of surmising what was going on in Wlad Emeryk's head—in the subconscious terrain of his psyche—particularly as he stood there watching Dagny play billiards with Count Avalov. One thing I can tell you is that on that very day he finally made up his mind *to kill Dagny, and afterwards to kill himself.* He stood there in the billiards room and mentally drafted the letter he later sent to Anton Keller, asking him to "see that no autopsy is performed on Mme Przybyszewska, for there will not be any doubt that I killed her, an autopsy is therefore unnecessary . . . my remains anyone can have . . . cover Mme Przybyszewska and her entire casket with fresh flowers, preferably roses." He decided to kill her in order to free himself from an *angelic whore*, and then he punished himself for killing a *demonic nun*. Compare this oxymoronic drive with the expression "to die in each other's arms" as a metaphor for mutual orgasm—a pretty commonplace euphemism in early seventeenth-century English "metaphysical" poetry. Such a comparison would prove Emeryk's *oxymoronic* drive actually *moronic.*

Facing bankruptcy, Emeryk was obviously suffering from a nervous breakdown.

As "anatomists" of melancholia such as Richard Burton teach us, such breakdowns have the power to substantially deform a fragile mind—both exacerbating crude, aggressive urges, and stimulating monstrous fantasies. Emeryk's desire for an erotic union with Dagny manifested as a double suicide—having, in his delusion, convinced himself that Dagny wanted it too—only, "the mother in her gets the upper hand, as she loves her son Zenon far too much" (as he wrote to Stach). Therefore, he had to kill her at a moment when she least expected it—which he actually did. Thus Emeryk conceived of an act more usually committed by desperate lovers (on a beautiful island in Japan, or in an untidy hotel room in Berlin, for instance), and which portrayed Dagny as his mistress, which she'd never been. The revolver Emeryk had inherited from Dagny's lover Wincent Brzozowski symbolically bound his penis to that of Wincent's, and with this phallic substitute he resolved to "penetrate" Dagny.

"Bravo!" exclaimed Count Avalov, as Dagny, with perfect aim, sent a ball into the corner pocket opposite.

"*Olé!*" Dagny blushed with excitement. *Olé*—it was a joyful word, used to encourage the dancers and singers she'd seen performing in Spain, where she'd spent a few weeks with Stach in a little fishing village. The sun, the ocean, the smell of roses . . . yes, they were together, and yes, they had loved each other and been tender. She had even been able to write there—some poems . . . *Sing me the Song of Death and Life* . . .

It seems to me that upon hearing Dagny utter that Spanish word, Wlad Emeryk would have thought of the last scene in Bizet's opera *Carmen*; the wanton gypsy woman, Carmen, throws her wedding ring at the feet of Don José, who then draws a knife and stabs her twice . . . This was another sexually charged fantasy in poor Emeryk's head: the ring vaginal, the knife phallic. He loved that opera and had read the story by Prosper Mérimée upon which the libretto was based. The epigraph to the story reads: "Every woman is evil. / Good she can be but twice— / Once, in the bed of love, / Once, on the bed where she dies." Carmen is the epitome of a femme fatale, as iconic as Gustav Klimt's masterpiece *Judith*—just look at Judith's lowered eyelids, her half-naked breasts; holding Holofernes's severed head, this woman is more than the liberator of the Israelities—*she is a demon of seduction.*

And yet, in Emeryk's feverish vision, Dagny was a divine creature—the very same angel of the Schwarze Ferkel; though, instead of a cigarette in her mouth, she had a billiard cue in her slender hand—much like the fiery spear of ecstasy, which was about to go through his heart . . .

"You look pale Wlad, are you all right?" the angel asked him.

"It's humid in here," murmured Wlad.

"Then I suppose we require another bottle of chilled champagne—don't you think so, count?" (The angel was direct.)

"But of course, Mme Przybyszewska!" said the count, looking for the waiter.

"Let me take care of it," suggested Wlad, sweating and trying to drag himself out of the necrophiliac-erotic swamp of his senses.

"How kind of you, darling," said the angel, accepting his services. "We'll be sitting at the table under the willows by the river. Let's go down, count, I've been longing to tell you about my closest friend, Maya Vogt. I do hope you'll meet her some day. Her brother Nils is a very good poet." She walked out with Avalov.

"Speaking of poets, there's another—very famous and very strange," Avalov said.

"Where?"

"Over there, playing billiards at that table. He calls himself Vazha-Pshavela, and he comes from the Pshavi highlands." The count spoke as they continued to walk. "He writes in very crude, unrefined language."

"I think I've heard of him," said Dagny, recalling her conversation with the Englishman in the train to the Black Sea. "I would like to meet him. Could you introduce me, count?"

"I could try . . . although, I have not had the pleasure of

becoming acquainted with him myself. Why don't you go take a seat at their table? I can see Emeryk coming now with the champagne."

Though surrounded by several enthusiastic young men, Pshavela was completely absorbed in the game, analyzing the balls on the table for what would prove another tricky hit. He'd mastered billiards in St. Petersburg, where he'd lived for a year while studying jurisprudence at the university; an impoverished student, the game helped him earn some cash for food. Once he won a dinner in a restaurant for him and his cousin, but the loser played a dirty trick with him—he booked a table, they dined and drank wine, and when the bill was about to come, the guy managed to slip out the back door—leaving Pshavela and his cousin with the check. Refusing to pay, they were rushed at by waiters and several customers, the whole thing ending in a fistfight of two against many. Witnesses tell how Pshavela, standing in the corner, knocked down his attackers one by one. A German boxer who happened to be there later approached Pshavela in the street, telling him how impressed he'd been with his fistfighting skills.

"The women of the Pshavi highlands differ from those of the lowlands," Pshavela explained to Dagny, his healthy eye half-shut. They were sitting with Avalov and Emeryk at the table under the willows. "They have more liberty, and they can walk or ride alone, roaming miles away from home in light, worn-out garments which disguise their figures, their feet clad in soft slippers. Our people still believe that some of these women have love affairs with man-eating giants called the *Daevi*, who live in remote highland caves and visit their lovers by night. That's why the Georgian word for "woman"—*kali*—is related to the Georgian for "sprite"—*ali*. I've seen several of these wandering maidens sleeping in the forest, and who knows what visions and thoughts invade their dreams as they rest beneath the sky, lying as if expired upon their beloved giants' chests."

"Could you pour me more wine, Wlad?" said Dagny to Emeryk.

"But here I assume," Pshavela continued slowly, as if telling some odd, quaint dream he'd had the night before, "that this goes back deep into the past, when our women were married to gods. The highland word for wife, *jalabi*, relates to what in Europe is called "religious hetaerism," or "temple prostitution." The average Pshavi man now finds such women in the realms of love and of poetry. And let me tell you why. . ."

"You're in your element, Dagny, my dear," Wlad says, giving her a shrewd wink, though secretly unnerved.

Pshavela pretended not to notice him.

"We have a custom in the Pshavi highlands, as rare in nature as a tulip tree grown in the desert, called *tsatsloba*. It goes like this: a girl, as soon as she matures, chooses a young man as her *love-brother*. Young men, reaching puberty, are supposed to make the same kind of choice—picking a *love-sister*. They can be related to each other or total strangers, no matter. The couples do not have to hide away or conceal their affair: they roam together at nights, give gifts to each other and, what is most curious, they are supposed to lie in bed together. However, there are certain restrictions they have to observe when doing this, namely that there can be no contact between their limbs or torsos—only the girl's head is permitted to rest on her love-brother's chest. Thus, there is no sexuality present between them in the physical sense, although verbally it is there. She might tell him something like this: 'how beautiful art thou, how refined are thy hands, how sweet are thy lips; let me, let me put thy tongue into my mouth, and let me, let me drink the water of thy mouth . . .'"

"I think this man has had too much to drink," Wlad whispered to Dagny. "Or else he must be deranged."

But for Dagny, Wlad might as well have not been there; she asked for more wine and smiled at Pshavela. "Please, continue."

"Through lying together, they overcome their bodies and open up their minds to the flow of celestial energy, the channeling of which is the function of all humans populating the Earth. The celestial stream of vibrating energy comes from remote planets, and, passing through us, continues on. It is obvious that highlanders, who live much closer to the skies than lowlanders do, have more refined planetary sensibilities, and overall are innately suited to this practice. However, plants and animals happen to be incommensurably greater transmitters than humans are, although only through us can planetary influences verbalize themselves. Thus poetry is born."

"Indeed!" This time, Emeryk winked at Avalov.

"Yes," agreed Dagny, staying close to the highlander; leaning towards him, she recited: "'She wished for no eagle, whose proud wings could fly her to the clouds, nor for a nightingale to sing her beauty's praise. She would fill her life with the rainbow colored cobwebs of her own dreams.' I wrote that while in Spain—*Olé!* Eh, Count Avalov?"

The sparkling wine, the evening breeze from the river and stories of love traditions in the highlands were carrying Dagny away—she heard the poet speak through the dense, dim aura which enveloped her:

"The spring of immortality pouring from the golden pipe . . . wish I could be replenished, inundated with thy body—our limbs entangled . . . I am the crop field for the scythe of thy rib . . . I am the dagger stuck in thy heart . . . I am the silver bowl filled up with wine for thee to drink—the wine red as our blood, the intoxicating juice of life . . . I am the woolen shirt soaked with the sweat of thy breast . . ."

"They grew up everywhere, they crowded around her, fluttered around in her parlor like birds of a thousand wings and a thousand colors ..." Dagny began to murmur her poetry in Norwegian. "Radiant lilies licked her with burning human tongues, orchids, chrysanthemums, cacti, oleander ..."

Pshavela, who had been speaking French (rather extraordinary, as he spoke no other language besides Russian) now switched to his native Georgian.

"I gaze upon thy smiling face and long to press my lips to thine, though well I know I ne'er will hold thee in my arms, O dearest mine ..."

"... Brown, yellow, mysterious red, blue like the fairy tale's glowing grotto ..." Dagny kept on reciting.

"Over the rushing waters wild, my voice takes wing and towards thee flies," Pshavela continued. "But mingling with the deafening roar in raging depths it swoons and dies ..."

"The fragrance bewildered her . . . now she saw the whole flower flock stride towards her . . . they pushed at her, pressed against her, they breathed their awful breath into her face . . . she was choking . . . she was choking . . . oh!" Dagny really was choking then, but Pshavela leaned towards her and squeezed her arm with his strong hand.

"Enough!" Wlad Emeryk lurched at him, prepared to drag him off by the sleeve.

"Come now, gentlemen, this is becoming ridiculous, don't you think?!" Count Avalov stood between them.

But suddenly, a crashing rumble of thunder halted them all in their tracks! A downpour fell upon them, as if out of nothing and nowhere. Pshavela stood frozen, his one-eyed gaze directed towards the riverbank, where a man strode along dressed in a yellow robe and holding a long staff. The man had clear-cut Mongolian features—narrow eyes, prominent cheekbones, a shaved head. Startlingly, a black raven was perched on his right shoulder, its strong claws piercing the man's yellowish-brown skin, its wings fluttering from time to time as it struggled to keep its balance. Saying nothing, Pshavela ran towards the stranger. Who was this man? Among Tibetan monks, he was known as the Leader of the Seven.

Tigran Poghossyan was baffled by the change that had come over his friend, the Black Greek. While he knew that Gurdjieff was fluent in various foreign languages, he'd taken it as a given that a man with Armenian blood in his veins would be multilingual. But something happened one morning that nearly knocked Tigran down. They'd been having breakfast and were talking about the weather, when suddenly Gurdjieff went into an elaborate meditation on music in general and the music of Bach in particular. What was strange, however, was that Gurdjieff was speaking in impeccable German, the kind that Tigran would hear in the *Kircha* neighborhood of Tiflis. (As a matter of fact, Gurdjieff spoke German that day with an Alsatian accent, which Tigran surely would not have recognized.)

"Bach is a terminal point," Gurdjieff declared with enthusiasm. "Nothing comes from him; everything merely leads up to him. This genius was not a mere individual; he had a collective soul."[25]

Tigran, who at that moment had just taken a sip of hot tea, choked and burned his lower lip.

"Bach's immense strength functioned without self-consciousness, like a force of nature; for this reason, his music is as cosmic and rich as nature," Gurdjieff added.

With a napkin covering his lower lip and chin, Tigran asked, "what is it that you just said, Sev Houyn-jan?"[26]

"For him, art was religion and so was distanced from the world or worldly success. It was an end in itself. Bach included religion in the definition of art just generally. All great art, even

---

25. Gurdjieff's musings on Bach here and below bear a striking resemblance to those in Albert Schweitzer's writings . . .
26. "Sev Houyn" is the Armenian for "Black Greek."

secular art, is religious in his eyes; for him, tones do not perish but ascend to God like praise too deep for utterance," said Gurdjieff, draining his cup of tea.

"Are you feeling all right this morning, Jhora-jan?" Tigran's voice trembled.[27]

Gurdjieff stood up, approached his friend's upright piano, pulled the chair closer, and sat down. Hesitating for a moment, he suddenly rushed at the keyboard, diving into an extremely complex, fiery fugue.

Tigran had seen his friend play before—trifling with the keys, producing very simple tunes and harmonies—a sort of eclectic mixture of traditional Armenian, Russian Orthodox, and pentatonic Oriental music. This time, however, Tigran was treated to a polyphonic tour de force of amazing stamina. The poor fellow just sat there and listened, trying to come up with some kind of an explanation. Going to the cupboard, he grabbed a bottle of Armenian Shustov brandy and took a huge gulp straight from the neck. He was very well aware that Armenians were the most talented people on Earth—and yet . . . could this mysterious, sudden talent have been caused by excessive contact with Dervishes, magicians and lamas? Was this man the same Gurdjieff he had known for so many years?

"Where did you learn to play such great music, Jhora-jan—in Switzerland?" inquired Tigran.

Gurdjieff could not hear him. He went on playing; the fugue was as mesmerizing to him as the siren song was for sailors. At last he straightened up, turned to Tigran and spouted yet more musicological speculations.

"Nowhere so well as in the *Well-Tempered Clavier* are we made to realize that art was Bach's religion. He does not depict natural soul states, as Beethoven does in his sonatas; there is no striving

27. "Jhora" is the informal Russian-Armenian for "George" (derived from the French).

and struggling towards a goal, only the reality of life as felt by a spirit ever conscious of being superior to life—a spirit in which the most contradictory emotions are simply phases of a fundamental superiority of soul." Here, he played some movements from *Prelude in E-Flat Minor*, before moving on to *Prelude and Fugue in G Major.* "Whoever has once felt this wonderful tranquility has comprehended the mysterious spirit that has here expressed all it knew and felt of life in this secret language of tone."

"Jhora-jan, you look slightly . . . *changed*," said Tigran, searching for the right word for what had come over his friend.

"Changed, how?!" Gurdjieff was surprised. "I was talking about what I call *objective consciousness*, attainable only by the Sacred Individuals, of whom Bach was certainly one."

Tigran was relived, mostly because Gurdjieff had switched back to speaking Armenian.

"But you spoke German, Jhora-jan—even von Zemmel the apothecary cannot speak such pure German!" said Tigran.

"Did I?" Gurdjieff said, his eyes misty. "I didn't notice." He began to play the *Well-Tempered Clavier* again.

He continued playing for an hour, maybe more. Yes, music was an end in and of itself for him, as if he believed that the tones "do not perish, but ascend to God like praise too deep for utterance," as Schweitzer put it. Then, exhausted and short of breath, he fell asleep still sitting in front of the piano, his hands in his lap.

Tigran was totally at a loss—*could it be that the Black Greek had contracted some bizarre disease in Central Asia?* He could not leave Gurdjieff sleeping upright in a chair—he might fall down and hurt himself. *His head! His enlightened head!* Thus, Tigran decided to send the neighbor boy to fetch a doctor. He was just moving towards the door, when suddenly a pounding came—bah! bah! bah! bah! It was exactly like the Commendatore pounding on Don Giovanni's door, though Tigran had never seen that opera. "Mamma-jan!" thought he. "What could possibly come next?!"

Nervously, he asked, "who is it?"

The pounding continued, though softer this time.

"Open up, Tigran!" Gurdjieff called from the sitting room. Encouraged by this, Tigran turned the key and opened the door.

He saw the thin, unshaved face of a man staring back at him with one, squinting eye, the other one stuck wide open; the man wore a light shepherd hat and was smiling. Nodding to him politely, the stranger stepped aside to give way to someone behind him. This turned out to be a Mongol dressed in a worn robe, holding a staff. A huge raven sat on his shoulder.

"*Barrrrev*, Tigrrran-jan, *barrrev!*" exclaimed the raven.[28] Tigran felt woozy. He had seen talking parrots and magpies, but had never heard a raven speak before . . . and in Armenian, no less. He stood as if struck dumb, and then murmured something in response.

"I hope you won't mind, my friend, if we crash here? I've traveled through twenty-four worlds, and I'm exhausted," said the raven, as the Mongol moved towards the Ottoman chair.

"My God! Gornahoor Harharkh!" Gurdjieff was both amazed and overjoyed. "And you, the greatest of all living Sacred Individuals—the Leader of the Seven!" Gurdjieff approached the Mongol and fell to his knees.

The Leader smiled at him and made a deep, courteous bow in response, keeping his palms together.

"Hey! Hey! Not that deep! Not that deep!" the raven shouted, trying to stay upright on the bowing Leader's shoulder. "As a matter of fact, I'm not *the* Gornahoor! As a matter of fact, I'm his great-grandson's terrestrial double. As a matter of fact, I passed through twenty-four worlds to materialize here—that's the distance between Saturn and Earth. You can call me Ferdinand— I'm a linguist, yes—Ferdinand Humboldt. I'm here on a very special cosmic-philological mission, very special . . . *a search for*

28. *Barev* is the Armenian for "hello."

the Perfect Language, if you please." (His Armenian was perfect.) Tears welled up in Tigran's eyes—he still could not believe it. Gurdjieff went and hugged the man that looked like a shepherd (that was Pshavela).

Everybody sat down and remained silent, until the raven, Ferdinand, produced another linguistic surprise. In high medieval Georgian, he began reciting two quatrains from Rustaveli's *Vepkhistqaosani*: "*Nakhes utskho moqme vinme, jda mtirrrrali tskhlisa pirrrrsa; shavi tskheni sadavita hqva lomsa da vitha gmirrrsa . . .*"

The direct English translation of these quatrains is as follows:

> They saw a certain stranger knight; he sat weeping on
> the bank of the stream, he held his black horse by
>   the reins,
> he looked like a lion and a hero; his bridle, armor and
> saddle were thickly bedight with pearls; the rose of his
> cheek was frozen in tears that welled up from his
> woe-stricken heart.

> His form was clad in a coat of tiger's skin with the
> fur on the outside; his head, too, was covered with a
>   cap of
> tiger's skin; in his hand he held a whip thicker than
> a man's
> arm. They looked and liked to look at that wondrous
> sight.

Not only Tigran, but even Pshavela and Gurdjieff stared at him amazed. The raven shouted, "yes, *confusio linguarum*, the confusion of languages! Undoubtedly a second Babel is at hand! The Cow's flight to the moon will be the second Babel!"

The Leader nodded at this remark, but said nothing. The raven went on:

"We need to stop that stupid animal, just like a millennia ago you humans were stopped from building your tower-to-the-sky! Yes, we need another confusion of languages to disrupt the second Babel! But I came here to resurrect language, not to confuse it . . . I came for the Cipher of the Golden Fleece, also known as the Lazarus Code! It is hidden in a text written in the Georgian tongue, a poem—more precisely, a poem about a panther's skin."

Pshavela and Gurdjieff looked at each other, slightly confused, and then turned to the raven.

"I know the poem," said the highlander. "You just recited some lines from it. It is Georgia's national treasure, and every Georgian knows it by heart—"

"I know it is your *treasure*," the raven interrupted, "but you Georgians are so preoccupied with your nationalist project that you cannot read the poem correctly and ascertain the true treasure hidden in it . . . beware, my highlander—one fine day, all this damned nationalism will exhaust your shamanic powers!"

Hearing this, Pshavela went pale, his healthy eye becoming as unfocused as his glassy one.

"I know the panther's skin poem and I know the legend of the Fleece," Gurdjieff said, "but what's the connection between the two? Speaking frankly, I've received some vague hints about the poem—the Voices said something about it, but I did not receive their message as a coherent, continuous whole."

"It's not your fault!" the raven said, "even though you are featherless bipeds and your minds are not fully developed. The message delivered by the Voices happened to be incomplete."

"How come?" Gurdjieff inquired.

Here Ferdinand the raven paused and then muttered, "because Gornahoor's apparatus, the lingvo-chronotopos accelerator, was damaged; to be precise, it was the space sub-block that was damaged. Due to that damage, a highland goatherd was able to speak French, and you, Black Greek, you spoke German with an Alsatian accent this morning. As a matter of fact, it was the cantor Albert Schweitzer from Strasbourg who spoke through you. The damage to the space-block caused tangible lingvo-topographical deformations, certain displacements, and dimensional irrelevancies. I was created and sent here to help my Saturnal father—Gornahoor Harharkh IV—to tackle the quantum discontinuity fracture!"

"As it happens, I loved speaking French yesterday," Pshavela acknowledged.

"Same with me and German . . . although I have no idea who that Schweitzer is," Gurdjieff admitted.

"Well, the *space out of joint* thing is proving rather entertaining, I agree! How about my Georgian and my Armenian, Tigranjan?!" the raven said, turning to Poghossyan, who sat there in dumb amazement.

The Leader woke him with a punch.

"Perfect! Perfect!" Tigran said, wiping his eyes.

"Now, let me get to the gist of my mission!" Ferdinand declared. "The whole problem with the crazy Cowmeme flight boils down to the *breach*—or the *Obligatory-Gap-Aspect*—in the unbroken flow of the Great Cosmic Octave. There is a dissonant gap between the notes *F* and *E*. The *Obligatory-Gap* was originally meant to be filled up with the joint consciousness of all human beings populating Earth. You know the story, my Black Greek—the breach impeded the flow of megalocosmic vibrations from the sacred substance Askokin, which comes from His-Most-Endlessness. On Earth, the Askokin Vibrations are also known as *The Love that Moves the Spheres*, and here I refer to Dante Alighieri, as you might have guessed."

"O, yes, yes!" Tigran affirmed with pathos.

"The Ashok of Tuscany . . ." Gurdjieff said.

"Enough of him," said the raven abruptly. "Here comes my major point. Originally, you humans filled up the breach pretty successfully—thanks to the Golden Fleece, the ideal transmitter of megalocosmic vibrations. Yes, certain unique featherless bipeds were given the Fleece in order to secure the harmonious flux of energy between *F* and *E*—between the world of the planets and the world of Earth. This was the sole reason why a position in the cosmos was designated for mankind. Moreover, the golden curves of the Fleece made up a text which transmitted information about the Primordial Contradiction between existence and nonexistence and their Reciprocal Maintenance—a ubiquitous quantum process, which here on Earth is considered the mystery of Resurrection, and which among Initiated Individuals is called the *Sacred Almznoshinoo* . . . how poetic!" At this, the raven pecked the Leader's bald skull and the latter nodded.

Ferdinand went on. "The text of the Fleece included a description of quantum particles, which are waves and corpuscles simultaneously. The frequencies of the waves and the structures of the corpuscles were also described." The raven paused, and then, with a lordly mein, declared: "Here comes another major point! The text, or the Cipher of the Golden Fleece, was written in the tongue of the first featherless biped, later inherited by another a single survivor of the disaster of Atlantis, here known as the Flood, who in turn passed it on to his son, Japheth. Consequently, the tongue is called *Japhetic*. Marrrr . . . Marrrr . . . Marrrr . . . Nicholas Marr, the famous linguist . . . he wrote on Japhetic . . . is he available, by the way?!"

"It should be possible, I met him a couple times," said Pshavela, fascinated by the raven's story. He was going to add something, but Ferdinand had become impatient and, with a grave countenance, shouted at the highlander: "I don't give a damn about Marrr! I care about the tongue which was desecrated by your people!"

Pshavela looked at him, nonplussed. "Which tongue?"

"The Georgian tongue, you fool, which comes from the text of the Golden Fleece; Japhetic, or proto-Iberian—which was spoken by tribes living in Colchis! The Magi and mystagogues of Colchis learned it from the wine-drinking panthers, which would congregate around a very unusual featherless biped—a truly Sacred Individual—who died and resurrected annually, was permanently drunk and taught his goats how to sing utterly ruthless songs. Alas, the tongue was lost in the great confusion of languages caused by the misguided construction of Babel . . ."

"But this confusion is not the fault of my people," Pshavela said with humor in his voice, amused by a reply so aptly spoken.

"Of course not, my highlander," the raven agreed, nodding, "and you know why? Because your people did not take part in the construction of Babel! No, you stayed home instead, drinking and feasting . . . ha-ha-ha! Therefore, you survived the confusion and retained the original Japhetic—but it is Georgian by now, distinctly Georgian; you did not maintain it in its pure form; you drank it away, along with your wits. Ha-ha-ha! Consequently I can assert that the Georgian language, my highlander, is *intoxicated Japhetic*, that's what it is!"

"Shall I serve some tea, my dear guests? You must be thirsty," Tigran politely interjected.

"No," the raven objected, "birds like me do not take tea; we usually prefer blood, clotted blood. We are scavengers . . ." and the raven's eyes filled with *all the seeming of a demon's that is dreaming* . . .

Tigran sat back, looking pale. Ferdinand went on.

"Let's get back to our sheep—or *the sheep skin*, to be more precise; I mean of course the Fleece and its Cipher. As the original Japhetic was lost, the Cipher of the Fleece became unreadable; it was forgotten and eventually lost, too. The local legend about a Colchi witch-doctress, who gave it to a bunch of sailors coming from a distant land, is a total hoax. As a matter of fact, what she gave to the captain of the sailors was not the Fleece, but a very different hairy thing, which female humans possess and which the Buddha—that most enlightened individual—euphemistically designated the "gates of life." It's as simple as that."

Here the Leader nodded, though stayed silent.

"The cipher was rediscovered after almost two millennia, thanks to the self-sacrifice of a Sacred Individual from the Brotherhood of the Essenes, who once publicly performed the act of Sacred Almznoshinoo. There was a certain El-Azar, whose reason remained suspended for four days between his dead, or past-being body, and his Kesdjan, or future-being body. It was the aforementioned Individual who managed to reverse the time-flux and produce an enormously strong charge of energy from his own heart, injecting it into the Kesdjan body of El-Azar, making it function as a living body once more. Such a reversal halted the quantum process of fleshly corruption, and when El-Azar was being washed by his sisters, one of the two, known for her contemplative nature, noticed certain unusual signs made by the maggots that had eaten her brother's flesh. She was so fascinated by the signs, that she took a clay tablet and copied them down. The written signs made up seven semantic units; these constituted the recovered Cipher of the Golden Fleece—the aboriginal Japhetic cipher."

Here the raven paused, but then began to speak again. "Now, what's so special about it? As I said already, the Golden Fleece was the most ideal transmitter of the megalocosmic flow of Askokin. And yet, this faculty was not in the lambskin itself but in the text it made manifest: the text explained, and simultaneously performed, the process by which words are transformed into the things they name, and how these things disclose their hidden meaning through the words that name them; it showed *how to do things with words*, and *how to make the things speak for themselves*.

Exactly like the reality of quantum particles when, at the same time, waves are corpuscles and corpuscles are waves."

"I think I need a drink," Pshavela murmured.

"How about a shot of Armagnac?" Gurdjieff suggested.

"Anything," said Pshavela.

"But of course my highlander needs a drink!" exclaimed the raven, cocking his head. "Aren't you the descendants of the wine-drinking panthers?! Aren't you the members of an ancient linguistic group, and don't you speak 'intoxicated' Japhetic?! Damn it—what indeed makes me mess about with this tipsy nation?! Alas, it is my penchant for linguistics, undoubtedly— metaphysical linguistics makes me do it!"

And here the raven calmed down and spoke to Pshavela directly.

"Actually, I shouldn't be cross with you, my highlander, you are unique amongst your people—you speak the language of the beasts of the field and the fowl of the air, and they speak unto you in response. And that language in particular contains substantial structural elements of aboriginal Japhetic! That's why you are here, that's why you have been summoned—your lingvo-animist skills are meant to play a significant role in the Work we are fated to accomplish."

"Work?" Gurdjieff said.

"The Work—a piece of a new and advanced art!" exclaimed the raven. "But before I explain it, let me ask you a question, my highlander: have you ever heard of the hymn called *Praise and Glorification of the Georgian Language?*"

"Is it a new piece by Prince Ilia Chavchavadze which I haven't had a chance to see yet?" asked Pshavela, who had drunk a substantial portion of Armagnac.

"No, my highlander, your 'father of the nation' has never even heard of it. He has other priorities—he's been listening to the crying of nationalist stones.[29] If he were less preoccupied with

29. "The Stones Themselves Cry" is an essay by Ilia Chavchavadze, which contested Armenian nationalism.

domestic issues, he would have learned that more than forty years ago, in a major Russian city, a text written in old Georgian script was discovered, translated and published by a French-speaking biped.[30] I've been to Paris and that's how I know this. You speak French, don't you, my highlander? Ha-ha-ha . . ."

Pshavela cast a gloomy glance at the bird and sipped more Armagnac.

"Very well," said the raven, "you keep drinking and I'll tell you the story."

"Go ahead, please," Gurdjieff said.

"Now," the raven went on, "some three hundred years after the public Almznoshinoo, the clay tablet containing the Cipher which El-Azar's sister had copied ended up in Eastern Georgia. Do not ask me how—I only know that female Sacred Individuals were involved, and that they realized they should take it to the land where some remnants of aboriginal Japhetic were still spoken. This happened at a very special time for the featherless bipeds then living in Georgia: their king and queen, by dint of some obscure revelations and signs, had become convinced that their individual souls were but small elements of a *Great World Soul*, which consisted of stars and earthly objects alike. This was *the Love that Moves the Spheres*, which I have already mentioned. Later on, that very *Love*, misinterpreted, drove them to destroy the Houses of Fire which before they had worshipped as the chief source of life.[31] But enough of that . . . let me go back to what I was saying before . . . yes . . . the royal court . . . ah yes! At the royal court, there was a philosophizing featherless biped who called himself a *gnostic*, and it was he the Queen ordered to read the

30. Here, the raven refers to the fact that the tenth-century *Praise and Glorification of the Georgian Language* by Ioane-Zosime was discovered in a Saint Petersburg library and translated and published in French by Marie Brosse in 1858. It became known in Georgia much later.

31. The raven is referring to the conversion of Zoroastric Eastern Georgia to Christianity in 337 AD.

mysterious inscription on the clay tablet made by El-Azar's sister. The Gnostic had great trouble with the text, as he was using the resources of his intoxicated Japhetic to read and interpret aboriginal Japhetic; plus, he was usually a bit drunk himself. Lastly, he had never heard of the megalocosmic functions of the Golden Fleece. Contemplating the seven semantic units and quantum formulae, the only thing he could figure out was that there was a 'mystery' hidden in the Georgian tongue and that this 'mystery' had to do with El-Azar's Almznoshinoo—which in the future would be re-enacted on a much broader scale, encompassing all humans and all tongues. To his credit, however, it should be mentioned that the Gnostic managed to come up with the numeric value of a few semantic units, which hinted at a solution to the Primordial Contradiction between existence and nonexistence. As it happens, the letters of intoxicated Japhetic—or the Georgian alphabet—have numeric equivalents, as in Hebrew and many other ancient languages. Since the Gnostic was pretty well acquainted with the gematria system of Kabbalistic interpretation, he played with some figures and concluded that the numeric value of the 'mystery' oscillated between 94 and 4,000. He couldn't specify what the whole damned numeric thing was about, only that the figure 4,000 referred to the four days of El-Azar's suspension between his past and future bodies, and that in the alphabet, this figure is the numeric equivalent of the Georgian phonetic sound *tsilie* and is pronounced . . ." and to Pshavela's surprise, the raven reproduced this weird sound impeccably.

"So what?!" Tigran said. "We have the same kind of sound in Armenian too, but we never flaunt it; we never make such a fuss about it."

"Good for you!" the raven declared in the same forbidding manner as his poetic analogue declared "Nevermore!" once upon a midnight dreary. He continued:

"Thanks to good wine, good food, and the healthy climate,

the Gnostic did not succumb to a mental breakdown because of his interpretative failure. Quite the contrary—the inventive fellow sat down and composed a hymn called *Praise and Glorification of the Georgian Language*, into which he poured all his findings from the clay tablet, spicing them up with certain rhetorical figures known to hymnography. The hymn was pretty well-received at the royal court, while the clay tablet was cast aside due to its impenetrable complexities. Nevertheless, it remained valued, passing from king to king as a relic of the great ancestors. Things stayed like this in Georgia for another eight hundred years, until a Cross-crazy featherless biped named Baldwin visited the local king and took the tablet away. That Baldwin fellow was commissioned by other Cross-crazy bipeds who lived in the West, but, driven by a particular kind of Cross-craze, were swarming down to Jerusalem—a place near El-Azar's Almznoshinoo. My guess is that they needed the tablet as a sort of a weapon against the non-Cross-crazy featherless bipeds living there. Because of such a stupid misappropriation of the power of the Golden Fleece, and also because they couldn't decipher it, the tablet did not work. The Cross-crazies suffered severe defeat. The trauma was so devastating that it made them forget about the tablet itself, transfiguring it in their fantasies into a magic chalice known as a 'gradal.' Ha! A hundred years later, when the Cross-crazies were drinking from the magic chalice in their dreams and pissing their sheets, the true 'gradal'—the clay tablet—was found by another speaker of intoxicated Japhetic, who called himself Rustaveli."

Tigran, who took a shot of Armagnac just as the raven uttered that name, choked and spilled the liquor. Coughing, he went out to the bathroom. Gurdjieff looked at Pshavela with amusement. The highlander had had enough alcohol to listen calmly to the raven's revelation about Rustaveli—and what a revelation it was! Ferdinand the raven went ahead, speaking emphatically:

"Listen my highlander, and you—my Tiger of Turkistan; Rustaveli managed to crack the Cipher of the Golden Fleece. In the monastery of the Holy Cross in Jerusalem, he heard Voices which endowed him with a facility for aboriginal Japhetic, enabling him to read and interpret all the semantic units, all the symbols and figures of the clay tablet text. However, the flow of inspiration enveloping him was so strong that it shattered the tablet into minuscule pieces and knocked Rustaveli unconscious. He stayed like that for seven days, stretched out on his bed and displaying no sign of life other than breathing. When he eventually recovered, the clear vision of a poem containing the Cipher of the Golden Fleece pulsated in his head. And so he sat down and put it in writing: 1,669 quatrains, each line made up of 16 syllables, with tonic accents and eight trochaic feet divided by a caesura. Line by line, syllable by syllable, he scattered the Cipher of the Fleece throughout his poem like spots scattered over the skin of a panther. Thus, he ended up with not only a poetic text, but a mysterious kind of 'fabric'—the sacred *Panther's Skin*, which harbored in itself the same information as the lost Fleece. Hence the title of the poem, *Vepkhistqaosani*, or *The Pardivested*. The trick is that the title refers to the poem itself, not to that featherless biped hulk Tariel, the knight of the poem."

Having said this, the raven suddenly fluttered up in the air, hung upside down from the chandelier like a parrot, and, swinging from it, started quoting in Georgian the introductory quatrain of *Vepkhistqaosani*:

> rrromelman   shekmna   samqarrro   dzalita   mit dzlierrrita,
> zegarrrdmo arrrsni sulita qvna zetsit monaberrrita,
> chven, katsta, mogvtsa kveqana, gvakvs utvalavi
>   perrrita,

karrr ... karrrr ... karrrr ... marrrr ... marrrr ...
marrrrr ...[32]

The Leader sat with his eyes closed, murmuring a mantra.
Gurdjieff joined in, while Pshavela repeated the poetry recited
by the raven. Tigran's head was swinging in unison with the
chandelier—he was worried that the big black bird would pull
it down.

Then there came a knock at the door.

The crazy morning goes on, thought Tigran, *Astvats, ichu
hamar*.[33] And he opened the door.

Two men stood there. One of them was surely an Englishman;
fair-haired with a neatly trimmed mustache, he wore a white,
spiked collar, a brownish bowtie, a sports jacket, britches, checkered
socks, and untidy shoes. The other man looked poor; he wore a
black hat, a mottled shirt, black pants and worn soldier's boots. A
big mustache hung down over his lips, and there was an apology
nestled in his eyes. He carried a painter's case over his shoulder.

"Here come my visual artists!" the raven exclaimed, flying down
from the chandelier and landing on the back of the Ottoman
chair.

"We extend our apologies for the intrusion," the Englishman
said in perfect Kurdish. "However, it was suggested that we come
here and introduce ourselves. My name is Gene Morris and I'm
a professor of optics, and this is Niko Pirosmani, a local artist,
whom I had the pleasure of meeting the other day."

Pirosmani took off his hat and muttered something that
nobody understood.

"Come in, come in, my friends, you are most welcome here!"
The raven invited them in. Pshavela and Gurdjieff also greeted

32. "He who created the firmament, by that mighty power / made beings
inspired from on high with souls celestial; / to us men He has given the world,
infinite in variety we / possess it ..."
33. Armenian for, "Oh God, why?"

them with excitement, and even Tigran was *"enchanté"* to meet them.

"No time for formalities, dear friends," the raven said. "We need to begin the Work. You two make yourselves comfortable and permit me to continue speaking." The newcomers were offered seats and Armagnac, which they greatly appreciated.

"What is the earthly word for the passage of megalocosmic vibrations of Askokin?" the raven inquired, although he did not wait for an answer. "The word is *Passion.* Yes—Passion is the passage, and that was the gist of the Golden Fleece Cipher. Now, as I already mentioned, the Gnostic in his intoxicated interpretation of the clay tablet gave us two numbers—4,000 and 94. The latter one has proven more difficult to tackle. The Gnostic writes in his hymn that 'as the miraculous omen,' the Georgian Tongue 'has the advantage of ninety-four years in regard to other tongues.' But what is this 'miraculous omen?' And what about the other number, 4,000? The Gnostic refers to an old Hebraic calculation, citing 'one day like one thousand years.' But if one day is like one thousand years, then how long is the time unit of ninety-four years? Given that an average earthly year is made up of 365 earthly days, then the 94 years of the hymn is actually 94 times 365 times 1,000, equaling 34,310,000. Do not be scared—this figure has nothing to do with time. According to the measuring equipment on Saturn, this is the frequency of the waves of the passage—or, alternately understood, the flow of megalocosmic vibrations of the sacred substance Askokin. And 4,000, according to that very same Saturnal equipment, is the length of the very same waves. That is all and nothing more."

Here the raven halted for effect, and then continued.

"Actually, there is one thing more. According to Gornahoor's calculations, the figure of 34,310,000 is the numeric value of the aboriginal Japhetic word for *Passion.* Yes, he got exactly that value. Compare the intoxicated Japhetic, or Georgian, equivalent of the word—*vnebai*—and you find its value is seventy-four. Ha-ha-ha—the figures speak for themselves, my highlander, don't they?!"

The raven was becoming very worked up.

"But the figures are dumb! It's all numeric idiocy, no matter how large! We need the Word itself; we need the aboriginal Japhetic for the Passion—only this and nothing more! We need to figure out or reconstruct the Word in its indigenous Japhetic form, because its morphemes and phonemes don't just denominate the act of Passion, but—and this is most significant—they *enact* the Passion by denominating It! This was written in the seven semantic units of the Cipher of the Fleece—the Word made up the whole Cipher! We need the Word itself, because by enacting the Passion, we will restart the megalocosmic flow of Askokin, the passage of vibrations, the transmission—and thus we will prevent the second Babel from happening! We need to *resurrect* the Word!"

"How do you imagine this linguistic Almznoshinoo will happen?" Gurdjieff asked.

"The Word will come with the Work!" quoth the raven, cooling down.

"And the Work is about *tanning* the *Panther's Skin*, right?" tipsy Pshavela joined in.

"It's not just about tanning," the raven responded. "It's more like how they used to extract gold from highland rivers. They would put a lambskin into the stream and particles of gold would stick to it. Our task is to *soak* the *Panther's Skin* in a very special kind of stream. And the stream is going to be the music of the Passions."

"And the music of the Passions is by the Shaman of Eisenach, right?" Gurdjieff said, recalling the Voices' incomplete message.

"Corrrrrect!" croaked the raven. "And it should be processed through your objective consciousness, my Tiger of Turkistan."

"You mean the objective consciousness discovered by Ashiata Shiemash—the Highest-Most-Saintly-Common-Cosmic-Sacred-Individual?" Gurdjieff asked.[34]

"Corrrrect!" the raven croaked again, adding, "it is hidden in the depths of the human mind—it is the Unconscious—and it is the sole force driving you to deliberate suffering. By the way, the Shaman of Vienna has wrongly capitalized on a lot of this."

"Excuse me," the Englishman said, again in Kurdish, "I can't determine how this dialogue between you and Mr. Black Greek bears much relevance to me. Could you please be more precise and provide us with some particular details of the Work?"

"By all means!" the raven exclaimed. "Here come the details."

Perching comfortably upon the shoulder of the Leader once again, the raven spoke the following.

"Cracking the Cipher of the Golden Fleece is going to be a group endeavor, a *collective improvisation*, if you will, making use of two remarkable texts—the *Panther's Skin* by Rustaveli, and the *St. John Passion* by the Shaman of Eisenach—plus some mystical pictures we will project onto a wall using a magic lantern. Therefore, this is going to be a synthesizing opus, based on audio-textual-visual synergy. The event will be held in the hall of a place called the German Garden here in Tiflis; however it will be controlled from above, via Gornahoor's lingvo-chronotopos accelerator, located on Saturn. Yet the most essential part of the Work will need to be performed locally. And now I ask for your attention—no more alcohol, please! My highlander, your task will be verbal and interpretative; you will have to translate the text of the *Panther's Skin* into the language of animals and plants, which you speak, and which, as I said, carries some structural traces of aboriginal Japhetic."

34. Ashiata Shiemash was a Messenger from Above, incarnated into a human body resident in Babylon. Thanks to his Holy Labors, the existence of human beings resembled for a time the existence of higher beings on other planets in the great universe. Beelzebub adored him.

"But that's a tall order!" Pshavela seemed perplexed. "The poem consists of 1,669 quatrains! How can I translate such a huge text during one night in a concert hall?!"

"It's 1,669 quatrains, or 6,676 lines, or 106,816 syllables, to be exact about it," the raven said calmly. "Do not worry, my friend, you will not have to do the whole text. The *Panther's Skin* is composed in such an intricate and organic way that every part contains the whole. Just choose any chapter. I'm certain that just like many of your countrymen, you know huge portions of it by heart. As you know, the performance includes the magic lantern show, which will feature illustrations of the poem made by a Hungarian-speaking featherless biped . . . what's his name? Ah, yes, Zitch . . . simply coordinate your part with those. Are we ready for the show now, Mr. Morris?"

"Absolutely, sir!" the Englishman answered.

Quoting from the poster on the German Garden gate, the raven announced, "Mr. Gene Morris, the well-known traveler, for the second time in town . . . Positively the grandest and definitely the most—" The raven broke off, asking the Englishman, "what brings you here for the second time?!"

"I'm not sure I can explain it, sir," the Englishman replied. "I'm skilled in optics, not psychology."

And here Tigran leapt up and spoke in English, which he had never done before: "What is the force that makes people wander, that they shall not cease from exploration?"

The raven looked at him with appreciation, and then said, "let's get back to optics." He turned to Pshavela, and spoke almost wryly:

"To fuel your lingvo-shamanic powers, my highlander, Mr. Morris will not only be projecting mystical illustrations of the poem, but a series of other drawings by Mr. Zitch—his erotic sketches, to be precise. Yes, very impressive pieces of pornographic art . . . even shocking, I should say."

"But the audience will go mad," Pshavela protested, worried. "This is not England, this is Asia!"

"We should all go slightly mad during the event," the raven rebutted. "Besides, the audience will be controlled from Saturn. But this is not for you to worry about. Just contemplate the mystical pictures and let your shamanic mind flow through the *Panther's Skin*, like a highland stream carrying particles of gold . . ."

As Pshavela said nothing to this, the raven turned to Gurdjieff.

"Now, my Tiger of Turkistan, here comes your turn. At the exact same time as the magic lantern show, a choir of German-speaking bipeds and a small orchestra will perform the *St. John Passion . . . Herrrr, unserrr Herrrrscherrr . . .* it is music full of anguish, chains of unrelenting dissonance linking the oboes and flutes to the turmoil of the rolling sixteenth notes in the strings' section, invading the bass, sustained in *B-flat . . .* such vibrations ideally harmonize with the megalocosmic frequencies."[35]

Responding to this, Gurdjieff sang with his eyes closed, "*Zeig uns durch deine Passion . . .*"[36]

"Yes," said the raven, seeming pleased with the quote. "With the cantor Schweitzer in your head, and your experience and knowledge of cosmic sounds and Sacred Movements, which you've learned from Initiated Individuals, you will process these sounds by the Shaman of Eisenach. Now you know that this is not just mere music, because that *German-speaking-sausage-eating-beer-drinking-woman-fucking* Sacred Individual produced the genuine *Ars Combinatoria*—music which discloses the hidden sacred meanings buried in words. The cantor in your head knows how the Shaman of Eisenach encoded the hidden meaning of his name into his music, leaving this world and ascending from his past-

35. "Lord, thou our Master . . ."
36. "Lead us through thine Passion . . ."

body to his future-body by descending semi-tones: B-A-C-H..."

The Leader, still meditating, repeated these sounds as he would a mantra. The raven pecked his bald skull once more and said: "The major work, however, will take place in this particular head. The Leader of the Seven is here to perform the *synthesis*. He will be communicating with the awakened objective consciousness of you two, my Tiger and my highlander. Thus, he will combine the semantic content of the translated *Panther's Skin* with the vibratory sequences of the musical *Passion*, forming one unified semantic system; he will let the music flow through the poetic texture, and, according to gold extraction model, the Cipher will be similarly extracted from that very flow. And thus the Word will be reconstructed, or *resurrected*, in the Leader's mind."

The Leader opened his eyes. His gaze was extraordinary; it made the whole room seem to expand beyond its limits. At least, that was how Gurdjieff felt.

"However," the raven continued, "to make the whole Work complete, the Leader will have to pass the Word to somebody else without uttering it—by no means may he utter it! Doing so would make the Word materialize as in any ordinary language, exhausting the cosmic polysemy accumulated in its 'inner form.' Neither is it possible to let the Word remain unuttered for too long—in earthly time, that is—as this would deplete its denominative powers, rendering it meaningless. Therefore, the Leader will have to communicate the Word through an act of 'copulation' with another body, and this should be the body of a very special kind of female featherless biped—a *woman who has loved much*. Although, here I must confess that the necessity of such an act is based on conjecture; it is a mere hypothesis, drawn from our analysis of the intoxicated Japhetic; the Georgian for 'word' and 'copulation' share the same root: *tqu*."

"Indeed!" asserted Pshavela, as if proud of the erotic treasures hidden in his native tongue.[37]

"Besides," the raven went on, "any true word is dialogical—requiring at least two people to disclose its meaning."

"As my great-aunt would put it—you cannot clap with one hand!" Tigran asserted. To this, the Leader responded by clapping with his right hand only. Nobody was able to catch just how he did it.

"Having said all this," the raven declared, "I'm ready to entertain your comments."

Silence. Pshavela's good eye was still riveted on the Leader's right hand; Gurdjieff, though physically present, was mentally absent, his mind moving upon a rushing stream of sixteenth notes played by the strings of an orchestra in his head; Tigran, who had received such irreverent treatment from the raven and the Mongol, seemed too discouraged to come up with anything else; Gene Morris took out a cigar, smelled it, sneezed, and then searched his pockets for a handkerchief.

At last, Pirosmani spoke—though making his statement in brilliant Japanese:

"You know what I want to tell you, brothers: let's raise some money, build a house by the river in the Ortachala Gardens, set up a large table in it with enough room for everybody, put a samovar on that table, drink tea, and talk about the arts . . ." he looked around apologetically.

The Leader stood up, approached Pirosmani, knelt in front of him, and bowed. The raven, still balancing on the Leader's shoulder, said: "Thank you, my simpleminded maker of images of mere Being—my primitive genius. We'll do what you've just suggested later, once the Opus Almznoshinoo—the Work—is

---

37. In his place, I would not have been so proud, since even contemporary Georgian translators painstakingly try to come up with a stylistically adequate equivalent of the common English idiom: "to make love."

accomplished. During the event, however, you'll be staying with us; you'll sleep on one of the benches of the German Garden and dream of your beloved, Margarita. Merely this and nothing more."

And then then raven spoke in the direction of Gurdjieff and Pshavela: "by the way, have we got the woman—the one who has loved much?"

"I think so," Gurdjieff said. Pshavela nodded.

Dagny stood in the middle of the hotel room—devastated. Emeryk was kneeling and embracing her legs, sobbing into the skirt of her dressing gown. He murmured fearfully insane words about death as the greatest happiness for her; he suggested committing a double suicide, and with the pathos of a rejected lover, he implored his lady to marry him. Poor fellow—looming financial ruin had driven him out of his wits.

However, that morbid proposal was the least shocking thing for Dagny, as in his delirium, Emeryk had confessed a far more macabre thing: he'd given money to Przybyszewski to take Dagny away, he'd bought her from him—yes, Stach had sold her, yes . . .

I see tears in her eyes, and I can hear her thinking of the humiliation: she is a fallen woman, she deserves her suffering, which was good for Stach—through that transaction he was cured of his "malaria," exorcised of his "infectious demon" . . . yes, she is a demon, an insatiable vampire, fed up with the blood of mortal males and seeking intercourse with God! *And now she heard His sick heart full of lust throb inside her own; and she felt Him put his long arms around her and press her to this heart that was dying* . . . Wretched woman, she is beginning to feel delirious . . . in the doorway, she sees a hand stretched out—long, dead—she kisses it . . . then the door opens, and she sees that the doorway is like the jaws of a beast, and the stench coming from it is the stench of the poisonous flowers of poetry. Ironically, Stach used to be revered by his Polish sycophants as a deity, a "demonic author." But the deity sold her off, exchanged her for hard cash, which he was attracted to, just like he was to virginal thighs and buttocks . . .

Or maybe I'm misreading her mind at this very crucial moment. What would an ordinary woman married to a sexually promiscuous, insane drunkard—married and divorced, though still attached—think at such a time? After all, to put it in terms of modern evolutionary psychology, women have an inherited interest in conjugal fidelity, which guarantees them helpmates during child-rearing; this goes back to hunter-gatherer times. "Stasiutulek, come soon! I long for you! I'm terribly nervous and neither Zenon nor I am really well yet"—she actually wrote this in one of her many letters to Stach.

And yet, to my mind, Dagny Juel was not that kind of a creature—I mean, a hunter-gatherer-prototypical female. Though disgusted by Emeryk's confession, she stood strong—sarcastically murmuring that simple duet between Pamina and Papageno from Mozart's *The Magic Flute*: "*Mann und Weib, und Weib und Man, reichet an in Gottheit an . . .*" Charming ditty, isn't it?

Emeryk, ashamed and embarrassed by his melodramatic-schizoid episode, rushed out of the room; he was a weak man, and his nervous system was further shattered by alcohol abuse. He slammed the door, however, to demonstrate his macho power. It seems that his balls must have still been producing testosterone, as he felt that they were slightly swollen: *testo-thanato-steron*, more likely. Either way, his exit was most welcome to Dagny.

With a shiver of disgust and moving like a zombie, she went out onto the balcony. Her room in the Grand Hotel overlooked the river and a part of the Mikhail Bridge. The bridge that stretched out of memory, into nothing . . . *a pier* . . . she saw herself standing there and screaming, her deformed face squeezed between her palms. She screamed for no one and nothing—that very same *nothing* made her scream. She had been sold like a slave—sold to *nothing*. She was suspended in that very *nothing*, and she felt it getting thicker and denser, materializing as hot, humid, sticky air; sweat from her forehead dripped into her eyes and she could not see ... the thick, watery air was getting into her nostrils, her lungs—she became short of breath, her head reeling, and in that foggy whirlpool she had a vision of herself lying naked on a feast table—*a slave prostitute*—surrounded by a group of drunken, laughing males, some of them masturbating over her, coming onto her face, breasts, armpits, belly and thighs. She was the mock-goddess of fertility, and their sperm poured onto her like saliva from death's greedy mouth. And amidst that mysterious rite of humiliation she climaxed, like how a woman being raped might experience an involuntary fit of pleasure through disgust and pain. She almost fainted, but something brought her back to her senses again: the noise of the turbid river running below, as turbid as her thoughts running through the riverbed of nothingness; she had the urge to jump into that river, to wash away the filth ... wash away? But what was left of her besides that filth?! She was no longer there—she was dead, oh, how beautiful— she died young, in her early thirties, yes, so young!

And then she heard a giggle coming from inside the room. A high-pitched voice said, "when women grow old and cease to be women, they get beards on their chins, ha-ha-ha-ha!"

It was August Strindberg who spoke. He looked weird: a very small man, just a couple feet tall, he sat in a deep armchair dressed in a flamboyant suit, holding a whip in his right hand and smoking a cigar.

"You miserable devil of a woman!" said he, wielding the whip. "Infernal creature—damnation upon your sex! Ha-ha-ha-ha-ha!"

"Why do you hate me?" Dagny asked.

"Well, as a matter of fact, I loved you once, didn't I?!" Strindberg replied wryly. "For three weeks, to be exact. For a whole three weeks I was screwing you while my Frieda was away. And then I bequeathed you to my dearest friend, Bengt ... ha-ha-ha ..."

"Bengt Lidforss, that poor syphilitic! He was keener on young men than young women," Dagny said, grinning.

"You hate him because he understood your literary activities only too well. My God, I loved it: 'Juel has now chosen her occupation and seized the pen instead of the prick!' I loved it, yes indeed—'She's writing short stories about love, whoring, murder and other depravities.'"

"Why do you hate women, *Father*?" asked Dagny.

"I believe that you—women—are all my enemies!" Strindberg replied. "Do you know what makes you dangerous? How unconscious you are of your instinctive dishonesty! It is risky to take anything on good faith where a woman is concerned. The only woman I could trust was my mother!"

"Grow up, old fool, grow up," Dagny said, launching an attack. "You're simply afraid of love and sex, and to hide this you come up with your fictions about screwing me for three weeks. Bullshit! You can't screw anybody, all you can do is sit and masturbate along with the other members of your fraternity, just like Bengt. All you covert homosexuals!"

"But you are an *overt* prostitute, aren't you, my dear Aspasia, my Henriette?!" Strindberg rebutted. "Oh, that night in the Schwarze Ferkel when you invited me to a black mass—lying on the table, lifting up your skirt and poking fingers in your pussy! Oh, my God! Remember, you stayed in that room on the street where all the prostitutes were, and you were almost taken away by the police—you thrived in your moral insanity. *My fictions*?! It was you who suggested those fictions—whole novels, I should say! You destroyed families and destroyed men—neurotic men, but not without talent—you made them squander their money and leave their homes, duties and professions! Now you want to go beyond that and seek ways to *copulate with God*! What for, are you going to destroy Him as well?! You won't, my darling, you won't, because God loves virgins—yes, it is upon their bosoms that he sleepeth at midday, placing His head between their virgin breasts. Yes, quiet is His sleep upon a virgin bosom, where no spot might soil His snowy fleece ... and you, my *seeker of God*, what happens to your kind?! Passing into abnormal womanhood, you end up in slime and mud, ha-ha-ha-ha!"

"Your passion for virginity and virgins is ill-founded, old fool," Dagny said. "Let me tell you why: as soon as your passion is awakened, you seem weaker to yourself, and feel your protective walls crumbling. So then you start despising the very virgin you admired. It comes from the premature ejaculation which is your genuine forte in bed, ha-ha!"

"Oh, how profound an analysis!" Strindberg was getting really piqued. "Now I have evidence you truly *seized the pen instead of the prick*! Listen, need some advice? What about *seizing a prick as a pen* and writing with it?! Ha! Just cut it away from your man, dip it into his blood, and write with it on his own breast; yes, scribble some ecstatic lines: divine the name of your god, combine copulation with exegesis ... I would suggest something like this: *Let me drink your sperm, Adonai.* You wouldn't even have to cut his head cut off—just his dick! Ha-ha-ha-ha-ha-ha!"

Strindberg choked on his own laughter. Then he jumped up and started to dance, grimacing and singing:

> Ah woe is me, how sad a thing
> Is life within this vale of tears,
> Death's angel triumphs like a king,
> And calls aloud to all the spheres—
> Vanity, all is vanity. Yes yes! Yes yes!

Looking at the spectacle of Strindberg grimacing and

dancing, Dagny wondered why men couldn't just be natural with women. Why do men first demonize and then humiliate women? How ridiculous! There is no room for women in the minds of such small creatures as men, no room for love, just the mere gratification of immature sexuality. That was why in her sexual fantasies she sought God, and why she wanted to write about such a union. Yes, write—because writing had become for her the ultimate form of eroticism, a transcendent sexual expression . . . yes, the mocking Strindberg was right—Dagny must have been a woman of metaphysical hyper-sensuality, and yes, she could have used a man's penis for a pen, a man's blood for ink, and a man's breast for a sheet of paper, and she could have written on it a hymn to God, her God! (I wonder what Dagny's reaction would have been to that movie by Nagisa Oshima, *In The Realm of the Senses*, its quasi-pornographic mysticism culminating in the severing of a penis and the writing of a poem in blood? Was not Dagny the first among the pre-modernists to resexualize writing and textualize the erotic senses?!)

> Dip his pen into his blood,
> Write about the slime and the mud,
> Where you copulate with your God!
> Yes, yes, yes . . .
> Damn, writing is a very tough Art!
> Fart, fart, fart . . .

Dancing and grimacing, Strindberg kept singing until he began to evaporate, eventually disappearing into the thick air.

Dagny stood still, listening to the distant booming of thunder. Suddenly, a bolt of lightning streaked through the air, followed by rain, pattering down stronger and stronger. The cool, swirling wind blew in from the river, lashing the rain against her balcony. She went out and stretched her arms into the thick curtain of pouring water—it was so thick, she couldn't see through it. Exposing herself further to the rain, Dagny slid down her robe and bared her breasts so that the rain might wash away the sweat of despair and delusion. Just minutes ago she had been feeling so small, so humiliated; now, as she bathed in that heavenly shower, luminous images exploded in her mind. Oh, she was Danaë, conceiving from the golden sperm of Zeus! She was Mary Magdalene, contemplating her Savior and immersed in the light and brilliance coming from Him . . . the flowers in His garden of Love grew lushly around her, their fragrance choking her breaths, their tendrils winding around her life . . . *Love, thou art the absolute sole end of life!*

Yes, the End must be near!

All of a sudden, the downpour came to a halt and the clouds parted, just as if an invisible master of atmospheric ceremonies had lifted the curtain of water. Dagny took a deep breath of ozone-charged air, which filled up her lungs like the intoxicating smoke of hashish. It made her dizzy. She stood there like a young actress just before her debut performance . . . she was hovering over a black crevasse . . . spontaneously leaning forward, she— oops—lost her balance, and fell from the balcony right into the river. *Splash!*

It took quite an effort to drag the woman out of the river: Gurdjieff, Gene Morris and Tigran Poghossyan made up the rescue team. Along with some other companions, they happened to be floating by on a raft and feasting.

Feasting on a raft was once a popular pastime in Tiflis. The rafts would launch from one end of the city and slowly float down towards the other end, before turning back; those aboard ate light refreshments and drank lots of wine while singing, dancing, reciting rhymes, or listening to a barrel organ. They would make occasional stops along the bank, inviting others to drink and share the fun.

As stated at the very beginning of this book, alcohol is my element and I am open to all forms of its consumption. Now, from the chronotopic (or time-space) perspective, there are two modes of consuming an alcoholic beverage: a *static* mode and a *dynamic* mode. The static mode occurs in the context of a set table, a buffet reception, say, be it indoors or outdoors. The dynamic one, however, implies drinking in or on any kind of mobile vehicle—an automobile, a train, a boat, an airplane, etc. It is dynamic drinking I most enjoy—much more than that accompanying a buffet or potluck. Any kind of movement doubles and triples the strength of the beverage, while the alcohol itself makes things more intense; you get an extremely rich sense of your surroundings, and spaces seem to grow larger while time dwindles, as if ridiculed by infinity. You know, I hate transatlantic flights, but what make them tolerable for me are the free drinks served—plus the small bottle of scotch I prudently buy from the duty-free stores . . .

Along with the three men who retrieved Dagny from the brownish waters of the river Mtkvari that evening, the raft also contained: the Leader of the Seven with a big raven named Ferdinand on his shoulder; Pirosmani, along with the lady of his heart (Margarita, a French chanson singer from one of the Ortachala restaurants); a *doudouk* player named Djivan; Pshavela the highlander; and three men wearing black national dress and conical "paprika" hats: they belonged to the fraternity of the *Qarachokhaely*—a very unique order of people native to Tiflis, who deserve a word of reference (and *reverence*) here.

I would compare the Qarachokhaely to the medieval German *Meistersingers*, or, "singing artisans." As a matter of fact, their origins go back to thirteenth-century Tiflis, to a sect of hedonist mystics called the *Rhinds*, who identified themselves as a marginalized branch of the Sufi school. Actually, "*rhind*" is the Persian word for feaster/drinker. These were men seeking mystic communion with Endlessness through Love and intoxication. Hafiz, who associated himself with the Rhinds, describes the metaphysical benefits of such a communion in his poetry, which praises love and wine. Some scholars hold that wine and drinking had a purely symbolic meaning in the Weltanschauung of the Rhinds, which I reject as pure speculation. The empirical manifestation of transcendent properties is crucial for any mysticism. Besides, sometimes wine is just wine, like a cigar is just a cigar.

The Rhinds were renowned for their skillfulness, outspokenness and disdain towards usury.[38] Their neighborhood in Tiflis was open to all kinds of creative, marginalized peoples—bards, artists, dancers, wandering Dervishes and odd religious visionaries—be they Judaic, Zoroastric, Christian, or Muslim. The Rhind neighborhood was so popular in those days that even King Lasha-Giorgi, heir to the great Tamar, would frequent it—much to the dismay of the royal court, which considered such visits scandalous. Alas, Lasha-Giorgi was an unwilling leomeme; he cared little for power and was deeply in love with a Kakhetian layman's wife, who bore him a child.

Like the descendants of the Rhinds, the Qarachokhaely were true adherents to the *belle esprit*. Heavy drinkers, good singers, poet-improvisers, and courageous fistfighters, they were also a generous and compassionate people. Plus, they were excellent artisans. Even though unlike their predecessors, they sometimes put excessive emphasis on the sensuous effects of wine and alcohol, they still used drinking to regularly perform the mysterious rite of the Rhind communion with Endlessness.

The stream had divested Dagny of her dressing gown, and so she ended up on the raft in her underwear, totally soaked. As she refused to be taken back to the hotel (she would never go back to that terrible place), she had to take her wet stuff off and wrap herself in a blue, Tiflis-style tablecloth, which happened to be on the raft. She did not mind that. Margarita helped her change, and

38. The Georgian for knight, "*rhaindi*," was possibly derived from "Rhind."

then she sat alone, catching her breath and occasionally shivering from psychical aftershock.

Tigran Poghossyan came over and offered her a small, clay chalice of red wine, which he claimed tasted "like a kiss from Bacchus." Then he related the Armenian origins of viticulture, substantiating his point with the obvious fact that Noah, who was known as the first winemaker, anchored his ark by the slopes of Mount Ararat. And Mme Przybyszewska had just survived the "flood," hadn't she?! The bowl of wine was timely.

"What made you jump into the river, beautiful woman?! Life is such a precious thing," said one of the Qarachokhaely, a man called Paepo. "You're not a stick of celery that can come into this world twice, are you?!"

Another man, whose name was Ghizho (meaning "mad"), observed the curves of her bare body through the blue tablecloth and sang: "I stand in water and I'm on fire, / Getting higher and higher in my desire . . . / Yes, I am a flaming fountain and a weeping fire!"

"Welcome aboard, Mme Przybyszewska!" Gurdjieff declared, a cup of wine in his hand.

Djivan began playing his *doudouk*, accompanied by Gene Morris on a very unusual barrel organ—it sounded like a pneumatic one, though it still had a grinder on it. The music was melancholy and lovely.

The Leader stood up, approached Dagny, and took her hand. Bowing, he touched it to his forehead, then sat by her side and muttered, "good vibrations . . . good vibrations . . ."

Ferdinand the raven fluttered down onto Gurdjieff's shoulder.

"Just look at those two," said the raven, referring to the Leader and Dagny. "What a funny analogue of the primary cosmological couple of the Tibetans: the Meditating White Monkey and the Mountain Witch!"

Gurdjieff smiled and nodded. "Then may the world of the new sublime art be born from them!" he said, and drank his wine.

"What, the raven speaks?!" said Dagny in surprise, wondering if she was still hallucinating.

"He's not a raven," explained Gurdjieff. "More a transfigured shaman."

Dagny was about to ask more about the extraordinary creature, but a third member of the Qarachokhaely, a man by the name of Hapho, interrupted her with a song.

> God, who hath made all things that come and go,
> And hath fashioned me out of this love *afar*,
> Give me power, such as I have not in my heart,
> So that in a short space I shall see this love *afar*.
> And desirous of this my love *afar*, for no other joy
> Would delight me so greatly,
> As the enjoyment of my love *afar* . . .

"*Afarrr, afarrr, afarrr . . .*" the raven repeated.

As Hapho was singing, the other two Qarachokhaely poured wine into horns and drank slowly, very slowly. Backed by Djivan's *doudouk* and Gene Morris's organ, Hapho went on:

> Star-summit of Being!
> Not reached by any wish,
> Not soiled by any No,
> Endless Yes of Being:
> I affirm you endlessly,
> For I love you, Endlessness . . .

"Sounds like a piece by Nietzsche, doesn't it?!" the raven suggested to Dagny, who sat there misty-eyed, rather like Alice after taking a deep puff from the Caterpillar's pipe.

Gurdjieff too began to sing:

> A vessel must be empty, if you want to fill it up with
> wine.
> Know emptiness and be compassionate:
> Make love to the Endless!
> Let your naught conceive the infinite numbers!
> This is the true Work.

"Love, endlessness, compassion . . . what rubbish! I've had it!
Enough of this," said Dagny, with a bitter, tipsy grimace.

"*Nevermore* say such things again!" the raven reprimanded her.
"Time is just an ugly flow streaming from the guilt of the past
towards the fear of future punishment, while the *here and now* is
only the bad conscience inbetween. Do not be afraid! Time is just
a disease; deliberate suffering shall cure you."

The Leader, his eyes closed, slipped his hand into Dagny's lap
and rested it on her sex. Then he took her hand, and, placing it on
his sex, said, "the Shaman of Vienna called it *Libido*, the Mantic
woman Diotima called it *Eros*, and Saul-Paul called it *Agape*. I
call it *emptiness inundated with compassion!*"

Dagny felt the Leader's penis getting harder and harder. She
had a spacey urge to kiss it . . .

Meanwhile, the Qarachokhaely were drinking from unusual
wooden vessels called *chinchila*, which has long thin necks that
permitted the wine to enter their mouths little by little; the effect
was like a direct kick to the brain.

The Leader spoke again. Although he spoke in his native
Tibetan, Dagny, to her amazement, could understand every bit of
it. His speech sounded like throat singing.

"Under non-repressive conditions, Libido tends to grow into
Eros. That is to say, the progression is toward self-sublimation
through lasting and expanding relations (including work relations)

which serves to intensify instinctual gratification. Eros works to eternalize himself in permanent order; the order is beauty and the work is play. In attaining this objective, Eros transcends it, and, searching for deeper gratification, develops into Agape—a Love Supreme. Through deliberate suffering, Agape intensifies the endless delay of gratification by channeling the flow of cosmic energy against the flow of time and shrinking the latter down to nothing. Through deliberate suffering, Agape can then grow into emptiness inundated with compassion!"

Uttering this last word, he shuddered; through her palm, Dagny could feel something *passing* through the Leader's body. Sensing this weird tremor coming over her too, she jerked her hand back, startled. The Leader smiled broadly at her and she burst into laughter.

"*Bene!*" croaked Ferdinand, reappearing between the two of them. "This is exactly the laughter of the Witch, my comparison was corrrrect! Corrrect! She is the Bride and he is the Groom— *Hierrrrosgamos*! *Hierrrrosgamos*! The Marriage of the Meditating White Monkey and the Mountain Witch! We must celebrate! All celebrate!" With that, the "metaphysical linguist" went fluttering up above the heads of the feasters.

It was getting dark. Pirosmani and Margarita lit the lanterns which hung from poles at every corner of the raft; the Qarachokhaely stuck tapers to the clay chalices and filled them up with wine yet again.

Djivan stopped playing his *doudouk* and Gene Morris started playing a different tune: *Brindisi* from Verdi's *La Traviata*, which Margarita eagerly picked up on, beginning, "*Libiamo* . . ." Pirosmani, drunk, started dancing in the middle of the raft. Hapho was reciting:

> Father Eternal, you are wrong
> And well should be shamed,

Your well-beloved son is dead,
And you sleep like a drunk.

So far, Pshavela had seemed detached from the rest of the feasters. He sat apart, caressing the brown-striped cat which sat in his lap; her name was Nestan, after the female protagonist in *Vepkhistqaosani*. Pshavela had been meditating on some of the stanzas of that very poem, occasionally exchanging views with the cat.

"True, Rustaveli's poem itself is like a panther or tiger skin," speculated Pshavela. "True, this kind of skin resembles a written page; this is a very profound metaphor, much like the one which compares language to a river."

The cat purred and said, "regarding the Code hidden in that poem, I would focus on the symmetry suggested by Rustaveli in the introduction; that is, the symmetry between the three types of minstrelsy and the three levels of Love. I suspect that the clue to the Cipher of the Fleece must be sought in the intermingling of writing and affection, which is so uncannily rendered in Nestan's letter to Tariel, in stanza 1291."

Pshavela knew the letter by heart and recited it. It's worth quoting here too, though, I'm afraid its poetic charm is lost in the English translation:

> Oh mine own! This letter is the work of my hands;
>   for pen
> I have my form, a pen steeped in gall; for paper I
>   glue
> thy heart even to my heart; oh heart, sad heart, thou
>   art
> bound, loose not thyself, now be bound!

Nestan the cat narrowed her eyes and said:

"Now, shift your focus and compare that passage to stanza 657, in which Tariel speaks to Phridon about his love for a beautiful tiger which, for him, evokes Nestan—*purrrrhhh*! And also why he is clad in a tiger skin . . ."

This time, it was Hapho who quoted from the poem, as if he were part of the conversation between the great highland bard and the cat:

> Since a beautiful tiger is portrayed to me as her image.
> for this I love its skin, I keep it as a coat for myself . . .
> . . .
> The tongues of all the sages could not forth-tell her
> praise. Enduring life, I think upon my lost one. Since
> then
> I have consorted with the beasts, calling myself one of
> Them . . .

Nestan the cat purred and narrowed her eyes. She continued, "getting back to your darling metaphors, my highlander: why would a man compare his beloved to ruthless beasts (though they are my cousins) like panthers or tigers?! What about doves or pheasants or fawns?! I surmise that Rustaveli's work here is covertly self-referential—he is inscribing Love and writing into each other, and furthermore I suggest that the poem is self-referential too. Thus it is about writing as a dissemination of difference, like the black and white spots on the panther's skin."

"But the Cipher of the Fleece, or the Lazarus Code—those were not merely about the *writing*," maintained Pshavela. "We speak of them as the ideal transmitters of the megalocosmic flow."

The cat narrowed her eyes again and said, "I would not go that far . . . instead, I would rather consider the passage in which the happy Tariel, after rescuing Nestan, goes back to the cave of his insane isolation and recovers numerous treasures hidden there. It is noteworthy that the episode begins with a reference to Dionysius the Areopagite, stanza 1492."

"That was exactly what I had in mind," Pshavela said and quoted:

> This hidden thing Divnos the sage reveals: "God sends good. He creates no evil. He shortens the bad to a moment,
> He renews the good for a long time, and His perfect self He
> makes more perfect. He degrades not Himself."

"See?!" the cat looked into Pshavela's good eye. "Rustaveli was a *progressive* scholar of literature. In this stanza he symbolically suggests the idea of reinterpreting the classics, of *rereading and rewriting*. Yes, indeed! And what does reinterpretation involve?! It involves parody, because through the art of parody, you dismantle the thing you want to interpret and notice content previously unnoticed. I give you my word for it, the panther's skin poem is a parody of the Golden Fleece Cipher and the Lazarus Code! Go ahead, my highlander, cast a purrrodic—sorry—*parodic* eye over Rustaveli's text, and you'll uncover the treasure hidden in it. To quote the fellow himself:

> They explored the hill abounding in caves, merry they played; they found those treasures sealed up by Tariel, uncounted by any, apprehended by none . . .

"Rustaveli's text is like a hill abounding in caves; to explore it, one should play merrily and thus find the thing apprehended by none."

"What?!" Pshavela sounded confused. Suddenly he had a weird fit. Somebody else began to speak through him, as had happened earlier to Gurdjieff; he recited in German:

> All other creatures look into the Open
> with their whole eyes...
> What is outside, we read solely from the animal's gaze,
> for we compel even the young child to turn and look
> back at
> preconceived things,
> never to know the acceptance so deeply set inside
> the animal's face. Free from death.
> It is all we see. The free animal
> always has its decline behind, its god ahead,
> and when it moves, it moves within eternity the way
> fountains
> flow ...

"Good!" the cat purred. "You've just verbalized an elegy, which comes from afar—Lake Duino, in Italy. This might enhance your interpretative skills."

"Yes, I do know the animal's gaze . . ." said the highlander, slightly nonplussed.

"Then look into the *Open!*" suggested the pussycat, and, purring, she sang an old Tiflis ditty:

> Wish I never looked at you!
> You broke my heart, I am forlorn ...
> Purrr purrrr purrrr ...
> To whom shall I complain?!
> Rustaveli is dead and gone ...

But enough of this. Nestan the cat was bored of Rustaveli. She jumped down and lapped up some wine from Pshavela's chalice, which he had not even touched yet. Eventually, the cat tipped the chalice over—oops, she looked sorry, she shouldn't have had so much wine . . .

Pshavela sat looking nowhere: like Caesar's mind when it "moved upon silence," his uncanny fancy moved upon the fabric of the *Panther's Skin* and was enriched by the unusual music coming from Djivan's *doudouk* and Gene Morris's organ. Together, they produced an unusual tune, somehow resembling the introductory aria of the *Goldberg Variations* by the Shaman of Haizenakh.

Gurdjieff was enjoying their interpretation very much, and asked them to go on with the rest of the *Variations*. When he spoke, it was with Schweitzer in his head:

"Bach originally composed the aria which you've just played as a *sarabande* for Anna Magdalena. It's based on a tune called "*Bist du bei mir*," or "When You Happen to Be with Me." To appreciate these variations, one has to grasp the art of counterpoint as Bach himself did. It's not just about the natural beauty of musical sounds, but the absolute freedom of movement, which provides happiness and gratification!"

Mangling the well-known Buddhis mantra, Poghossyan declared, "*O mani petme houng!*" looking absolutely happy and gratified.

The musicians went on playing, wine was poured and drunk, the moon was high and bright, and the raft slowly floated downriver.

"How lovely the night is!" Margarita said. "May I tell a little story?"

An ecstatic Pirosmani kissed the striped stockings which covered her ankles. The rest of the crew were also eager to hear Margarita's story, and so she began.

"I'm going to tell you about a little girl named Gatta. She grew up in a brothel, as her mother worked there and they had no other place to live. Gatta was so cute, so beautiful, that everybody in the brothel was very fond of her. The prostitutes kept her away from the whoring life; the girl would help in the kitchen and with the laundry.

"And yet, when Gatta was sixteen, she was raped by a group of soldiers from a nearby regiment who had thrown a rowdy party in the brothel.

"After that, she ran away, seeking shelter in a convent located in the highlands. And there too the nuns took a liking to her. However, one night she was awakened by sounds of sighing and panting, which came from the chapel. She slipped in and discovered all the nuns, including the mother superior, stark naked and making love to a big ebony crucifix laid on the chapel floor, one by one ...

"Dumbstruck by this scene, Gatta left the convent and ran into the fields just as a fierce thunderstorm broke overhead. Taking refuge under a green oak tree, she was struck by lightning. Gatta did not die though—she fell into a lethargic sleep, and later on the stigmata appeared on her hands and her feet and her side, and wine came out of it— wine which enlightened those who drank it.

"Those who drank the wine came to know about love the way the fields know about light, the way the forest gives shelter, the way an animal's divine raw desire seeks to unite with whatever might please its soul, without a single thought of remorse. The years passed by. Gatta remained asleep under the burnt green oak, while peasants from faraway provinces congregated around her to drink her wine.

"And then the day came when she was awakened by a kiss. She opened her eyes and saw the face of her God smiling at her.

"'My Love,' Gatta said, 'where have you been for so long?'

"And He spoke to her, saying, 'you saw me long before; I was one of the soldiers that raped you.'

"Here's to Gatta and to the wine of her stigmata!" Hapho suggested, improvising a toast, and the other feasters joined in, exclaiming, "Hear hear!"

Gene Morris rushed up to the Qarachokhaely, asked them to pour him more wine, and, standing between them, declared:

"Ladies and gentlemen! Brothers and sisters! Let me recite a poem written by an Englishman who lived in the seventeenth century. Though originally composed in English, this poem sounds Georgian, it's truly amazing! Just listen, it's called 'Drinking.'"

And he recited one of my favorite poems by Abraham Cowley:

> THE thirsty *Earth* soaks up the *rain*,
> And drinks, and gapes for drink again.
> The *plants* suck in the *earth*, and are
> With constant drinking fresh and faire.
> The *sea* it self, which one would think
> Should have but little need of *drink*,
> Drinks ten thousand *rivers* up,
> So fill'd that they o'erflow the *cup*.
> The busie *Sun* (and one would guess
> By's drunken fiery face no less)
> Drinks up the *sea*, and when h'as done,
> The *Moon* and *Stars* drink up the *Sun*.
> They drink and dance by their own light,
> They drink and revel all the night.
> Nothing in *Nature's sober* found,
> But an eternal *health* goes round.
> Fill up the *bowl* then, fill it high,
> Fill all the *glasses* there, for why
> Should every creature drink but I,
> Why, *man of morals*, tell me why?

The feasters concurred with shouts of pleasure and appreciation.

"To the meeting of East and West in our beautiful city of Tiflis!" Tigran Poghossyan exclaimed, raising his chalice and singing along with the Qarachokhaely, "If I drink a lot, my friend, so what?!"

"Good vibrations . . . good vibrations . . . our brother from Albion is a good man," the Leader remarked, and went on to mumble a mantra deep in his throat.[39]

Dagny sat there, content and numb, words and images soaking in her brain like pieces of bread in a bowl of wine.

Sorry—there is one more important thing I forgot to mention. The man steering the raft, who was hired by Poghossyan for a hefty fee (though Gurdjieff took care of it, of course), was none other than Camo; yes, the very same Simon Ter-Petrossyan who should have been, if not canonized, then at least beatified by the likes of the Red Brigades or the IRA.

Koba was sitting on a bench in the Ortachala Gardens. Although the moon shone bone-white, Koba's face could not be seen, as he sat hidden behind the large branch of a fir tree. The drunken sounds of revelry came from a nearby restaurant—laughter, singing, the clinking of glasses and plates, waiters shouting orders, soft melodies played on *doudouks* accompanied by drums, a barrel organ, and the high-pitched trilling of *zournas*. But Koba didn't give a damn about this mini-Babel of inconsequential drunk people—

It was all just *convergences* and *divergences* . . . *as long as capitalism endured, the bourgeoisie and the proletariat would remain*

39. Ironically, the Leader of the Seven died a couple years later, during Francis Younghusband's military expedition to Tibet. When the invasion began, the Leader convinced Tibetan rulers that resisting the enemy by force was wrong, as in the eyes of God, all life is equally precious and the death of so many would only further increase the great burden that He carried as a result of our abnormal existence on Earth. Therefore, the Leader went out unarmed to meet the invaders and, together with the monks that accompanied him, was shot dead by the English troops.

bound thread by thread to the fabric of a single capitalist society.

He was waiting for his liaison man to arrive with new information. As he sat there, his mind dwelt upon how he might use terrorism to overthrow the existing government and create a new power. How could he expose the corruption of the current regime to the light of day, and then smash it to smithereens? He looked down at the river; the man was supposed to arrive by raft. They could have met in one of Koba's "safe houses," but the future chief of the world proletariat planned his conspiracies idiosyncratically, in order to confuse the police. Besides, a breath of fresh air would do him no harm—it was hot and muggy that summer in Tiflis.

The "underground" life Koba had been leading for the last three months proved not only necessary in these bourgeois surroundings, but pretty exciting too. Of course, it wasn't very comfortable or convenient, but somehow he'd begun to feel like a genuine recluse, an anchorite of sorts, pondering the eschatological science of the revolution of the oppressed and exploited classes; the messianic science of the socialist victory in all countries; the millenarian science of building a communist society. But he also felt like a progressive artist, contemplating new expressive forms and aesthetic ideas which nobody else had ever dreamed of. And like a diabolical fish, he occasionally swam in the waves of the populace, appearing at demonstrations and rallies to shake the beliefs and souls (if they had any) of the propertied classes—and his brethren workers too. Yes, he *acted*, he *performed*, because if not, then "what avails me of the knowledge of the philosophizing of the philosophers?" The words he silently quoted were Avtandil's, from Rustaveli's poem of love . . . *Love?* What was that?! No time for that paltry thing— unless Camo showed up with a couple of whores. Koba had read about a professor, Freud, who had masterfully dismantled that which the bourgeoisie call "love." True love would come only after the complete emancipation of the proletariat!

Koba's drowsy ruminations were interrupted by "emancipated" female laughter coming from the riverside. Vaguely, he made out a noisy company of feasters clambering onto the bank from a raft. Squinting, he saw a tall Qarachokhaely striding ahead of the group with a woman carried in his arms. The woman must have been wrapped in a tablecloth or something similar. That was her only apparel—he could see her bare leg hanging down, a pretty, long and slender leg, as well as her bare arm and shoulder. She was obviously drunk—her laughter gave her away. The two were followed by a couple of men with shaved heads; one was dressed in a European suit, while the other wore a light-colored gown and held a staff; a dark bird sat on his shoulder. Two more Qarachokhaely walked with another woman between them, and among three or four more drunken revellers, Koba noticed the highland bard Pshavela. The episode in the Persian restaurant flashed in his mind, and he grinned his wicked grin.

Koba sat still and kept his face hidden behind the branch as the feasters leisurely passed him by. His man was supposed to be on the same raft, but Koba had not spotted him as of yet.

"Hello there, Koba-jan," he heard from behind him; it was Camo.

"You conspiratorial son of a bitch," Koba said, "How did you manage to get over here invisibly?!"

"I'm working on it, Koba-jan!" Camo said, with humor in his voice. "The revolution will need invisible men in its service."

"And they will be called the 'Soldiers of the Invisible Front,'" Koba suggested. How prophetic he was just then—this would become the romanticized name for the KGB. "Did you enjoy serving the morally corrupt bourgeoisie?"

"You mean piloting the raft? Yes, Koba-jan, it was very enjoyable, and plus they paid me well."

"Well, the bourgeoisie cannot support their way of life without wage-laborers at their command, and the proletariat cannot survive unless they hire themselves out to the bourgeoisie," stated Koba grinning. Then he said seriously, "well, my invisible man, what are the tidings?"

"Should we talk here or go to your hideout?" Camo inquired.

"The night is dark, and the police lack imagination. Therefore, we can stay here and enjoy the cool breeze," Koba said. "Now tell me what you found out."

In his confused way, Camo tried to cut a long story short and thus made it even longer; nevertheless, he managed to convey first what he'd learned from Tigran Poghossyan and second what he'd observed during the feast on the raft. Koba occasionally interrupted him with remarks.

Poghossyan, Camo reported, had defected from the Dashnak party and was eager to join Koba's underground Marxist circle; moreover, he was extremely keen to be introduced to Koba himself.

"I would be more careful in trusting the Dashnak, be it active members or defectors," Koba stated.

"Why, Koba-jan? You do not trust them because they are Armenian?" Camo asked, somewhat insulted.

"No, brother," said Koba, "because they are nationalists. Furthermore, they are bourgeois nationalists, just like our Georgian National-Democrats. The proletariat has no nationality—only capitalist chains which they need to destroy. It cannot be otherwise. Lenin recognizes the existence of two cultures under capitalism—bourgeois and proletarian—and therefore the slogan of national culture under capitalism is a nationalist slogan. All this is true and Lenin is absolutely right about it."

Though Camo had not read much Lenin at that time and the reference Koba made was not all that clear to him, he was still satisfied with the answer and went on with his story. He tried to convey the gist of the meeting which took place in Poghossyan's flat that morning, involving many of the same bizarre people he'd seen again later, feasting on the raft. Koba was amused by the talking raven.

"Of course the raven spoke Armenian, ha-ha-ha!" he said. "Didn't I just tell you never to trust those Dashnak nationalists?" "No Koba-jan, no," Camo said. "Listen to me. Tigran said that the raven spoke many languages. Strangest of all, that devilish bird knew the entire text of *Vepkhistqaosani* by heart! I saw that bird on the raft myself, I swear by my mother!"

Koba burst into laughter and looked into Camo's eyes, saying, "you speak like a drunk! Did those Qarachokhaely hulks pour wine down your throat?! Huh! A raven quoting *Vepkhistqaosani* by heart! It must have been a wind-up bird, a mechanism, a gadget produced somewhere in England or China—it could not be otherwise. Undoubtedly this proves that bourgeois culture is in decay and decline—*decadence*, my brother, *degeneration!*"

As Camo himself already kind of doubted that the talking raven had been real, he did not argue the point. He went on, explaining about a gilded lamb skin stolen by the Greeks; about Noah getting drunk with some wine-drinking tigers and speaking Georgian on Mount Ararat, proving that the Georgian language had Armenian origins and is called by some people "Procho-Japhetic"; and about a secret cipher invented by Shota Rustaveli, who turned out to be the first conspirator ever known to this part of the world.[40]

"Koba-jan, just as we write our confidential messages in milk on paper, the blessed Shota Rustaveli wrote with a special combination of black dots and white spots, just like the body of a leopard. If you read those dot-spots in his immortal poem, your brain gets bigger and bigger until it explodes, and then the dead will come out of their graves, drink wine, and shoot down flying cows."

40. A slip of the tongue. Meaning "proto," Camo said *procho*, which comes from the word *prochi*—the Georgian for "asshole".

"Nonsense!" Koba seemed irritated. "I was right; you've had too much wine, shit-for-brains! How can Georgian be derived from Proto-Japhetic, or whatever they called it?! Who can say for certain where our language comes from? Linguistics is no trifling matter."

The young Stalin said this forty-nine years before he gave a notorious interview called "Marxism and the Problems of Linguistics," which was printed in *Pravda*, the official newspaper of the USSR. It is truly a remarkable interview, prefaced by the following *apolloguising-apologising* (to appropriate from James Joyce) introductory note:

> A group of younger comrades have asked me to give my opinion in the press on problems relating to linguistics, particularly in reference to Marxism in linguistics. I am not a linguistic expert and, of course cannot fully satisfy the request of the comrades. As to Marxism in linguistics, as in other social sciences, this is something directly in my field. I have therefore consented to answer a number of questions put by the comrades.

The main "comrade" Stalin was referring to was the half-Georgian, half Scottish professor Nikolay Yakovlevich Marr—the very "Marrrr" mentioned by Ferdinand the raven. It was Nikolay Yakovlevich Marr who came up with the extraordinary idea that Georgian, North Caucasian, Basque, Pelasgian, and Etruscan, among other languages, shared a Proto-Japhetic source. Marr would later declare that "Japhetisms" could be found in every language, thus concluding that all language developed out of the Japhetic source, following stages he called "sudden explosions."

In the interview, Stalin objected to the idea of "sudden explosions," although his criticism went farther, too. Marr had come up with another crazy idea Stalin didn't like; he suggested that with the abolition of class structure, the material language that humans use will disappear and an abstract language will develop in its place, enabling people to communicate through their thoughts, unencumbered by the "matter" of language. Claiming to translate Marr's "gibberish into simple human language," Stalin then accused him of landing in "the swamp of idealism."

Though rudimentary and ideologically biased, Stalin's linguistic speculations, as well as his criticism of Marr and his teachings, are plausible to a certain extent. Stalin's emphasis on the material aspects of language, often neglected by pre-Humboldt philosophers, is absolutely valid from the perspective of structural linguistics and semiotics. I don't think Stalin ever read Hjelmslev or Ferdinand de Saussure, but his ideas were similar.

Nevertheless, Stalin's preoccupation with revolutionary Marxism and Leninism, combined with his morbidly ambitious character and lust for power, clouded his insight into what Marr was essentially proposing. Niko Marr was affiliated with the Pardimemes; he envisaged the advent of a perfect language based on a kind of shamanic semiotics, which would enable humans to transcend material differences and understand each other with greater ease. The perfect, abstract language would foster the shamanic capacity of individual consciousness to mingle with the collective consciousness—the amphibious consciousness, the consciousness of sea creatures, the Crystal Consciousness, the Bright one, the Deep one.

There was another hidden motivation which made Stalin embark upon an anti-Marr campaign. Marr also happened to be a Rustaveli scholar, and had hypothesized that *The Knight in the Panther's Skin* was the fourteenth-century Georgian translation of a Persian original. Such an attempt to deprive Georgians of their national treasure would have insulted even Stalin, who by the time of the *Pravda* interview was as detached from his homeland as God Himself.

As Niko Marr died in 1934, the grapes of Stalin's academic wrath poisoned Marr's followers only; in his campaign, Stalin was categorical: "The removal of these plague spots will put Soviet linguistics on a sound basis, will lead it out on to the broad highway and enable Soviet linguistics to occupy first place in world linguistics."

But let's get back to the young Koba sitting on a bench in the Ortachala Gardens, bored by Camo's incoherent account. The excited fellow was speaking of *maghalo-cosmic vibrations*, which were produced by some musician up in the sky, who played a barrel organ and thus made the planets go round, or "circulate."[41] He also spoke about the event in the hall of the German Garden the following night, where some foreigners were planning to play the music of the "circulation of the planets." Georgia's "great bard," Vazha-Pshavela, was going to recite Rustaveli as an accompaniment, and an English traveller, Gene Morris, intended to show mystical pictures of naked women and men fucking. Finally, a famous magician named Gurdjieff was going to ventriloquize, while a Mongol who'd been especially invited would attempt to be hit by a bolt of lightning. And so on and so forth.

Koba was amused by all this "maghalo-cosmic" nonsense. *Yes, undoubtedly the bourgeoisie was stuck in the swamp of its morbid imagination.* It should be noted, however, that while listening to Camo, Koba had a flashback of the vision he had seen in the observatory a couple months before. But how could that rubbish attract the attention of a man who'd committed himself to the revolutionary fight?!

"Look here, Camo-jan, my brother," he said, yawning, "listening to you, I realize that excessively close contact with the

41. Camo says *maghalo* instead of *megalo*, which comes from the Georgian *maghali*, meaning "tall," "high," or "above."

bourgeoisie is poisonous. The atmosphere of ideological and moral decay that clings to them might seriously damage your brain. See what happened to Pshavela, our distinguished poet—he's gone completely crazy, hanging around with a bunch of charlatans, drunks and whores! Speaking of which, who was that drunken woman wrapped in a tablecloth?"

"I don't know, Koba-jan. She fell into the river from the Grand Hotel balcony and we dragged her out."

"*Decline and fall!*" Koba emphasised. "How bourgeois of her! And who is the 'famous magician,' Gurdjieff?! What a name he's got! 'Gourji' is what the Turks call Georgians. Is he local?"

"Poghossyan says Gurdjieff's mother was Armenian, but his father was a Greek from Alexandropole. He speaks very good Georgian though, and many other languages besides. A very educated man."

"Educated men don't stoop to cheap tricks like ventriloquism. That Gurdjieff of yours must be an ordinary charlatan, out to steal poor people's money. He might be a Dashnak agent too," asserted Koba. "As for your Englishman, Morris, he's surely here on an espionage mission. The English have always been active in the Caucasus; they want to weaken Russia's influence here. But this is good—rivalry between capitalist powers is nothing but advantageous for the international proletariat. It cannot be otherwise. You say the Englishman is going to project some indecent pictures tomorrow?"

"Yes Koba-jan," Camo said, with some embarrassment. "Naked bodies fucking and other erotic obscenities of all kinds. And, you know what, Koba-jan? This is going to be really advantageous for us, as you just said. The pictures will shock the public and when my explosion comes, the effect is going to be huge, is it not?!"

"You come down to earth at last," Koba said with appreciation. "This magic lantern thing sounds interesting. I saw a similar show in Gori last year. People were hypnotized, watching drawings by

Zitch projected onto a white screen. Generally speaking, images have a very strong impact on the human imagination, and we should definitely repurpose such instruments for our revolutionary propaganda."

(With this comment, Koba anticipated Lenin's statement about cinema being "the most important" of the arts to the new regime.)

"You just wait and see, Koba-jan," Camo said, with a touch of inspiration. "I'm thinking of a distinctly . . . *theatrical* explosion. Just imagine a devilish mixture of *saltirical-petre*, *sulfurical* acid, *nitratical* acid . . . and shit!"

"Shit?!" Koba inquired.

"Yes, Koba-jan, I'm going to explode a bag of shit in the hall of the German Garden!" Camo said emphatically. "It'll show those capitalists where they are and who they are! Yes, and then I'm going to scatter a huge bunch of revolutional proclamational leaflets all over the hall, which they'll have to use to wipe the shit off their bourgeois faces. Isn't that rich! After all, the revolution is about wiping all that shit off us, isn't it?!"

Koba looked cross. Getting worked up, he said, "Listen, you! A right Bakunin or Kropotkin you are! Before you think of anything else, go home, lie down and sleep away that drunken 'shit,' do you understand?! And remember, tomorrow in the German Garden I don't want any casualties or serious damage—it's about terrorizing people only—just terror! Understood?!"

"I understand, Koba-jan, I understand, please calm yourself." Camo had become docile, as if he really were sobering up.

"Very well, go have a rest," Koba said, cooling down, "Every good student is supposed to have a decent night's sleep before his first examination."

As he walked away, Koba fantasized about sharing his thoughts with Ketskhoveli and Tsulukidze, his closest associates among the local Marxists. *Though it seems minor and doesn't involve a big group of people, this is still going to be an international event, comrades, I mean—foreigners will be present.* Here he produced a generous fart, a result of what he had digested earlier. *Lenin too, proceeding from Marxist theory, had come to the conclusion that the simultaneous victory of the socialist revolution in all countries, or in a majority of civilized countries, was* . . . another fart . . .

Prostrate between Earth and Saturn, Gornahoor Harharkh IV was feeling somewhat flustered, even resembling Mime, the dwarf from *Der Ring des Nibelungen*, nervously forging the magic sword . . .

The damage to the lingvo-chronotopos accelerator's space-block made it difficult for Gornahoor to tackle the cosmic warp through which he was supposed to conduct the unfolding of the Opus Almznoshinoo, also known as the Celestial Love Feast or the Agape. Thank goodness his terrestrial double—Ferdinand the raven—was so adept at handling the quantum discontinuity fracture and the minor lingvo-spatial confusions.

Now that the space-block was fixed, Gornahoor could stick to his original plan and "play" by sheet music rather than improvise. As it happened, improvisation was not greatly encouraged on his planet and within the adjoining spheres; that objectivity and discipline yield better results than idle imaginative play was commonly accepted there. The creative value of differential variation was not totally rejected, however; it was even considered useful when it came to filling in gaps or breaches in the Cosmic Octave.

Why was he feeling flustered then?! Because a short time ago, the Voices had delivered a message notifying Gornahoor that his boss was about to arrive on a project implementation assessment mission. This was the Archangel Looisos himself: the Chief-Common-Universal-Arch-Chemist-Physicist and the Deputy Chief of the High Commission of Sacred Individuals!

The Great Looisos's interest in the project was motivated by the fact that he was the one who intervened in the featherless bipeds' existence soon after they came into being, in order to establish the role designated for those bipeds in the solar system's overall Planetary Maintenance. Commissioned by the Most Great Archangel Sakaki, it was Looisos who devised and actualized a special organ called the Kundabuffer to keep the bipeds busy with their task—maintaining the moon in its orbit around Earth. The moon and another planet called Anoolios, already lost, were two cosmic bodies that resulted from a collision in the Solar System, which happened due to the erroneous calculations of Dhemi Urgush, who was concerned with matters of world-creation and world-maintenance. The featherless bipeds were born and given their task in order to impede the destructive consequences of that very collision. The Kundabuffer was implanted right at the base of their spinal columns so that they would remain ignorant of their purpose, just like the fowl of the air and the beasts of the field are also ignorant of their planetary functions. Such ignorance enables every creature to live according to its true nature. However, in the case of the featherless bipeds, things went astray: the Kundabuffer metamorphosed into what Gornahoor IV described in the terrestrial tongue as *free will*, and the bipeds started to come up with various fantastic stories in which the moon was their deity; they even started killing each other in order to make sacrificial offerings. They also built temples to their deity and adored the idols set up there. Gornahoor's linguistic expertise made him interpret such a metamorphosis as the *displacement of the signified by the signifier*—or, *Paradise Lost*! (Here the Saturnal raven liked to quote a blind featherless biped from Albion.)

Looisos had to intervene for a second time, removing the Kundabuffer organ, but even this removal could not succeed in abolishing free will. The entire moon-maintenance venture was about to collapse. The High Commission desperately sought a solution, which eventually came from the bipeds themselves. Free Will underwent another metamorphosis and autonomously transformed into the *Will to Power*, which, eventually, proved self-consuming and blocked its own development: its ubiquity resulted in Entropy.

Entropic stagnation gave the Commission room to maneuver: the task of planetary maintenance was reappraised, redefined and reassigned to that particular breed of featherless biped known as Shamanic Individuals, who through their sublime arts managed to open up space for the Infinite in the folds of entropic totality. The change proved successful, although only for a time; suddenly, there came the premonition of dangerous developments capable of arising due to the above-mentioned stagnation. The "Cow's flight to the moon" would cause collisions surpassing the original in terms of devastating consequences.

And now, here was Looisos once again, shining like one thousand Lucifers, his eyes like gigantic, crazy diamonds. Gornahoor humbly welcomed his boss—"*Your Conformity!*"— and immediately delved into elaborate descriptions of the project implementation unit, sticking to all presentational formalities observed in the celestial academe.

"Let's skip it," interrupted Looisos. "We have watched your activities regarding the Opus both here on Saturn and on Earth. So far we haven't observed any deviations from the major goal—the formation of the objective consciousness through the liberation of the sacred substance Askokin, which the three-brained beings, known to you as the featherless bipeds, perceive in the guise of what they call *Love*. Now I would like to go through some details with you, namely the project implementation assets, tangible and intangible."

"Your Conformity," Gornahoor politely suggested, "shall I brief you on the *artistic* aspects of our Project?"

"Yes."

"From our point of view, the Opus Almznoshinoo is a piece of what could be called *hybrid art*," Gornahoor commenced. "Through a simultaneous application, drama, the poetic word, musical intonation, and visual imagery interact. We are, sort of, elaborating on the patterns suggested earlier on planet Earth by an unusual featherless biped named Richard Wagner. Now, why are we doing this? As Your Conformity has just mentioned, our goal is the formation of the objective consciousness, which is supposed to radically shatter the entropic stagnation caused by the predominance of mechanistic instincts among the featherless bipeds. By the way, a few of those bipeds whom we consider Shamanic Individuals have upon several occasions verbalized the very urgent need of such a consciousness, which would critically disrupt the opaque layer produced by those very mechanistic instincts. Let me give just a few examples: a certain Charles Baudelaire called for an art which would 'register the passing moment without doing violence to its fleeting transience'; someone named Walter Pater urged others to 'snatch moments of intensity from flux'; the rather interesting thinker Henri Bergson speaks of a need for 'representations which would not falsely spatialize the purely temporal flow of consciousness'; others seek an art which would record the intensity of inner experience on its own terms ... etc. It is absolutely obvious that to implement such an intention would require a special kind of 'unified sensibility,' or an acute and multifaceted awareness of a particular moment of experience. To render and express an experience acquired through the practice of unified sensibility, the bipeds need a synthetic vehicle capable of comprehending and transmitting those complex impressions accumulated during ordinary processes of perceiving. I call this necessary synthetic vehicle the 'Objective Correlative,' which is the formula for a particular and excessively diverse experience. To quote from George Santayana's recent book: we need to unite 'disparate things having a common overtone of feeling.' Therefore, to realize all this, we are

combining different artistic forms in our Opus Almznoshinoo . . .
I beg Your Conformity's pardon, but I'm concerned I might have
lost you." (Gornahoor still couldn't help feeling flustered.)

Looisos sat with an odd expression on his luminous though
gloomy face; his crazy diamond eyes cast glances everywhere at
once.

"Proceed!" the Archangel said.

Gornahoor resumed his presentation.

"Now I would like to draw Your Conformity's attention to
the above-mentioned Bergsonian idea of 'spatializing the purely
temporal flow of consciousness.' This will take us a few terrestrial
centuries back to a form of science called alchemy, which was
devoted to transforming base metals into pure gold (a substance
the featherless bipeds held in exaggerated esteem). As it happens,
the science of alchemy can be understood as a metaphor for
liberating the sacred substance Askokin through objective
consciousness—a metaphor nourished by various allegorical signs
and symbols. Only a few Shamanic Individuals realized that. For
our purposes, however, we consider it expedient to use alchemy to
help the featherless bipeds fulfill their task and attain the extreme
existential mode of *emptiness-full-of-compassion*. In this particular
mode, they will be able to overcome the Entropy loosed upon
their world. Thus, I suggest a neo-alchemical supplement to the
Opus—the *Transformation of Time into Pure Space through Music*,
which I have tested on several critical occasions. Actually, I am
referring here to what I have designated in chemical terms as
sublimation. It would improve the ability of creative featherless
bipeds to come up with those semantic systems and models
which would substantially reduce the density of self-destructive
mechanistic instincts, instead channeling their efforts towards
higher pursuits."

Carried away by his own words, new ideas flooding him even
as he spoke, Gornahoor finally came to a conclusion.

"Having said all this, I am absolutely positive that a new age is about to dawn on planet Earth, which will encourage new cultural and artistic forms; in other words, new semantic systems. I propose calling this new age 'modernism'; the word derives from one of the dead terrestrial languages."

Gornahoor paused, and then delivered the conclusion of his presentation.

"This is where we are as of today, Your Conformity. I know my brief presentation could not cover all the details of the implementation of the project, and I might have bypassed some important observations and findings, which might have been worth conveying and clarifying here. Therefore I'm ready to entertain any questions you may have, Your Conformity."

In the silence that followed, Gornahoor noticed that Looisos's pupils were dilated from anxiety and distress. A heavy groan came from the depths of the Archangel's huge form, and at last Looisos spoke.

"Something here brings me into darkness, not into light, as if my strength and my hope are about to perish. You'll need to be extra careful, Gornahoor, extra precise and extra meticulous with your calculations—dividing times by times and measuring space by space—because even the tiniest of lingvo-chronotopic irregularities, augmented by warps, planetary disturbances, and discontinuities, could channel the sacred substance Askokin in the wrong direction. Then the gold of your alchemy will grow dim—even the finest gold can change! Even your modernism project will alter and deform, breeding and inspiring so-called political Shamanic Individuals—the kings of the Earth, the false prophets and the priests—all those who will make the Cow fly to the moon! And for the sins of those prophets and the iniquities of those priests that have shed the blood of the just in the midst of the earth, all will wander as if blind through the streets; they will pollute themselves with blood, so that no one will touch their garments. Behold, I see the morbid sublimation of repressed desire, the cruellest flowers of unreason bred from the dead land. Yes, the misappropriation of Askokin could generate a monstrous creativity: those false king-prophet-priests shall manipulate the bones, flesh and entrails of the masses in order to accomplish ruthless feats of all-devouring hybrid art, fully controlling the sensibilities, feelings, memories and affections of those they enslave. Behold, I see this happening, and therefore my eyes do fill with tears, my bowels are troubled and my liver is poured upon the ground like the souls of children poured out upon their mothers' bosoms . . . My Gornahoor, you know that the Opus Almznoshinoo is not about this solar system only. Under the great Law of Reciprocal Maintenance, even minor planetary displacements can bring about a much larger number of irreparable calamities, which will haunt our steps so that we cannot go out into our streets, and they will pursue us unto the mountains and lay in wait for us in the wilderness! The featherless bipeds were meant to fill up the gaps in the Megalocosmic Octave and help the Music of the Spheres—which transforms time into space— flow smoothly through this small part of the universe. However, if one single cosmic interval in the whole Octave fails, such music will tear the joy from our hearts and turn our dance into one of mourning. Behold, I almost see that happening! Behold, art's power to heal shall be exhausted; the crowds shall wage the wars! Behold, I see the Song of Songs decomposing into an acronym, SS, wreaking ruthless torture upon the daughters of Jerusalem! Oh, Most Great Archangel Sakaki, why have you forsaken me?! Sometimes I feel like I am about to commit suicide. Fare thee well, my Gornahoor! Remember me! Adieu! Remember me!"

And having poured forth his bitter discontent, Looisos began to "recede like the unpurged images of the day"—becoming unseen, unknown, abstracted, secret . . .

"Strange . . ." thought Gornahoor, thankful for the departure of his boss. "Things must be hectic in the High Commission now that the Great Archangel Sakaki left it, having been made one of the four Quarter-Maintainers of the whole universe. *Remember me . . .* remember you?! No, no, my memory is a table and I must wipe away everything unessential and get back to my task."

Thus Harharkh the raven returned to his lingvo-chronotopos accelerator, becoming fully occupied by the complexity of his work. And here again I see Mime the *Nibelung* in him—fatally absorbed in the tricky challenges of the task immediately before him, forging and hammering the miraculous sword for the mighty Siegfried: tan tata ta ta ta tan tata, tan tata ta ta ta tan tata, tan tata ta ta ta tan tata . . .

> *You have overcome your slavery and spiritual sleep,*
> *escaped from the vicious circle.*
> *There are postures proceeding from a higher order of laws,*
> *which will open you to a different order within yourself*
>   *and thus free you,*
> *and unify you,*
> *and awaken you to the real meaning of your life,*
> *so that your real being will act and make itself heard . . .*
> *learn the science of Movements . . . haiiiiaaaaaaa . . .*
>   *aaaa . . .*
> *the sacred art of Love! haaaiiiaaaa . . . aaaaa . . .*
> *In the images it produces you can read exactly the feeling*
>   *which animates*
> *you—*
> *the sensation coming from beyond, coming from within*
>   *you,*
> *from where the center overlaps the circumspection,*
> *coming from afar . . . haiiiiiaaa . . . aaaaaaa . . .*

Dagny hears the chanting voice of the Black Greek encouraging her, sounding like a Tibetan priest reading from the Book of the Dead, directing souls departing from their bodies through the labyrinth of Karmic sway. Wrapped in a blue tablecloth, she is dancing on a table, surrounded by intoxicated men and women. The table is suspended in the middle of an illuminated space. Her senses mingle: the intense, dazzling light fuses with the sounds of string instruments, oboes and flutes playing a Middle Eastern tune, to which she dances, moving in fits of indescribable pleasure, which surge through her alongside the waves of music ... haiiiiiaaa ... aaaaaaa ... then the drunken crowd rushes at her and drags her down, beginning to consume her flesh ... she gives her body to them ...

Awakening suddenly, Dagny opened her eyes and found herself in a room full of roses. There were hundreds of them; they covered her, the floor, and the walls. The scent of the flowers inundated her, stealing her breath away. She felt spacey, the sensation of the dream still grimly lingering inside her. *What happened last night*?! She could not tell.

But all these roses! Amazing! I must be dreaming still ... how is it possible?! There must be thousands of them here. Through the open door, she could see roses in the adjoining sitting room too, spread all over the tables, the armchairs, the sofa ...

She got out of bed and stepped cautiously between the flowers, the thorns lightly scratching her ankles. Draped in a blanket, she went into the sitting room. Margarita stood at the window, looking into the street.

She turned around, welcomed Dagny with a smile, and said, nonplussed, "my God, these Georgians are completely mad! Just look." She beckoned Dagny to the window. Looking out, Dagny saw a dozen carts lined up along the street, with even more approaching. All of them were loaded with baskets full of red roses.

"Where are the roses coming from?" asked Dagny.

"Pirosmani," Margarita replied. "This is lunacy! The florist said he'd been paid by a painter named Niko Pirosmanashvili to deliver *one million roses* to my place. My God!" She giggled.

"Is he so rich?" Dagny could not believe it.

"Of course not! All he has is a small store somewhere in a sleepy village. It looks like he's sold it and spent all the money on these roses. I'm in a daze ... he has destroyed himself. Why?! For a mere chanson singer? Why?! What a whim! Shall I sell them back to the florist and send the money to Niko? I feel lost ... crazy, crazy man!"[42]

"Indeed, this is truly mad!" Dagny said, amazed by the fantastic gift. Suddenly she felt gloomy, as the memory of another "gift" flashed in her mind: Emeryk "receiving" her from Stach ...

What happened last night? Intoxicated by the revelry, she hadn't given a damn about anything. Even Zenon, her little boy! Well, she didn't have to worry about him just yet—he was staying with the Kellers for a couple days. Emeryk had arranged it—as a matter of fact, he'd insisted upon it. Why? Had he really been serious about the double suicide?!

Yes, of course—he wanted the boy far away from the bloody scene he was plotting, starring Dagny ... the whorish mamma ... but Emeryk, poor Emeryk—she'd destroyed him too. Some animals destroy each other through the violence of their passion.

---

42. Pirosmani did in fact deliver this surreal gift to Margarita. A few other Georgians have also done things of this sort; take for example the Svanetian prince Dadeshkeliani, who fell in love with a young and lovely English baroness who was visiting the Svaneti highlands. Dadeshkeliani made several advances, but she turned him down. And thus deranged by unrequited love, he presented the lady of his heart with Mount Ushba, the highest and most sacred mountain for Svanetians. The gift was confirmed by a notary and the relevant papers are still kept today by the descendants of that English beauty. As Carlyle would put it, prince Dadeshkeliani's act was "an error which the violence of passion may excuse." And to paraphrase Orwell: "All Georgians are crazy, but some Georgians are crazier than others."

Was Emeryk's choice any crazier than selling all you have to send a million flowers to a beloved woman?! Love is behind both deeds . . . love destroys . . .

I try to read the hazy look in Dagny's large green eyes as she looks at the hoard of roses around her. But let her own writing speak for her, once again (notice the floral motif):

> But then when the roses withered, she was happy. She loved to see the leaves yellow at the edges. She filled both hands and let them fall, one by one. She shook the bush so a shower of dull, pale leaves rustled above her head. And she saw that the roses were black with charred leaves . . . she was cold; she felt her heart like a cold white crystal. Its shine blinded her and she longed for secret flowers no sun had ever shone upon, dangerous flowers that carried poison in their veins, sleep-inducing and ungraspable . . . and one night she found, deep in the forest, in the shade where no ray of sun could penetrate, a dark, fateful plant with hirsute leaves and heavy-hearted bells of a colour taken from the sky and the earth. Avidly she read its veiled eyes, she pressed it to her heart, and she felt she loved its poisonous breath . . .

Thoughts like this "secret," "dangerous," and "poisonous" flower blossomed in her head, now aching from the night before. Margarita brought her a cup of coffee, which was black and smelled of roses: a poisonous, floral brew. She heard her new friend saying something, but she did not understand what. *Margarita wants to go downstairs and stop that insane flow of petals and thorns* . . . Dagny noticed a painting on the wall.

"Is that one by him, by Pirosmani?"

"Yes. It's called *A Boy on a Donkey.*"

The painting had been done on black oilcloth; a little boy sat on a donkey, as if trapped in total darkness with nowhere to go. *And where has the donkey between my own legs wandered off to?!* Dagny thought. *I don't even have a dress to put on . . . ha-ha! Rejoice and be glad, O daughter of Edom, that dwellest in the land of Uz; the cup also shall pass through unto thee: thou shalt be drunken and shalt make thyself naked!* It was only at this moment that she realised she was totally naked—protected by nothing more than the blooms of insanity.

"What can I do? I need to leave this place and find my son!" (Yes, Zenon remained the only beacon of light in the dark oilcloth painting of her life.)

"Oh, you don't have to worry about that, my dear," said Margarita encouragingly. "The Black Greek found a lovely dress for you and asked me to provide you with underthings. Why don't you put them on and then come downstairs? I'll try and settle this matter with the florist and then we'll go and see our friends."

"What friends?" Dagny asked, stepping carefully over the rose bouquets, feeling relived now that she knew she had a dress.

"Why, the ones we were feasting with on the raft last night— the Asian monk and the rest. Wasn't it gorgeous?!" Margarita replied, smiling innocently. "They're gathered in a small basement restaurant not far from here. Surely the Black Greek will help you find your son and whatever else you need done, my dear."

An Asian monk, the Black Greek . . . really, what had she done last night?! Dagny pulled the dress over her head.

"What makes a Tibetan monk go to brunch?!" she asked. "Isn't that unusual?"

"They are *rehearsing*," Margarita said.

"Rehearsing *what*?"

"The Love Feast."

"But surely last night's feast was lovely enough?!" Dagny asked, lacing up her boots. *How will I pay them back for these things?!* she thought; her finances were completely dependent upon Emeryk. *Yes, I truly am the boy on the donkey in the darkness.*

That morning, the donkey of her fate ended up bringing Dagny to the restaurant where the organizers of the Love Feast were rehearsing.

The restaurant was closed to customers—Gurdjieff had arranged it. He was planning to experiment with a couple of verbal, musical, and meditative combinations along with the Leader, the raven and Pshavela—a sort of Opus Almznoshinoo in miniature.

Mumbling, the Leader of the Seven sat on a kilim rug laid out in the middle of the restaurant hall. He had been immersed in deep meditation ever since early morning, a mantra spinning in his head. It worked well; through the mantra, his mind swiftly transcended its empirical existence, achieving the pure existentialism of *I am It.* In the self-annihilating ecstasy of objective contemplation, a peculiar awareness of *Being-there* occurred to him, like the potentiality of the tree occurs to the seed. Reflecting upon sundry fragments of thoughts and impressions, he compounded these into the imaginative correlates of an impersonal emotion, which mounted in him like a flame. This particular kind of emotion, which he usually experienced while meditating, was extremely strong and ambiguous, as it carried within it an intrinsic combination of pleasure and pain. It was known as the "sentiment of the sublime," which structures consciousness by exposing the mind to deliberate suffering and pure compassion. Certain Shamanic Individuals, like the Leader, could produce patterns of abstraction that disclosed the intangible and the incomprehensible, visibly representing the unrepresentable in its very remoteness; they could break through and traverse the incommensurability of the finitude of sense perception up to an infinity of the intelligible through an unperceivable and absolute "otherness"—this by yoking the incommensurate together in the dual acts of suffering and compassion. And that was what Shamanic Individuals called "the art of the sublime."

The meditating Leader did not notice Ferdinand the raven, who was flitting around the room, occasionally landing on a piece of furniture or the Leader's shoulders or bald head; he did not even see the bird swing from the chandelier while croaking in Georgian: "*Baqhaqhi tsqhalshi qhiqhinebs! Baqhaqhi tsqhalshi qhiqhinebs!*"[43] or bursting into multilingual chatter, such as: "Ni hao! J'aime Sabbath fornications Ruach Elohim spiritus vini et uisge-beatha-whiskey cum Heiliger Brahmaputra... Ammahim und la livid raptura of a Zurbaran Saint-Onan por favor caesura khoshgyaldi! Scoozi-spinooze me! The Gracehoper jigging ajog-agigue, hoppy on Kant's cunt in his joyicity to play pupa-pupa and policy-pulicy and jhopa-jhopa!

"Arigato Ishmael-san! Jai guru Hare Krishna, vo istinu akbar! Matte kudasai, prje proshe pani, plus précieuse que la vie, dirty dog! Bismillah! Moulin Khmer Rouge! Kulu Sé Mama!

" Sator Arepo Tenet Opera Rotas: Schwindsucht and pollution Opera naturale cum grano salis.

"Merhaba, Sebastian-bey!

"Winkelmusik of Szopen oder Pichon cum Chopinek i-jhe Chopinetto . . ."

Gurdjieff had been playing music while the raven was croaking, but it was not that of "Chopin" or "Chopinek" or "Chopinetto." The Black Greek sat barefoot before the upright piano on a low stool, and, dressed in a light summer suit, played some sort of toccata similar to the one that opens Bach's *Suite No. 6*. His fingers roamed over the keys and he accompanied the music

---

43. This means "a frog is croaking in the water" and it is the toughest tongue twister for non-native speakers.

with shamanic droning.[44] In a zombie-like state, Schweitzer's reading of the score echoing in his head, he searched through Bach's suite—the succession of dances—for the abstract musical equivalent of the movements he had discovered during his travels and encounters with Central Asian shamans and Dervishes. He was warming up for the collective improvisation that he, Pshavela, and the Leader had planned for that morning, with Ferdinand the raven transmitting Gornahoor's lingvo-chronotopos signals.

Pshavela was late. He was supposed to bring a draft of some passages of the *Panther's Skin* translated into the language of plants and animals, as specified by the Voices in charge of the Opus Almznoshinoo. Gurdjieff was totally engrossed by his baroque-shamanic variations; therefore he did not notice when Dagny and Margarita entered the restaurant hall and sat at a small table in the corner. Dagny, still embarrassed about the night before, didn't dare interrupt the others to explain her motherly concern for Zenon. She just sat there, with no idea what was going to happen next. She felt slightly nauseous, due to a post-revelry blend of hangover and self-disgust. No, let me put it another way: she was hungover with the poison of alienation. She asked for a shot of absinthe and some water.

Pshavela entered, shouldering an embroidered highland-style saddlebag, and offered a melancholy greeting to the ladies. Lost in thought, he stumbled upon a chair in his path and kicked it aside.

"Enter the highlander," croaked Ferdinand the raven. "The hermeneutic hunter! I hope your translation efforts have yielded some interesting results."

Ignoring the raven's welcome, Pshavela sat next to the Leader, opened his saddlebag and pulled a well-thumbed volume from

---

44. Interestingly, decades later, the Shaman of Toronto, Glenn Gould, would play Carnegie Hall barefoot, sitting on an unusually low stool and performing Bach's *Suite No. 6*. He incorporated droning into the counterpoint, as he also did in a few other outstanding recordings.

it, along with a few sheets of paper covered with crisscrossed inscriptions.

"Does anyone fancy raven for breakfast?" Pshavela asked wryly. "Are you sure, my ebony friend, you will be able to survive the transmission of celestial waves and not get fried in the process?"

"We'll see, my highlander!" replied Ferdinand, perching on the Leader's shoulder. "You don't seem very enthusiastic about the versification element of the Opus."

"My enthusiasm is beside the point." Pshavela was abrupt, as he sometimes could be.

"Why don't we just begin," Gurdjieff said, turning from the piano to his companions, though his fingers still roamed over the keyboard.

"Rrright you arrrre!" the raven nodded. "And here we go! But first, I suggest we hear at least one stanza of the highlander's bio-poetic rendering. I would like to synchronise some verbal matters we have at hand, to get a better sense of the whole thing. Do you follow me?"

"Not exactly, I'm afraid," Gurdjieff said, and started playing again, as if not very interested in the raven's point.

"Well, my Black Greek," the raven said, sounding slightly irritated, "I happen to espouse the idea that any kind of translation is a two-way movement, a dialogical thing, so to say—that is, the renderrrred and the renderrring: one usually impacts the other. The former undergoes a certain deconstrrruction, while the latter undergoes a certain reconstrrruction, and vice versa. The true meaning is somewhere in between the rrrendered and the rrrendering. Therefore, it is always worthwhile to do a reverse translation from one to the other and the other way round, and by such indirection *find direction out*, or in other words, find *meaning*. Thus, I want to try and *translate* the text translated by the highlander into the language of the animals and plants *backwards*—into the tongue of the featherless bipeds. Then we'll see what meanings we get."

Broodingly playing with musical statements, counter-statements, and drone, Gurdjieff simply nodded.

"Now my highlander, which stanza would you prefer to present?" the raven asked Pshavela.

"The introductory one: 'He who created the firmament, by that mighty power / made beings inspired from on high with souls celestial,' and so on . . ." Pshavela said, looking through his manuscript.

"Do me a favour, please," the raven said, "utter your sounds slowly, so I may make my reverse rendering immediate."

The highlander began producing an unusual bio-phonetic combination of sounds, which Ferdinand the raven followed closely and translated quickly:

> Desire make earth eat sky . . . big snake swallow big
> bird . . .
> Much excrement and urine . . . we are the offspring . . .
> Desire make sky pour juice into earth . . .
> Light and darkness . . . come and go . . . many odor
> spots . . .
> The scent is strong . . . the strong scent makes all
> move . . .
> Hunger makes kill . . . saliva and blood . . .
> Seed makes many . . . mucus and the offspring body . . .
> milk . . .
> We grow from dark to light . . . our roots in the earth . . .
> our crowns in the sky . . .
> Desire passes through us . . . from earth to sky . . .
> from sky to earth . . .
> Desire makes clay shiver and breathe . . .
> Desire is strong . . .

Gurdjieff accompanied this uncanny declamation on the piano, but when the other two stopped he kept playing his shamanic drone. Perched on the Leader's shoulder, the raven suddenly fluttered and then shivered, clawing the Mongol's flesh so that a few drops of some dark, dense liquid appeared.

"What are those drops?" Pshavela asked.

"The meaning, my highlander!" the raven said, in a deep, hoarse voice, still shivering. "The meaning we just extracted from our translation."

Gurdjieff stood up, approached the Leader, and studied the drops rolling down his chest.

"My God, is this the *substance*?!" Gurdjieff looked amazed.

"The sacred substance Askokin," Ferdinand repeated, through another fit of shuddering. Then he calmed down: "but it's still a crude version tainted with admixtures: blood, humors, ichor, etc. We need pure Askokin, which is invisible and intangible."

"How did you make it?" Gurdjieff was roused.

"I didn't make it, it was my Father up there," the raven replied. My "Father who art in heaven," as you would say . . . although mine is actually on Saturn. Yes, Gornahoor Harharkh IV made it, by using his lingvo-chronotopos accelerator to generate meta-musical vibrations in the Leader's mind, using your shamanic counterpoint as transformative substance and the highlander's *vegeto-zoo-poetic* discourse as base matter; an effect similar to that your alchemists tried producing, though they usually failed. However, as I said, this is just crude Askokin. To obtain the pure kind, we need the Cipher of the Fleece, the Almznoshinoo Code of El-Azar—the Resurrection! And we are going to obtain it at the Celestial Agape when we transform the *Panther's Skin* through a full-scale shamanic counterpoint of the *St. John Passion!*"

The raven fluttered up, sat on the Leader's head and announced to Pshavela, "meanwhile, my highlander, we'll need to go through another round of our dialogical rendering and test one more time exactly how Gornahoor's meta-music works in the Leader's head. Why don't we try a vegeto-zoo-poetic version of Tariel's lament upon the loss of his beloved Nestan, after her abduction by the dark creatures called the *kajebi*?"

Pshavela consented wordlessly, rummaging in his bag and producing from it another sheet of paper covered by some unknown script.

"Very good," the raven said, and turned to Gurdjieff. "From you, my Black Greek, I'll need more clearly articulated turmoil of the rolling sixteenths as they invade the bass, sustained in B-flat. Would you please? May my Father on Saturn and the cantor Schweitzer help you!"

Gurdjieff turned back to his keyboard.

"Let Gornahoor be with us!" said the raven, tilting his head. And shuddering even more powerfully than before, he attended Pshavela's inhuman utterances, translating them:

> Earth, hey—earth! Open up!
> I want you to take my eyes and keep them,
> As you keep—or perchance you might've already
>   eaten—
> The sacred bones of my beloved.
> I know you'll turn my eyes into ashes,
> Like you turned the bones of my beloved into ashes,
> Let ashes be ashes—*in death's dream kingdom!*
> *Too close to death, one sees it no longer . . .*
> *Stare ahead instead, maybe with the wide eyes of animals.*
>
> You compose and you decompose—
> This is your sacred art.
> Take my eyes then, take them to that last of meeting
>   places:

Decompose them and make me see the bones of my
beloved.
Pierce my eye with the bone of my beloved's arm,
So I can see my beloved's body in bloom:
Let my eyes be on her like *the sunlight on a broken
column.*
*Continuously confronted by creation, we see there
Only a dimmed reflection of the free and open.
Or some dumb animal, with its calm eyes,
Is seeing through and through us.
That's our Fate, to be possessed by the opposite,
To see an inversion and nothing more.*

Open up, hey—earth! Open up!
Let my eyes look upon the sacred bones of my
beloved,
Like the *two multifoliate stars of the other kingdom.*
Let us—my beloved and I—*wear rat's coats, crow-skin*
And be like *the wind in the branches of a swinging tree,*
Let her shriek with delight,
Let her bosom swell with wild desire,
And milk and blood come on me . . .[45]

As the three were performing, some sparkling reddish drops
dripped from punctures made by the raven's claws in the Leader's
skull. The drops slowly rolled down the Leader's temples and
cheeks, like blood from the head which wore a crown of thorns.
Pshavela and Gurdjieff kept going, but Ferdinand had to stop—
he was convulsing, as if a high-voltage electrical current was
passing through his feathered body. Falling down on the floor,

45. Vazha-Pshavela did publish this short poem "Earth, Hey, Earth, Open
Up!" though not until 1908, and of course it did not contain the T.S. Eliot lines
from "The Hollow Men" or Rilke's "Eighth Duino Elegy." This is just an inter-
polation by Gornahoor Harharkh IV.

he raced around in circles like a chicken with its head cut off.

A sparkling, reddish aura enveloped the Leader's body, and the room filled with a strange freshness. Dagny thought that her second glass of absinthe was causing her to hallucinate. She rose up and walked towards the Leader. As she approached him, the atmosphere of freshness became even more pronounced. She knelt in front of him, embraced him, and licked one drop of the substance off his temple. It tingled slightly on her tongue. She tried to stand up and go back, but an invisible, mighty, vertiginous hand seemed to drag her down, and her head dropped into the Leader's lap.

No, she did not lose her senses; she just lay there with her eyes open. Strange visions loomed in front of her, and multiple Voices spoke of a carnivalesque rhapsody made up of bizarre images and phrases, encompassing and surpassing the space around and inside her, like a huge medusa jellyfish . . .

She strode into the grand Zodiacal fields like a circus performer spinning through the diamond sky . . .

A lilting Voice called out: *The Transformation of Nothingness into Beauty through Love!*

She was like Leda ravished by the Swan. Another Voice spoke of a *staggering girl . . . unable to push the feathered glory from her loosening thighs . . . caressed by the dark webs . . . mastered by the brute blood of the air . . . her nape caught in his bill . . .*

The shudder in her loins engendered there the Beauty which would destroy fortified cities and all-mighty kings. That was the Beauty of abstract forms—the clear-cut images of the unimaginable shaped by the brushstrokes of Love, which makes all things more acute at the moment of vanishing . . .

Then the intensity of the "Leda and the Swan" scene turned into the *Wonderland* fun of Alice and the flamingo: a little girl held a live flamingo as a mallet and tried to hit a live hedgehog as if it were a ball . . .

And then she turned into wide-eyed Europa, sitting on a magnificent white bull and crossing the wine-dark sea . . . Love is as strong as the god of thunder transformed into a robust bull, and it carries you away across the sea and further, to where you are beyond Being. Yes, she felt it was *more* than just being there: sitting on that bull, she felt penetrated by the ecstatic influx of life, which flowed through all seven cavities of her body, down to her armpits and her loosened hair. She sang of Love, which makes the fibers of your soul part one after the other and dismembers your body . . . only thus dismembered will you realize the truth and utter—*I am*. It is like the song which articulates silence, as the Passion articulates life in death . . .

She was caught in the twilight—a creature flying between day and night, both a swallow and a bat: "I'm black but comely," she said, flying above the Ponte Vecchio Bridge, where Love once welcomed a poet, and dazzled him with visions of heaven and hell.

She saw a procession crossing the bridge; there was Ganesh, the elephant-headed god, followed by dancers with ivy-garlands on their necks, and flute players. Garlands and flutes! They were journeying to Mount Calvary, where the great sacrifice look place. Next, she saw them moving up the slope, approaching the Crucifix at the top of the mount. And there Ganesh trumpeted, and she saw the Cross taking root and putting forth buds. And He came down from the cross and embraced the elephant-headed god. She turned back into a woman; sitting next to Him at a table as his bride, he took up the bread and said, "For as often as ye eat this bread, and drink this cup, ye do shew the Lord's death till he come."And He broke the bread and she was blinded by the light bursting from it *like a million suns*!

Dagny recovered from the trance, feeling hazy. She heard Gurdjieff speaking.

"You've just tasted an extremely crude Askokin. But we will

require the purest Askokin in order to pass through the planet's major nerve endings and into the minds of Shamanic Individuals; through the latter, we will reach the masses, saving them from sheer madness! To make the pure Askokin flow, however, we need the Cipher of the Golden Fleece, or the Word, as I was telling you last night . . . the Cipher will form in the Leader's objective consciousness during the Agape, and then he will pass it on to a woman like you—*one who has loved much*, who appreciates music and poetry, and who has also been exposed to deliberate suffering. This transfer of information must happen via the Sacred Movements which originate from the primordial union of the White Monkey and the Mountain Witch—to put it in the symbolic language of Tibetan cosmogony. Therefore, we will require your participation in the Love Feast. It is tonight in the hall of the German Garden. Will you join us?"

As if she hadn't heard a single word, Dagny just looked into Gurdjieff's eyes and said, "I need to see my son, Zenon."

She jumped up and rushed out into the street.

Gurdjieff tried to follow her, worried by that the crude Askokin might have disturbed her psyche. But he was stopped at the door by Pshavela's call.

"Where is the raven, Black Greek?"

Gurdjieff looked back and saw the highlander and the Leader searching everywhere for the ebony bird.

"I'll check behind the counter, that where I last saw him," Gurdjieff said.

Stepping behind the counter, Gurdjieff stumbled upon something. Actually, it was not *something* but *someone* the Black Greek knew only too well; Sohrab Addin, the mock-Dervish, was lying on the floor and snoring. But there was no sign of Ferdinand the raven . . .

Gurdjieff's kick awakened the mock-Dervish. He got to his knees slowly, stretching and yawning. Then, suddenly, with a dexterous summersault, he jumped up and landed right on top of the counter.

"*Si può? Si può? Signore! Signori Scusatemi, se da sol me presentoooo* . . . my name is epiloooogue!!!" Sohrab Addin sang. Then he jumped down and saluted everyone there. "How exciting it is to be here with you again, my friends, my sycophants of Love, my artists of the sublime, my hermeneutic Argonauts of the great Cipher of the Fleece! And how depressing is it to see that all of you, myself included, are in deep shit!"

"Hey, mind your tongue, you piece of shit!" Pshavela was pissed off.

Sohrab Addin drew back in apology. "*Mi scusi* . . . I do regret it. Would you please excuse this small outburst of mine?"

"Let him explain himself," Gurdjieff told Pshavela, and turned to the mock-Dervish, saying, "tell us what's going on—where is the raven?"

"Between Nothingness and Eternity!" Sohrab Addin exclaimed. "That bird has flown, yes indeed, back to his Father, if you will; he is reunited with Gornahoor Harharkh IV! Alas, Ferdinand the raven was annihilated by the overdose of lingvo-chronotopos acceleration transmitted from Gornahoor's apparatus during your little collective improvisation. That fellow on Saturn must have made his calculations a bit too hastily, and you know about haste making waste. Thus, our poor raven must now be turning and turning around somewhere—amongst the planetary waste . . ."

"You mean we've lost contact with Gornahoor and his accelerator?!" Gurdjieff asked, concerned.

"I wouldn't get melodramatic," the mock-Dervish said. "It can't be defined as a *complete* loss of contact. We really only dropped out of the Law of Reciprocal Maintenance, or speaking more simply, we lost the *correspondence*, the reciprocity between the two levels of planetary existence. The thing is, Gornahoor can still use *involution* to influence us from above, while we are left without any means of *evolving* and sending our messages up to him. Thus, even if we manage to get the Cipher of the Fleece, there is no way for us to pass the information on to Gornahoor, who is supposed to use the formula to open up the chronotopos channel for the flow of Askokin. Moreover, we had planned for the Black Greek to disseminate the etherograms by using Gornahoor's accelerator as a broadcasting base; this was going to be how the Askokin would reach the brains of Shamanic Individuals on our planet. In short, it looks like we are going to fail."

"How could Gornahoor have made such a mistake?!" Gurdjieff became discouraged. "This must be the same curse that destroyed his great-grandfather."

"This was not the work of a curse." Sohrab Addin belched, adding with a hint of pessimism, "it's just the nature of time, which from the very beginning demanded the slow death of the universe. The world is degenerating. Or maybe I'm exaggerating?"

He was going to say something else, but the Leader interrupted him, speaking with his mouth shut—*ventriloquizing*:

"To bring back reciprocal contact with Harharkh, we need the silvered mirrors and magnifying glasses which our brother from Albion has in his magic lantern machine."

"What's that?" Pshavela scrutinized the Leader with his sole eye, as he had done earlier when the Tibetan monk had clapped one-handedly.

"Let the Leader of the Seven speak," Gurdjieff said.

"I can make the machine emit highly amplified radiation on one or more discrete frequencies—a steady beam of coherent light made up of highly excited atoms and molecules. To produce such a light we need the quanta of electromagnetic energy, known as photons."

"How do you know that?!" the amazed mock-Dervish inquired. "Do you also study optics in Lhasa?!"

"No, we study emptiness and compassion," the Leader replied.

"But what has compassion to do with optical physics?!" the mock-Dervish asked with sheer incredulity.

"Compassion is the mother of all knowledge, be it scientific or otherwise," the Leader explained.

"Very true!" Pshavela said, with his eye riveted on the Leader.

The mock-Dervish bowed, clasped his face in his palms, and then spoke, tilting his head. "What's the light that I see there at the end of the tunnel? Is that the steady beam emitted by spiritual atoms and molecules excited by the discharge of electromagnetic compassion? Out, out, false radiance! No, this radiance is produced by the headlight of an oncoming train— that huge, powerful monster of steel, full of sound and fury, its engine fed with pressurized steam and its cars rushing towards us like tomorrow and tomorrow and tomorrow . . ."

"Shall we to talk to our Albion brother, Gene Morris?" proposed Gurdjieff, who was slightly confused by the mock-Dervish's weird soliloquy. "I'll send the message boy to bring him here."

"No, you needn't," the Leader stopped him. "I'll perform what I've just described at the Love Feast tonight." And with these words he shut his eyes, dozing off.

For a while they sat in silence punctuated by the Leader's even breathing. Then Sohrab Addin asked:

"What about the woman, the one who was supposed to play a metaphysical-lingvo-erotic part in our Celestial Agape, thereby beginning a grand, new kind of love affair? Did she . . . say *no?*"

June 4th, 1901 was marked by another heavy rainstorm in Tiflis. Several charity events planned for the day were even cancelled by the authorities. Dagny didn't mind the torrents flooding the city, though. As one of the Qarachokhaely told her at the feast on the raft, "through the rain heaven makes love to earth."

Yes, He—the Inconceivable, the Endless, the Miraculous—was haunting her in the form of rain. He was the White Monkey, and she the Mountain Witch. How does it feel to make love to a half-god, half-animal? Which positions do they prefer? Surely not the missionary position—that is human, all too human; the theriomorphic deities must prefer animal positions; doggy style, for instance. But all animals get sad after copulation, as some philosopher say . . . do the gods get sad too?! Dagny couldn't know—she had only been with men. Men usually became sleepy if they lasted too long, or got melodramatic if they came too fast. They were neither animals nor gods, and they didn't know what love was. She knew it—she knew what love was, she was the Priestess of Love. Men just wanted to turn her into a vessel, a container for their petty fantasies, desires, and sperm.

But some of them came up with more "advanced" ideas: they wanted her to conceive the Word of Resurrection, the Cipher of the Golden Fleece. Her husband, Stach, was writing a new play in which the Golden Fleece was the symbol of Love, which neither men nor women could handle because Love was stronger than they were, it was as strong as Death! But Dagny herself felt strong—she was feeling strong that very moment in June; yes, she was as strong as the month of June, which had pulled all the leaves from the trees and flooded the streets of a city populated with carefree, easygoing people . . . "*Madame, let me help you cross the flooded street,*" one of them suggested to her; or, "*let me carry you in my arms, so that you may not wet your angelic feet . . . You are like a doll; let me take you home . . .*" That last one seemed well-off, he was a shopkeeper; he would nourish her, adore her, inundate her with love and candies . . . she embraced him, kissing his temple and caressing his cheek, but then kept striding along the flooded cobblestones . . .

Her brain was still drunk on that unusual substance she had licked from the Mongol's temple—plus all the absinthe she'd had; a sweet, intoxicating feeling of freedom pushed her onwards, filling her with an invisible, radiant excitement. She had wisdom, she had the knowledge of the Golden Fleece—it was the pubic hair below her belly; the female pubic triangle was the miraculous Fleece, the texture of Love which men mythologize, taking long sea-journeys in their wet dreams, dying for it, accomplishing heroic deeds for it—for a triangle of pubic hair . . . oh goodness! Was she hallucinating still? No, her mind was definitely clear, she saw—yes—she saw her own vagina moving towards her—ha-ha! Just like in that story by Gogol: a government functionary loses his nose one morning and later sees it walking down the streets and riding in fancy carriages dressed as a minister.

Draped in the Golden Fleece, Dagny's vagina approached and they embraced. "How delightful to see you, sister!" she said, and it replied, "Oh, I'm overjoyed to see you, sister!" "Come, let's have a drink, let's celebrate the occasion," Dagny suggested. "Oh I'd love to have a drink with you," said her vagina. "I'm really thirsty, I could have a man-juice with you, the juice we squeeze from their balls . . ." "Good choice, sister," Dagny said, "that juice is what keeps us young, forever young and strong!" She kept striding along, conversing with her pussy. "What do you think of Medea, sister? She came from this country, did you know that? Yes, Medea the sorceress, who helped Jason get the fleece, then married him and murdered their children to avenge Jason's infidelity." "I don't care for Medea, it's the juice from Jason's balls that I'm in the mood for." "But I'm Medea, don't you see? I helped Stach and the rest of the artist-Argonauts get the Golden Fleece, and then he abandoned me, he sold me to a lunatic! Ha-ha-ha! Artists don't pay taxes, but still they're always short of money. But what do they need money for? They live in the fictitious world of their writing, where money is also supposed to be fictitious." "No sister," her pussy said, "they can't survive in that made-up world, they need reality to keep them going and we are that reality, but they have to buy it; that is why they need money . . . we are the mothers of realism!" "I was going to find my son, but I'm afraid I've lost my way!" said Dagny.

Yes, she had gotten lost; she had no idea where the Kellers lived, and because she had no money, she couldn't get a carriage back to the hotel—to the hotel where Emeryk was probably waiting for her, brooding on double-suicide. "Love is a rope by which the Devil drags men into hell," she recalled him saying, quoting Stach. No, love is a miraculous Golden Fleece: drenched, soaked in sweat and the juice of masculine balls— that was exactly what she would tell him before the "suicide," ha-ha-ha. Stach would have been impressed, too . . .

She must have been roaming the streets for hours. She stood in the evening twilight, avoiding the occasional advances made by men passing by: their excited glances undressing her, foreign tongues speaking to her, licking her body. The waves of alcohol and crude Askokin propelled her forward until she found herself standing in front of illuminated gates—the gates of the German Garden.

"Dinnertime, sister!" said Dagny, and walked in.

"Mme Przybyszewska!" It was Count Avalov. "How nice to see you here. You're alone?!"

"Well," replied Dagny, "In fact I'm not alone, I'm here with my sister."

"Your sister?" Avalov said, intrigued. "Where is she?"

"Can't you see her?" said Dagny, pointing to her vagina. "She is wearing the Golden Fleece!"

"Mme Przybyszewska, are you all right?!" Avalov seemed shocked.

But Dagny did not reply. She went ahead, cutting through the dense, humid air and the socialising crowd. A man who looked familiar offered her a glass of champagne—it was Oliver Wardrop, Her Majesty's vice-consul to Crimea. They had met on a train to Batumi a week ago ... how nice to see him again, she said ... and how nice of Mme Przybyszewska to come to this concert, where she might bask in an extraordinary fusion of European baroque music with Middle Eastern poetry, he told her. The vice-consul hoped she felt better than the last time he'd seen her? Oh yes, much better, much better ... actually she and her sister were somewhat hungry. Her sister?! Never mind her ... Oh certainly, she would permit Mr. Wardrop to introduce her to Mr. Nicholas Marr, professor of linguistics, who has just arrived from Mount Athon in Greece, where he'd been searching for ancient Georgian manuscripts. How do you do, professor Marr? It's a pleasure ... What's your next destination? Mount Sinai ... How interesting... Yes he's looking for a very special manuscript carrying a sort of a hymn to the Georgian language ... What's so special about the Georgian language? Ah, yes, it comes from the primordial language, which was spoken before the Indo-European invasion, and the Germanic invasion too. Sorry about the invasion, professor. I'm a Germanic woman and on behalf of all Germanic peoples, I do apologize. Ha-ha-ha. Would you care for another glass of champagne? Ah, here comes Prince Ilia Chavchavadze. Have you met before? The Prince is delighted to meet the wife of Stanislaw Przybyszewski, the distinguished Polish author and patriot ... I do very much respect the Young Poland movement ... Georgians could learn from them ... we have much in common. I hate the Polish patriots, Prince, they are suicidal drunkards, ha-ha-ha. ("This woman is acting strangely," the prince whispered to one of his companions.) We Georgians also are keen on wine, but when it comes to suicide—no way, we are hedonists! Here's to Georgian women and their hedonist men! Ha-ha-ha!

Dagny floated on. She saw Asian faces, some of them resembling that man, the Leader of the Seven. She noticed Gurdjieff talking to them, along with a couple of swarthy men who looked Arabic or Hindu. She heard Stach's fellow Poles, Germans, Russians, Turks, Armenians . . . a confusion of peoples and tongues like the confusion of senses inside her. Feeling dizzy, she sat on a bench in the corner of the garden. Just a bit of privacy . . . that was all she needed to pull herself together . . . no, she wasn't feeling drunk at all, not a bit; there was only that weird brew boiling in her blood, that thing called Askokin—the *elisir d'amore* . . . ha-ha-ha . . .

"Would you mind if I took a seat beside the two of you, Mme Przybyszewska? I mean, of course, you and your sister in the Golden Fleece."

Dagny looked up and saw a man dressed in a dirty, torn jacket, with a bow tie around his neck and no shirt. He stood there smiling and sipping wine.

"How do you know about my sister? And who are you?" she asked, surprised.

"I know many things about you, madame. Let me introduce myself—Sohrab Addin. I happen to work for the Iranian diplomatic mission here."

"How do you know 'many things' about me then? I've never had any contact with the Iranian diplomatic mission."

"It's a long story. Yes, a very long story, though it seems to be coming to an end."

"An end?! Look at that, yet another man who knows about endings," Dagny said sarcastically. "Yesterday, someone like you tried to 'end' me in a double suicide."

"The double suicide of the White Monkey and the Mountain Witch," Sohrab Addin declared. "Human suicide ends with death and nothing but death. Only the Divine Suicide gives life."

"What is the Divine Suicide?"

"Passion."

"What is Passion?"

"Pure Askokin."

"And who has seen the pure Askokin?"

"Well, several have that I could name: the author of the *Panther's Skin*, for one; the Shaman of Haisenakh . . . a certain Vermeer, a draftsman from the city of Delft—he even tried to capture its flow in his paintings. Even reading love letters or playing music—the radiance from that channels the flow of pure Askokin. Love letters are messages from beyond—from His Most Endlessness. You too will experience its flow tonight. A toast!" Sohrab Addin drained his glass of wine bottoms up.

"Thank you, I've already tried it. It's still flowing through my veins."

"It may destroy you unless you share it with somebody else."

"My god, the double suicide again . . . or is this a double seduction?!" she said, giggling. "I'd rather share it with my sister in the Golden Fleece!"

"You mean masturbate?" he laughs.

"Yes!" She bursts into laughter too. "Yes, I would call that truly modern: the immaculate conception via masturbation. A new Word made flesh through my body. Is that what the Black Greek wants from me?! Surely I am the new Madonna . . . which makes Eddie Munch a prophetic artist, ha-ha-ha!"

"Share it with anyone, even the man who brought you here— that poor deranged fellow who wants to kill himself through you. He'll change his bloody mind rather quickly, you can be sure of that, my dear."

"Wlad Emeryk?!" she said, bending over and choking with laughter. "Uuhhh! I got it right after all . . . the double seduction! You are seducing me on behalf of Wlad, that necrophiliac, who wants to kill me and make love to my dead body. No, spare me this! I'd rather share the sacred substance with you, sir. Come on, let's begin! My sister and I are hungry . . ." and she spread her legs, lifting her skirt up.

"Ducha! Ducha! What are you doing?!" Wlad Emeryk emerged

from behind Sohrab Addin, pushing him aside. "I've been looking for you, I got the police involved! Thank God, Avalov just sent me a message, telling me that you were here. Where have you been? Who is this man? Come, come with me, I'll take you home!"

"What do you want from me, you slave trader?" Dagny said in a stirring voice. "Leave me alone!"

"Please, Ducha, this is not the place for scandal. People will see," Emeryk implored her. "Let's go back to the hotel, please. You need a rest, you look ill."

"Sir, it appears the lady is rejecting your proposal," Sohrab Addin said politely. "Why don't you just leave?"

"Who are you, you dirty bastard? How dare you to speak to me like that?" Emeryk was furious; he lurched toward the stranger.

But suddenly Pshavela emerged between them, grabbed Emeryk by the shirt, lifted him up, and threw him into the bushes. "Slow down, my boy," said the highlander.

"Bad vibrations, bad vibrations . . ." asserted the Leader of the Seven, coming out of the bushes and moving ahead towards the hall.

"Police! Police!" Emeryk shouted.

"Listen, mock-Dervish," Pshavela told Sohrab Addin, "something's wrong with this woman—she must have a fever or something. Take her away from here. Go to Margarita's. Go through the back garden. I'll take care of her man."

And he did: squeezing Emeryk's mouth with his left hand, he then applied the index and middle fingers of his right hand to Emeryk's throat, sending the agitated fellow into a deep sleep. Having thus pacified him, Pshavela came out of the bushes and glanced around conspiratorially with his single eye, then strode off towards the hall. The police, late as usual, were nowhere in sight. He bumped into Count Avalov, who asked if they'd met before . . . (no, Pshavela has not seen Mme Przybyszewska . . . no, not Mr. Emeryk either . . . have a good night, count, Your Excellency). Mingling with the crowd of people, he greeted his colleagues from the Literacy Society and was "overjoyed to see Prince Chavchavadze at the event."

Meanwhile Sohrab Addin propped Dagny up, as she could hardly walk. They passed through the back garden and once on the street hailed a carriage. Helping Dagny in, the mock-Dervish told the driver: "Take us to the Grand Hotel!"

Koba, who would be Stalin one day, watched the whole scene from behind the fence, amused by yet another bourgeois skirmish. *That woman must be something, huh*?! he thought. But what was she to the highland bard, and he to her? Pshavela, who "spoke" to snowy hills, gigantic mountains, forests, rivers, and to the rain— what had he to do with that fallen woman?! Koba would later call writers "engineers of human souls." Could Pshavela with his bourgeois sympathies be equal to the task?! No, Koba would need new creative workers to craft artistic propaganda . . .

Actually, at that very moment he was less worried about the bard than he was about Camo and his infernal explosive, which had been set up under the stage right below the magic lantern. How would it work? He had to be extremely careful—there must be no serious casualties, just terror; terror and *lots of shit*. Ha-ha-ha! Let the upper crust—let the *aristocracy*—smell it . . .

Koba heard the bell ringing for the performance to start. The crowd leisurely moved into the hall. Prince Chavchavadze, surrounded by a group of young people, made a joke which was met with hearty laughter. *The Great Father of the Nation*, thought Koba. *Well, let Him smell the shit of His Sons* . . .

Everybody crowded into the hall. For a while, the noisy garden was completely silent except for the singing of crickets. Koba looked up; the starlit dome seemed unusually close to earth, as if some mighty cosmic hand had pulled it downward in order to enhance the influence of the celestial bodies. The night air became crystal clear and he took a deep breath. The sound of applause came from the hall, and then a voice said: "*Guten Abend, Meine Damen und Herren!*" There was more applause, and then the performance began. The hall windows were closed, so Koba couldn't hear very much of it. He stood there, waiting for *it* to happen . . . he hummed a tune, feeling on edge . . .

Some ten, maybe fifteen minutes had passed, when suddenly he saw a thin red beam above the roof of the hall, surging upwards and piercing the sky. And then: he couldn't understand it, he just felt something strange happening, something he'd never experienced before—the sensation of an earthquake passing through his body . . . *what is this?!* He tried to fathom it and nearly swooned. Then came the music in mighty waves, produced by an orchestra and a choir. He tried to look up again, but was blinded by powerful rays of light coming from the windows of the hall. The radiance was fused with the music, which flowed like a huge, turbulent river, and an incantation of rhythmic poetry in some inhuman language (though the poetic texture formed by the sounds was entrancing). All space inside him and around him was overwhelmed by that terrible recitative, fast developing into an all-consuming cacophony . . .

Koba fell to the ground and lay curled up like a fetus, cramped and shuddering, hiding from the awesome cascade of Voices rushing around him.

And then it all stopped.

Koba remained crouching for a while. When he stood up, slowly, and looked over the fence, the garden was quiet again; no sounds were coming from the hall, as if the performance was over. Feeling dazed and curious about what had happened, he tiptoed towards the hall breathing fast, his heart pounding, his temples pulsating . . .

When he got inside, a very strong light stung his eyes. He shaded them with his palm and looked around. A baffling sight greeted him—it was the weirdest thing he'd ever seen:

People were sitting in rows, stock-still—all alive, though motionless and dumb. Their eyes were open, and they blinked every once in a while and moved their heads slowly from side to side, as if looking at something which was not visible. There were traces of blissful excitement on their enlightened faces, and the air smelled of extraordinary freshness.

Koba moved down the aisle towards the stage. The members of the choir and the musicians of the orchestra—their instruments still in their laps—were frozen just like the audience, looking as if they were devouring with their eyes something invisible. To the left, backstage, he could see from behind a torn curtain that the magic lantern was broken into pieces; next to it, a group of people sat under the influence of the same insensible ecstasy as the rest of the crowd. There was Pshavela, with his big mustache and huge eyes, a half-naked Mongol, and a buttoned-up fellow. The stage floor in front of the group was wrecked, and through a big hole in it he could see his friend Camo, standing stock-still like a die-hard sentinel and covered in shit.

Koba stood nonplussed, contemplating how to help Camo, when suddenly he heard a growl come from behind him. He looked back and saw a huge, flame-bright leopard, creeping towards him down the aisle. Koba's gut loosened—there was no way for him to escape; there wasn't even any time for him to think about possible maneuvers, or where to find a weapon to aid in self-defense. The powerful beast was coming nearer, and it was both terrifying and enchanting. He stood there petrified, completely numb, feeling the warm urine leak through his pants . . . the leopard lurched, and, producing a thunderous roar, jumped at him. No, it was not a jump—it was a tremendous blast, targeted at him. And he fell down unconscious.

When Koba came back to his senses, he found himself in his underground headquarters, lying in bed, with absolutely no idea of either how he'd survived or how he'd made it home.

One thing he could tell, however, was that he felt extraordinary—refreshed and strong . . .

Gornahoor Harharkh was trying to figure out *what went wrong*. What was that minuscule explosion which came from the site of the Cosmic Agape, which had disturbed the lingvo-chronotopos waves he'd sent to planet Earth? Sure, the waves were strong enough to suppress the explosion—to implode it and reverse it upon its source . . . And yet, the tiny, pitiful blast must have been exacerbated by something else, thus causing this odd result.

At the beginning, everything went smoothly: the counterpoint between the oboes and the strings in the *Passion*, the fervent choir, the vegeto-zoo-poetic renderings of the *Panther's Skin* . . . and then all of a sudden . . . but *sudden?* No, if anything can go wrong, it will.

Gornahoor, he kept telling himself, *you should have been extra careful*. He'd guessed that excessive amounts of transmitted vibrations might fry his terrestrial double, Ferdinand the raven. Planetary reciprocity was likely lost because of that, and now it definitely was lost.

But who figured out how to imbue what on Earth was known as the Cipher of the Golden Fleece with the frequencies of the flow of Askokin? Who among the featherless bipeds managed to produce such an amplified light through stimulating an emission of radiation? It seemed the stimulated emission and the unidentified explosion must have interacted at some point, the former magnifying the latter . . . that was the problem. Of course, such an interaction could have happened in any place where there were silvered mirrors and multiplying glasses. A *parasitical explosion*—that's what Gornahoor would call it . . .

Call it what you will, idiot! The fact is that the Askokin flow was deformed, sent astray, misdirected! Moreover, why did the Ur-Leopard materialize as a mere hologram, vanishing in yet another stupid blast? At least it was a known anomaly, having manifested during other, earlier attempts to create artistic sublimity. Mulling over the error, Gornahoor thought of *Hamlet* (a dramatic composition by that allegedly feathered human known worldwide as the Swan of Avon); the protagonist's mind is dominated by an emotion which is inexpressible because it is in *excess* of the facts as they appear. Similarly, the leopard hologram must have autonomously formed itself from the uncontrolled energies of that very same excess of emotion. Exactly the same thing happens to the featherless bipeds when repressed contents of their psyche are incompletely sublimated.

Besides, exacerbated by the lingvo-chronotopos energies, there was a danger that the error erased clusters of Pardimeme information from the memories of the Shamanic Individuals who performed the Opus Almznoshinoo during the Agape. If that happened, they would forget the events that had taken place over the last three weeks—but no big deal; it was *tomorrow* they were working for, not *yesterday*. It was only because of high hopes for the future that they wrestled with the dead arm of the past . . .

Gornahoor looked at the dissemination monitor. The system was working efficiently, delivering surges of Askokin to . . . *to whom* . . . ? The question exploded in his mind, setting him ablaze.

To whom?! Could it be . . . to *false shamans*?! The sacred substance . . . feeding into *their* brains?!

Well, a priori, certain deviations were expected, due to dissonance and breaches in the Megalocosmic Octave, but the Askokin . . . draining away?

Gornahoor was shocked.

If those false Shamanic Individuals received the Askokin, then over time they would begin to develop an extremely dangerous and powerful quality called *charisma*, which attracts the love and admiration of huge masses of featherless bipeds . . . the politicizing of art would follow, with art being transformed into the terrible aesthetics of power. Gornahoor could even imagine that happening; diabolical pictures flashed in his mind like solar flares . . .

Furthermore, because of this awful error, the concept of "dehumanizing the arts"—initially formulated with the aim of restoring objectivity to artistic expression (by purifying art of banal interpretations of reality)—was also likely to degenerate into something . . . something . . . analogous to the dehumanization of vast swathes of hypnotized featherless bipeds . . .

This is the way the world ends: not with a bang, but a bug; not with a whimper, but a hamper . . . Gornahoor was losing his mind. Actually, it was turning into an alarm bell. Or was it a death bell? Ding-dong! Ding-dong! Ding-dong . . . no, it was a diving bell, a cracked one—cracked by blows from within, and from outside too . . . a double crack-up! The project of modernism would end: not with a Song of Songs but a *Scream* of Screams. Yes, some rogue demon would harness and fly the Cow to the moon—screaming!

With that outrageous vision in mind, Gornahoor realized that the curse which had destroyed his great-grandfather had reached the great-grandson too.

Archangel Looisos! The Greatest Archangel Sakaki! Why?!

And Gornahoor wept. Good old Gornahoor, poor old Gornahoor wept . . .

Meanwhile, on Earth . . .

Sohrab Addin, the mock-Dervish, walked cautiously away from Dagny's door. He tiptoed down the corridor, holding himself carefully—he was still drunk, drunk on her and the crude Askokin, which dripped from her drenched armpits, her hot mouth, her wet vagina . . . oh, yes, their bodies had been cemented fast with that balm.

No, "drunk" does not adequately summarize his state of mind

as he walked down the corridor. Rather, he'd put it as follows: He had read her body like a book in which the mysteries of love were written, and now, with her nudity in his head and the heat of her passion on his skin, he was repeating the passages he had memorized—as a tragedian in a provincial theater recites over and over again the text he's meant to learn by heart. Yes—that more closely described his mood.

The corridor seemed longer than he'd thought it was. Odd, the hotel was not that big. He must be hallucinating; it was as if with each careful step, the space around him grew larger. Flashbacks to that wild hour which had just concluded—of him and Dagny making love—caused him to stumble, but he went on, balancing himself against the walls.

Come now, steady up—he has to be extra careful, Emeryk might emerge at any moment: Emeryk the furious, Emeryk the deranged, Emeryk the imminent . . . he was determined to kill her and then blow out his own frenzied brains. Sohrab could see it happening— Emeryk's lips deformed in a lunatic's grimace, his shaking hand holding the revolver, and his penis growing hard . . .

My god, what a woman! Even death itself desires her! And yes, when she makes love to death, it will be the most passionate, erotic experience of her life—the ultimate, enlightening climax, permeated with the rapturous joy of self-transcendence—like Isolde's last song, which transcends the ecstatic music of Love. This was Dagny's destiny; it was exactly why Sohrab had brought her to the Grand Hotel instead of taking her to Margarita's, where she might hide.

Ertrinken, versinken, unbewusst, höchste Lust![46] The music of Isolde's "Liebestod" ringing in his head, Sohrab tumbled down the stairs and landed on the lobby floor, waking up the boy sleeping at the reception desk.

"Sir, are you all right?"

46. ". . . to drown, to founder, unconscious, utmost rapture!"

Of course Sohrab Addin was *all right*. He stood up, tilted his head, fixed his hair, and walked out—shuffling and moonwalking in a mock-elegant fashion, just like the Shaman of Harlem, Cab Calloway, would walk off the stage at the Cotton Club . . . *She had a dream about the king of Sweden! hi-de hi-de hi-de hi-de hooo!*

It was long past midnight and the street was empty; a couple drunks on the corner were trying to come up with some sort of tune. Sohrab looked at them appreciatively; "a few good ones left," he said, and stood there deciding where he should go next. He was in the middle of these vague deliberations when suddenly he caught sight of a powerful radiance coming from the Alexander Garden across the street. He decided to head straight over.

Going deeper and deeper into the Garden, he came across a remarkable scene.

It felt like déjà vu. The composition of the entire scene repeated Édouard Manet's *Luncheon on the Grass*, with the nude Dagny sitting in front and two men on either side of her, talking to each other in Polish. There was a third digging in the earth behind them. They were having bread and wine. The whole scene was glaringly illuminated.

When Sohrab Addin approached them, Dagny looked up and said:

"Hello, mock-Dervish, and welcome to my Love Feast! Please, meet my friends. The gentleman on my left is Stach Przybyszewski, my former husband. The gentleman on my right is Wincent Brzozowsky, my last lover. The one behind me, I believe you know him, that's Wlad Emeryk, and he's digging my grave. Come, have some bread and wine with me; let's celebrate my death!"

"Thank you, my lady," Sohrab said, "I'd love to sit with you and while away the time, drinking your wine." And he sat down in front of her.

Dagny took the bread, broke it, dipped it in the bowl of wine, and passed it to Sohrab. He ate it. She picked up the bowl of wine and gave it to him. He drank it. And then he heard the sound of a flute. The player was invisible, but the melody was well known: it was the tune from Mozart's *The Magic Flute*, which attracts strange animals and makes them dance.

"This is a Japanese flute," Dagny said, "made of bone taken from the thigh of a heron crazed by the moon."

"I suppose now we'll see some dancing animals?" the mock-Dervish proposed.

But he was wrong. Instead of animals, he saw an extraordinary group of people solemnly emerge from the dark side of the garden and enter the glaring light. Among them were Tariel, the knight in the panther's skin, and his beloved Nestan; Mary Magdalene, carrying a clay tablet; Lazarus, draped in unraveling mummy cloth; Jason, clad in the Golden Fleece; and lastly, Medea, looking as moon-crazed as the heron from which the flute was made.

The three couples then performed a dance to the music of the flute.

"The Sacred Movements, as discovered by Gurdjieff, the Black Greek, when he traveled through Central Asia and Tibet," said Dagny, as if trying to explain to Sohrab the odd entrance of the dancers. "They're cosmic messages transmitted by human bodies. Human bodies are the letters through which the Spirit writes."

In pairs, one by one, the dancers approached Dagny and the others, sitting around them in a triangular formation. They started eating the bread and drinking the wine.

Here Dagny spoke again:

"As death nears, I feel the power in my heart. I feel strong, much stronger than I ever felt in the company of men. I know death loves me, loves me with a love so tender, so subtle, it thrills me. You see, the men I had before—they were ruthless like mischievous boys, *les enfants terribles*, but they never grew up, they only dreamed pathetic dreams of their tiny dicks growing bigger. They teased and tortured cats with cruel, impetuous curiosity. Imprudent, misguided creatures—they were bewitched by flesh and anxious to undress its mysteries, but all they ever learned were scraps of knowledge. They will never know that the true mystery of the body is its *reality*. Only the body is real; my body exposed to death is real. From the shadows to reality I go . . ."

The men by her side, Stach and Wincent, started a skirmish, kicking and clutching each other; they ended up rolling across the ground like two boys, bunched into a ball of animosity.

Looking at them, Tariel burst into hearty laughter, then took out a spike and pricked Nestan's thigh. She growled like a riled panther. Another prick, another growl . . .

"I bore children to one of them," Dagny said, pointing at Stach. "And I helped him to obtain the Golden Fleece of Love." And she tittered.

"Kill them, kill the children you bore to him!" Medea said distantly, caressing Jason's shoulder through the Fleece.

"Delightful!" Jason said, nearly sobbing. "It's not my fault! I blame it all on women!"

Here Lazarus spoke:

> I spent four days in death's bed—
> four days like four nights of ardor and love
> in the bower of the Egyptian Queen.
> Death would kiss me with the kisses of her mouth,
> taking my breath away,
> and I penetrated her and left my seed in her.
> I felt her enveloping me, pressing her breasts against
> me,
> squeezing me with her arms and thighs,
> and the maggots of her passion ate my flesh.

She got intoxicated with the wine of my blood
and would ask for more and more and more.
And we would die together in each other's arms,
and I would rise again to die in her anew,
and she would rise again to die in me—
like perfect lovers do,
for theirs is the true knowledge of each other's body.
And thus we labored in her bed—
exhausting all means to make us one,
falling into the abyss of oblivion and blissful
    nothingness,
until my Father came and dragged me out,
like a caring parent would drag his beloved, errant
    son from a brothel . . .

As Lazarus spoke, Dagny crept up to him and carefully studied his body. Picking maggots off him, she put them in her mouth . . . and when Lazarus had finished, Dagny turned to Mary Magdalene and embraced her.

"Mary, sweet Magdalene, I am a woman who has loved much, like you. And now my love turns me toward Death. Tell me, what kind of a lover is death?"

And Mary Magdalene spoke:

There is only one death—the death of my Lord
    Jesus Christ.
That Death made all other deaths die.
It is like the mightiest of warriors, who slaughters
    the dragon.
I saw His Death and was astounded,
like an ordinary village girl
seeing the pharaoh's chariot rushing toward her.
Shining like a million suns, through the opened gates

of Infinity,
it blinded me.
And only through that sacred blindness
Could I see Him risen in his true body—
gorgeous as the Divine Groom emerging from the
wedding shrine.
O, verily so, we were conceived in that sacred
marriage
of eternal life and death,
and it recurs eternally in the Love that moves us.

"I see the Golden Fleece! The magic Lamb Skin!" Jason
exclaimed, pointing at Dagny's pubic hair.
"You want to grab that one too, don't you, my treacherous
prince?" said Medea darkly. Then turned to Dagny, saying:

Woman, you don't know what death is.
True knowledge will come when you murder your
darlings—
the offspring of thy womb:
the babes you bore, you fed with you breast, you
taught to play, to speak . . .
I slew them like I would slaughter sacrificial goat-kids!
O heart of mine, steel thyself!
First I did hesitate to do the deed that must be done.
But then I took the sword and I advanced to the post
where darkness besieges the strongholds of life.
The blood of my dear children stained my hands, my
breast, my face.
I flung myself into the darkness
and there I felt death's palms covering my eyes,
sliding softly down my neck, my breasts, my belly,
touching my thighs, squeezing my buttocks . . .

I gave in and *It* penetrated me, whinnying and
    neighing . . .
Even now I shudder as I speak of that intercourse.
It was not Its seed that death left in me.
No—it was a hidden truth that was revealed in my
    womb as I climaxed.
I knew the tongue which animals and plants and
    minerals did speak,
but in that instant I was inspired with greater
    knowledge,
which made me read anew what was inscribed
in the fabric of the Golden Fleece . . .

"What was inscribed there?" Dagny asked.

"I'll tell you what was inscribed there," Jason interrupted tauntingly. "It said: every woman is bitter as bile but each has two good moments: one in bed and the other in the grave."

"Three words were written on its golden folds," Medea said, ignoring Jason. "Only three words, which were as follows: *Baa . . . baa . . . baa . . .*"

"*Baaaa . . . baaaa,*" Dagny repeated, and the others joined in: "*Baaa . . . baaa . . .* baaa . . ." And they laughed.

"And then I died," Medea said, "and in death I was united with my children once more."

Dagny turned to Nestan and asked, "Tell me, beautiful woman, what's death to you?"

Nestan growled (as Tariel kept pricking her) and said, "Death is like my beloved Tariel, the knight who rescued me: a narrow road cannot keep Tariel back, nor a rocky one; by him, all are levelled, the weak and the strong-hearted, youths and graybeards."[47] She growled again.

47. Compare with Rustaveli's "A narrow road cannot keep back Death, nor a rocky / one; by him all are levelled, weak and strong-hearted; in / the end the earth unites in one place youth and graybeard."

Suddenly, Tariel became agitated. With his eyes wide open, he gazed at Nestan and exclaimed, "My panther! My panther! Your hot fires burn me! I want to kiss your lips! Let me kiss your lips!"

He lurched at her, trying to embrace her and kiss her. Nestan resisted furiously, scratching his face and growling. Tariel forced her to the ground, grappled with her, and, overcoming her with his powerful body, he strangled her, muttering, "Let me kiss you, let me kiss your lips . . ."

When it was done, he rocked slowly back on his heels, still gazing at her and panting. Then he started to sob, bursting into a groaning lamentation.

"Ahhhh . . . ooooohhhh . . . uuuhhhh . . . aaahhhhh . . ." Sobbing and keening like this, he lifted Nestan's lifeless body in his arms and staggered away.

The flute sounded again. Mary, Lazarus, Jason, and Medea rose up and followed the knight in the panther's skin into the darkness of the garden.

The mock-Dervish rose up and rushed after them.

"How about going to the sulphur baths?" he suggested. "Such elaborate meditations upon the nature of death remind me too much of life, and I need to wash it all off!" He stepped aside into the thicket, casting an abrupt, farewell glance at Dagny.

Dagny stood up, smiling. She straightened her back; her legs open, her hands behind her head, she was Munch's *Sphinx* incarnate.

Stach and Wincent seemed to have made peace, and were talking nonchalantly in Polish. Emeryk, in the rear, kept digging.

Looking at the night sky, Dagny said:

Be still! Be still!
The stars are singing a mysterious song

about one who's walking for the last time
Through the rose garden.
Be still, oh, be still!
I hear a loved voice calling . . .
do you see all the stars falling
over my life?
Be still . . .
The day has spoken far too many words.

"That's true enough, so shut up! Shut up!" Stach said to her brusquely. Then, to Wincent, "she grew up in wealth and luxury—*an aristocrat!* But I took her down a peg or two."

"Sick rose of mine . . . Ducha, I'm dead and I'm waiting for you. Please don't be too long!" Wincent looked at her with melancholy eyes. "You are *the grave where buried love doth live!*"

"Huh, you're like a pussy penetrated by a mighty cock! So shut up!" Stach said sarcastically, and then turned back to Wincent.

"No Stach, I can't stay dumb, I can't stay wordless because *It* wants to speak through me! Yes, my Golden Fleece speaks through me—the rainbow colors the cobwebs of my dreams, which restore to words their full significance. So you had better listen to me, you fool!

"I am the Gate of Life; the void pluralized; the Nothing about which there once was much ado; the *nihilo* of creation, the verb that propels nouns like spermatozoids are propelled towards the ovule; the door to exodus and exile . . .

"I am the mother of unreality, awakening her babies from the sleep of reality with a kiss at noon . . . the darkness comes at noon through that same kiss . . . like the silence uttered by the ineffable Word . . .

"There are three truths thrust within me—*things are, things are not*, and *things neither are nor are not*. They are otherwise: each comes out of the other two, like in a metaphor, which is *All*.

"We will sail together on a river, me and my children; we will sail to a land sunlit and far away, and we will dance a festive dance around the fire there ... those children, you know, always ask me for a drink; they're always thirsty for all kinds of juices. And as time passes, as they mature and seek pleasures of a different sort, they will pour those juices back into me.

"Thus, in nature nothing is lost. He who enters the kingdom of God must first enter his mother and die, because when God entered man's kingdom through His Mother He died for man. This is beautiful and the beauty is awesome. Sex is a big drama that symbolically stars the son and the mother.

"Yes, the new age is being conceived in me: the *Damsels of Avignon* will come out of Africa ...

"I see a poisonous, copper-green fly clinging to the sun's giant rose, which fades slowly over the horizon's arc ...

"God, playing with madness, produces the honey of poetry from the flowers of evil; my children, intoxicated with that honey, will adore Him.

"Drunken poets, hanging onto their women, will shoot along with the fire squad at tortured, hollow men ...

"The art of death will come after the death of art!

"I am the wound on the body of your perceived world; the wound is its mouth and it speaks a tongue you cannot interpret; the tongue is like secret flames behind high, dark walls in the whispering green of a garden ...

"There was a woman named Dagny, forlorn in a strange city like the jilted maiden, Sophia, who stepped through the looking-glass and fell into the resounding echoes of the material world ...

"What was she looking for? Where did she want to go? She closed her eyes and let herself drift unresistingly ...

"*In dem wogenden Schwall, in dem tönenden Schall.*

"And to her, everything in that strange city tasted of death.

Yes, she could discern in the taste of strong, matured wine the blood of the dismembered God fortified by passion.

"She died with that taste on her palate. The wine was still flooding her brain when the burning-hot bullet struck through it and dark red liquid rolled from her nostrils and she drowned in the universal stream of the world-breath ... *in des Welt-Atems wehendem All* ...

"She was the first among those who would come after— indeed, there will be others who will let me speak through them; speak about my wild, soft desires, and my cherished anxieties; speak the sound of the snow falling faintly through the universe, and the unconscious, utmost rapture of the river flowing down to meet the sea ... the sea ... *unbewusst, höchste Lust!* Oh, yes—the luster of lust."

Here she stopped. Dagny stood in silence for a while and then, falling back between Stach and Wincent, she crossed her long legs and declared with a careless, though elegant and queenly gesture:

"Wlad Emeryk, you wretched lunatic, go ahead—serve me my last lunch!"

ZURAB KARUMIDZE was born in 1957, and studied English at Tbilisi State University, where he was awarded a PhD for his dissertation on wit and conceit in the poetry of John Donne. Between 1994 and 1995, he was a visiting Fulbright Scholar at the University of Wisconsin-Milwaukee, where he studied postmodern American metafiction. He is currently an international fellow affiliated with The Center for the Humanities at Washington University in St. Louis. In addition to three novels, *The Wine-Dark Sea*, *Gigo and the Goat*, and *Dagny, or a Love Feast*, Karumidze has also published the short-story collection *Opera*. His nonfiction includes a history of jazz music entitled *The Life of Jazz*, which received Georgia's prestigious Saba award in 2010, and *Enough!: The Rose Revolution in the Republic of Georgia*, which he co-authored. *Dagny, or a Love Feast* was nominated for the 2013 International IMPAC Dublin Literary Award. He lives in Tbilisi.

GEORGIAN LITERATURE SERIES

In 2012, the Ministry of Culture and Monument Protection of Georgia collaborated with Dalkey Archive Press to publish *Contemporary Georgian Fiction*, a landmark anthology providing English-language readers with their first introduction to some of the greatest authors writing in Georgian since the restoration of independence.

Given the success of this project, the relationship between Dalkey Archive and the Ministry has evolved into a close, ongoing partnership, allowing an unprecedented number of translations of the major works of post-Soviet Georgian literature to published and publicized across the English-speaking world. Beginning with such contemporary classics as Aka Morchiladze's best-selling *Journey to Karabakh*, the Georgian Literature Series will provide readers with a much-needed overview of a vibrant and innovative literary culture that has thus far been sorely under-represented in translation.

MICHAL AJVAZ, *The Golden Age.*
    The Other City.
PIERRE ALBERT-BIROT, *Grabinoulor.*
YUZ ALESHKOVSKY, *Kangaroo.*
FELIPE ALFAU, *Chromos.*
    Locos.
IVAN ÂNGELO, *The Celebration.*
    The Tower of Glass.
ANTÓNIO LOBO ANTUNES, *Knowledge of*
    Hell.
    The Splendor of Portugal.
ALAIN ARIAS-MISSON, *Theatre of Incest.*
JOHN ASHBERY AND JAMES SCHUYLER,
    A Nest of Ninnies.
ROBERT ASHLEY, *Perfect Lives.*
GABRIELA AVIGUR-ROTEM, *Heatwave*
    and Crazy Birds.
DJUNA BARNES, *Ladies Almanack.*
    Ryder.
JOHN BARTH, *LETTERS.*
    Sabbatical.
DONALD BARTHELME, *The King.*
    Paradise.
SVETISLAV BASARA, *Chinese Letter.*
MIQUEL BAUÇÀ, *The Siege in the Room.*
RENÉ BELLETTO, *Dying.*
MAREK BIEŃCZYK, *Transparency.*
ANDREI BITOV, *Pushkin House.*
ANDREJ BLATNIK, *You Do Understand.*
LOUIS PAUL BOON, *Chapel Road.*
    My Little War.
    Summer in Termuren.
ROGER BOYLAN, *Killoyle.*
IGNÁCIO DE LOYOLA BRANDÃO,
    Anonymous Celebrity.
    Zero.
BONNIE BREMSER, *Troia: Mexican Memoirs.*
CHRISTINE BROOKE-ROSE, *Amalgamemnon.*
BRIGID BROPHY, *In Transit.*
GERALD L. BRUNS, *Modern Poetry and*
    the Idea of Language.
GABRIELLE BURTON, *Heartbreak Hotel.*
MICHEL BUTOR, *Degrees.*
    Mobile.
G. CABRERA INFANTE, *Infante's Inferno.*
    Three Trapped Tigers.
JULIETA CAMPOS,
    The Fear of Losing Eurydice.
ANNE CARSON, *Eros the Bittersweet.*
ORLY CASTEL-BLOOM, *Dolly City.*
LOUIS-FERDINAND CÉLINE, *Castle to Castle.*
    Conversations with Professor Y.
    London Bridge.
    Normance.
    North.
    Rigadoon.
MARIE CHAIX, *The Laurels of Lake*
    Constance.
HUGO CHARTERIS, *The Tide Is Right.*
ERIC CHEVILLARD, *Demolishing Nisard.*

MARC CHOLODENKO, *Mordechai Schamz.*
JOSHUA COHEN, *Witz.*
EMILY HOLMES COLEMAN, *The Shutter*
    of Snow.
ROBERT COOVER, *A Night at the Movies.*
STANLEY CRAWFORD, *Log of the S.S. The*
    Mrs Unguentine.
    Some Instructions to My Wife.
RENÉ CREVEL, *Putting My Foot in It.*
RALPH CUSACK, *Cadenza.*
NICHOLAS DELBANCO, *The Count of*
    Concord.
    Sherbrookes.
NIGEL DENNIS, *Cards of Identity.*
PETER DIMOCK, *A Short Rhetoric for*
    Leaving the Family.
ARIEL DORFMAN, *Konfidenz.*
COLEMAN DOWELL,
    Island People.
    Too Much Flesh and Jabez.
ARKADII DRAGOMOSHCHENKO, *Dust.*
RIKKI DUCORNET, *The Complete*
    Butcher's Tales.
    The Fountains of Neptune.
    The Jade Cabinet.
    Phosphor in Dreamland.
WILLIAM EASTLAKE, *The Bamboo Bed.*
    Castle Keep.
    Lyric of the Circle Heart.
JEAN ECHENOZ, *Chopin's Move.*
STANLEY ELKIN, *A Bad Man.*
    Criers and Kibitzers, Kibitzers
    and Criers.
    The Dick Gibson Show.
    The Franchiser.
    The Living End.
    Mrs. Ted Bliss.
FRANÇOIS EMMANUEL, *Invitation to a*
    Voyage.
SALVADOR ESPRIU, *Ariadne in the*
    Grotesque Labyrinth.
LESLIE A. FIEDLER, *Love and Death in*
    the American Novel.
JUAN FILLOY, *Op Oloop.*
ANDY FITCH, *Pop Poetics.*
GUSTAVE FLAUBERT, *Bouvard and Pécuchet.*
KASS FLEISHER, *Talking out of School.*
FORD MADOX FORD,
    The March of Literature.
JON FOSSE, *Aliss at the Fire.*
    Melancholy.
MAX FRISCH, *I'm Not Stiller.*
    Man in the Holocene.
CARLOS FUENTES, *Christopher Unborn.*
    Distant Relations.
    Terra Nostra.
    Where the Air Is Clear.
TAKEHIKO FUKUNAGA, *Flowers of Grass.*
WILLIAM GADDIS, *J R.*
    The Recognitions.

SELECTED DALKEY ARCHIVE TITLES

JANICE GALLOWAY, *Foreign Parts*.
   The Trick Is to Keep Breathing.
WILLIAM H. GASS, *Cartesian Sonata*
   and Other Novellas.
   Finding a Form.
   A Temple of Texts.
   The Tunnel.
   Willie Masters' Lonesome Wife.
GÉRARD GAVARRY, *Hoppla! 1 2 3*.
ETIENNE GILSON,
   The Arts of the Beautiful.
   Forms and Substances in the Arts.
C. S. GISCOMBE, *Giscome Road*.
   Here.
DOUGLAS GLOVER, *Bad News of the Heart*.
WITOLD GOMBROWICZ,
   A Kind of Testament.
PAULO EMÍLIO SALES GOMES, *P's Three*
   Women.
GEORGI GOSPODINOV, *Natural Novel*.
JUAN GOYTISOLO, *Count Julian*.
   Juan the Landless.
   Makbara.
   Marks of Identity.
HENRY GREEN, *Back*.
   Blindness.
   Concluding.
   Doting.
   Nothing.
JACK GREEN, *Fire the Bastards!*
JIŘÍ GRUŠA, *The Questionnaire*.
MELA HARTWIG, *Am I a Redundant*
   Human Being?
JOHN HAWKES, *The Passion Artist*.
   Whistlejacket.
ELIZABETH HEIGHWAY, ED., *Contemporary*
   Georgian Fiction.
ALEKSANDAR HEMON, ED.,
   Best European Fiction.
AIDAN HIGGINS, *Balcony of Europe*.
   Blind Man's Bluff
   Bornholm Night-Ferry.
   Flotsam and Jetsam.
   Langrishe, Go Down.
   Scenes from a Receding Past.
KEIZO HINO, *Isle of Dreams*.
KAZUSHI HOSAKA, *Plainsong*.
ALDOUS HUXLEY, *Antic Hay*.
   Crome Yellow.
   Point Counter Point.
   Those Barren Leaves.
   Time Must Have a Stop.
NAOYUKI II, *The Shadow of a Blue Cat*.
GERT JONKE, *The Distant Sound*.
   Geometric Regional Novel.
   Homage to Czerny.
   The System of Vienna.
JACQUES JOUET, *Mountain R*.
   Savage.
   Upstaged.

MIEKO KANAI, *The Word Book*.
YORAM KANIUK, *Life on Sandpaper*.
HUGH KENNER, *Flaubert*.
   Joyce and Beckett: The Stoic Comedians.
   Joyce's Voices.
DANILO KIŠ, *The Attic*.
   Garden, Ashes.
   The Lute and the Scars
   Psalm 44.
   A Tomb for Boris Davidovich.
ANITA KONKKA, *A Fool's Paradise*.
GEORGE KONRÁD, *The City Builder*.
TADEUSZ KONWICKI, *A Minor Apocalypse*.
   The Polish Complex.
MENIS KOUMANDAREAS, *Koula*.
ELAINE KRAF, *The Princess of 72nd Street*.
JIM KRUSOE, *Iceland*.
AYŞE KULIN, *Farewell: A Mansion in*
   Occupied Istanbul.
EMILIO LASCANO TEGUI, *On Elegance*
   While Sleeping.
ERIC LAURRENT, *Do Not Touch*.
VIOLETTE LEDUC, *La Bâtarde*.
EDOUARD LEVÉ, *Autoportrait*.
   Suicide.
MARIO LEVI, *Istanbul Was a Fairy Tale*.
DEBORAH LEVY, *Billy and Girl*.
JOSÉ LEZAMA LIMA, *Paradiso*.
ROSA LIKSOM, *Dark Paradise*.
OSMAN LINS, *Avalovara*.
   The Queen of the Prisons of Greece.
ALF MAC LOCHLAINN,
   The Corpus in the Library.
   Out of Focus.
RON LOEWINSOHN, *Magnetic Field(s)*.
MINA LOY, *Stories and Essays of Mina Loy*.
D. KEITH MANO, *Take Five*.
MICHELINE AHARONIAN MARCOM,
   The Mirror in the Well.
BEN MARCUS,
   The Age of Wire and String.
WALLACE MARKFIELD,
   Teitlebaum's Window.
   To an Early Grave.
DAVID MARKSON, *Reader's Block*.
   Wittgenstein's Mistress.
CAROLE MASO, *AVA*.
LADISLAV MATEJKA AND KRYSTYNA
   POMORSKA, EDS.,
   Readings in Russian Poetics:
   Formalist and Structuralist Views.
HARRY MATHEWS, *Cigarettes*.
   The Conversions.
   The Human Country: New and
   Collected Stories.
   The Journalist.
   My Life in CIA.
   Singular Pleasures.
   The Sinking of the Odradek
   Stadium.
   Tlooth.

JOSEPH MCELROY,
Night Soul and Other Stories.
ABDELWAHAB MEDDEB, *Talismano.*
GERHARD MEIER, *Isle of the Dead.*
HERMAN MELVILLE, *The Confidence-Man.*
AMANDA MICHALOPOULOU, *I'd Like.*
STEVEN MILLHAUSER, *The Barnum Museum.*
In the Penny Arcade.
RALPH J. MILLS, JR., *Essays on Poetry.*
MOMUS, *The Book of Jokes.*
CHRISTINE MONTALBETTI, *The Origin of Man.*
Western.
OLIVE MOORE, *Spleen.*
NICHOLAS MOSLEY, *Accident.*
Assassins.
Catastrophe Practice.
Experience and Religion.
A Garden of Trees.
Hopeful Monsters.
Imago Bird.
Impossible Object.
Inventing God.
Judith.
Look at the Dark.
Natalie Natalia.
Serpent.
Time at War.
WARREN MOTTE,
*Fables of the Novel: French Fiction
since 1990.*
*Fiction Now: The French Novel in
the 21st Century.*
*Oulipo: A Primer of Potential
Literature.*
GERALD MURNANE, *Barley Patch.*
Inland.
YVES NAVARRE, *Our Share of Time.*
Sweet Tooth.
DOROTHY NELSON, *In Night's City.*
Tar and Feathers.
ESHKOL NEVO, *Homesick.*
WILFRIDO D. NOLLEDO, *But for the Lovers.*
FLANN O'BRIEN, *At Swim-Two-Birds.*
The Best of Myles.
The Dalkey Archive.
The Hard Life.
The Poor Mouth.
The Third Policeman.
CLAUDE OLLIER, *The Mise-en-Scène.*
Wert and the Life Without End.
GIOVANNI ORELLI, *Walaschek's Dream.*
PATRIK OUŘEDNÍK, *Europeana.*
The Opportune Moment, 1855.
BORIS PAHOR, *Necropolis.*
FERNANDO DEL PASO, *News from the
Empire.*
Palinuro of Mexico.
ROBERT PINGET, *The Inquisitory.*
Mahu or The Material.
Trio.
MANUEL PUIG, *Betrayed by Rita Hayworth.*

The Buenos Aires Affair.
Heartbreak Tango.
RAYMOND QUENEAU, *The Last Days.*
Odile.
Pierrot Mon Ami.
Saint Glinglin.
ANN QUIN, *Berg.*
Passages.
Three.
Tripticks.
ISHMAEL REED, *The Free-Lance Pallbearers.*
The Last Days of Louisiana Red.
Ishmael Reed: The Plays.
Juice!
Reckless Eyeballing.
The Terrible Threes.
The Terrible Twos.
Yellow Back Radio Broke-Down.
JASIA REICHARDT, *15 Journeys Warsaw
to London.*
NOËLLE REVAZ, *With the Animals.*
JOÃO UBALDO RIBEIRO, *House of the
Fortunate Buddhas.*
JEAN RICARDOU, *Place Names.*
RAINER MARIA RILKE, *The Notebooks of
Malte Laurids Brigge.*
JULIÁN RÍOS, *The House of Ulysses.*
Larva: A Midsummer Night's Babel.
Poundemonium.
Procession of Shadows.
AUGUSTO ROA BASTOS, *I the Supreme.*
DANIËL ROBBERECHTS, *Arriving in Avignon.*
JEAN ROLIN, *The Explosion of the
Radiator Hose.*
OLIVIER ROLIN, *Hotel Crystal.*
ALIX CLEO ROUBAUD, *Alix's Journal.*
JACQUES ROUBAUD, *The Form of a
City Changes Faster, Alas, Than
the Human Heart.*
The Great Fire of London.
Hortense in Exile.
Hortense Is Abducted.
The Loop.
Mathematics:
The Plurality of Worlds of Lewis.
The Princess Hoppy.
Some Thing Black.
RAYMOND ROUSSEL, *Impressions of Africa.*
VEDRANA RUDAN, *Night.*
STIG SÆTERBAKKEN, *Siamese.*
Self Control.
LYDIE SALVAYRE, *The Company of Ghosts.*
The Lecture.
The Power of Flies.
LUIS RAFAEL SÁNCHEZ,
Macho Camacho's Beat.
SEVERO SARDUY, *Cobra & Maitreya.*
NATHALIE SARRAUTE,
Do You Hear Them?
Martereau.
The Planetarium.

FOR A FULL LIST OF PUBLICATIONS, VISIT:
www.dalkeyarchive.com

ARNO SCHMIDT, *Collected Novellas.*
Collected Stories.
Nobodaddy's Children.
Two Novels.
ASAF SCHURR, *Motti.*
GAIL SCOTT, *My Paris.*
DAMION SEARLS, *What We Were Doing and Where We Were Going.*
JUNE AKERS SEESE, *Is This What Other Women Feel Too?*
What Waiting Really Means.
BERNARD SHARE, *Inish.*
Transit.
VIKTOR SHKLOVSKY, *Bowstring.*
Knight's Move.
A Sentimental Journey: Memoirs 1917–1922.
Energy of Delusion: A Book on Plot.
Literature and Cinematography.
Theory of Prose.
Third Factory.
Zoo, or Letters Not about Love.
PIERRE SINIAC, *The Collaborators.*
KJERSTI A. SKOMSVOLD, *The Faster I Walk, the Smaller I Am.*
JOSEF ŠKVORECKÝ, *The Engineer of Human Souls.*
GILBERT SORRENTINO, *Aberration of Starlight.*
Blue Pastoral.
Crystal Vision.
Imaginative Qualities of Actual Things.
Mulligan Stew.
Pack of Lies.
Red the Fiend.
The Sky Changes.
Something Said.
Splendide-Hôtel.
Steelwork.
Under the Shadow.
W. M. SPACKMAN, *The Complete Fiction.*
ANDRZEJ STASIUK, *Dukla.*
Fado.
GERTRUDE STEIN, *The Making of Americans.*
A Novel of Thank You.
LARS SVENDSEN, *A Philosophy of Evil.*
PIOTR SZEWC, *Annihilation.*
GONÇALO M. TAVARES, *Jerusalem.*
Joseph Walser's Machine.
Learning to Pray in the Age of Technique.
LUCIAN DAN TEODOROVICI, *Our Circus Presents . . .*
NIKANOR TERATOLOGEN, *Assisted Living.*
STEFAN THEMERSON, *Hobson's Island.*
The Mystery of the Sardine.
Tom Harris.
TAEKO TOMIOKA, *Building Waves.*

JOHN TOOMEY, *Sleepwalker.*
JEAN-PHILIPPE TOUSSAINT, *The Bathroom.*
Camera.
Monsieur.
Reticence.
Running Away.
Self-Portrait Abroad.
Television.
The Truth about Marie.
DUMITRU TSEPENEAG, *Hotel Europa.*
The Necessary Marriage.
Pigeon Post.
Vain Art of the Fugue.
ESTHER TUSQUETS, *Stranded.*
DUBRAVKA UGRESIC, *Lend Me Your Character.*
Thank You for Not Reading.
TOR ULVEN, *Replacement.*
MATI UNT, *Brecht at Night.*
Diary of a Blood Donor.
Things in the Night.
ÁLVARO URIBE AND OLIVIA SEARS, EDS., *Best of Contemporary Mexican Fiction.*
ELOY URROZ, *Friction.*
The Obstacles.
LUISA VALENZUELA, *Dark Desires and the Others.*
He Who Searches.
PAUL VERHAEGHEN, *Omega Minor.*
AGLAJA VETERANYI, *Why the Child Is Cooking in the Polenta.*
BORIS VIAN, *Heartsnatcher.*
LLORENÇ VILLALONGA, *The Dolls' Room.*
TOOMAS VINT, *An Unending Landscape.*
ORNELA VORPSI, *The Country Where No One Ever Dies.*
AUSTRYN WAINHOUSE, *Hedyphagetica.*
CURTIS WHITE, *America's Magic Mountain.*
The Idea of Home.
Memories of My Father Watching TV.
Requiem.
DIANE WILLIAMS, *Excitability: Selected Stories.*
Romancer Erector.
DOUGLAS WOOLF, *Wall to Wall.*
Ya! & John-Juan.
JAY WRIGHT, *Polynomials and Pollen.*
The Presentable Art of Reading Absence.
PHILIP WYLIE, *Generation of Vipers.*
MARGUERITE YOUNG, *Angel in the Forest.*
Miss MacIntosh, My Darling.
REYOUNG, *Unbabbling.*
VLADO ŽABOT, *The Succubus.*
ZORAN ŽIVKOVIĆ, *Hidden Camera.*
LOUIS ZUKOFSKY, *Collected Fiction.*
VITOMIL ZUPAN, *Minuet for Guitar.*
SCOTT ZWIREN, *God Head.*